THE JANUS GATE

PRESENT TENSE

STAR TREK®
THE ORIGINAL SERIES

book one of three

THE JANUS GATE

PRESENT TENSE

L. A. Graf

**Based upon STAR TREK®
created by Gene Roddenberry**

POCKET BOOKS

New York   London   Toronto   Sydney   Singapore

An *Original* Publication of POCKET BOOKS

 POCKET BOOKS, a division of Simon & Schuster, Inc.
1230 Avenue of the Americas, New York, NY 10020

ISBN: 0–671–03635–1

First Pocket Books printing June 2002

10 9 8 7 6 5 4 3 2 1

POCKET and colophon are registered trademarks of Simon & Schuster, Inc.

For information regarding special discounts for bulk purchases, please contact Simon & Schuster Special Sales at 1-800-456-6798 or business@simonandschuster.com

Printed in the U.S.A.

Chapter One

THE GREAT STARSHIP TREMBLED, frame and struts wailing in distress as she careened into her own attenuated warp field. Behind her, the ice-blue sphere of Psi 2000 shattered like a bursting bubble, filling the *Enterprise*'s main viewscreen with glittering fragments that evaporated almost as soon as they were made. A planet in its death throes, chasing after a starship who just might be dying herself.

James Kirk gripped the arms of his command chair so hard his hands hurt. He'd never heard a ship howl like this before. As many times as he'd pushed this girl to her limits—and sometimes beyond—he'd never truly, in his heart, believed for a moment that she could fail him. But he'd also never imploded a small universe inside her belly, never sling-shotted all hundred tons of her through a dying planet's gravity well and flung her back out into space. Never felt her surge so convulsively ahead of herself as the fabric of space all around her thinned, stretched, twisted into a bright spinning whiteness that teetered just on the edge of comprehension—

Then, just that suddenly, it was over.

Kirk felt as though he bolted awake from a dream. Solidity returned with an almost audible *pop!,* and all around him his bridge crew stirred at their stations, casting half-glances at each other and touching the edges of panels and screens to make sure they were really still there.

Kirk forced himself to uncurl his grip on the command chair and straighten his shoulders. No matter how distracted the crew might seem by their duties, they would be aware of their captain's mood, just as he was always aware of theirs. They didn't need to sense any uncertainty in their commander after the chaos they'd all suffered these last few days. The movement made his upper arm throb where McCoy had only moments ago injected him with a dose of antiviral serum as he came aboard the bridge. Not for the first time, he wished the doctor hadn't ripped open his uniform sleeve to administer the injection. Sitting bare-shouldered in front of the crew made him feel ill-kempt and undignified.

"Are you all right, Jim?"

Kirk glanced aside at Spock, worried for just an instant that the Vulcan had somehow sensed his spasm of insecurity. He sketched a self-conscious nod as his first officer stepped up to the arm of the command chair. "You?"

The Vulcan paused a moment, as if it had only occurred to him to consider his condition because his captain asked. Then he nodded as well. A blur of surreal light still throbbed at the center of the viewscreen, and the ship beneath them thrummed in dangerous sympathy.

"We found a cure." McCoy, out of Kirk's view behind the shoulder of the command chair, sounded definitive but grim. As though his intellect knew this to be true, but his emotions weren't quite so sure despite the empty hypospray in his hands. "We're over that part of it."

It was the only part McCoy could influence, not to mention the part that had first gotten them into this mess. Kirk didn't have the heart to tell the doctor that developing an antiviral inoculation to counteract the infection they'd brought up from Psi 2000 was probably the least of their worries now. He still hadn't moved his eyes from the viewscreen, where blurred light had replaced the usual streaming view of stars, almost as if they had somehow all congealed into that formless glow. At first, Kirk thought the viewscreen had sustained some unspecific damage in their flight from the dying planet, ruining its ability to show them the space outside. Then a single spinning star, coiled almost like a tiny galaxy, peeled away from the mass and slid swiftly underneath their bow. That was when Kirk realized he *was* seeing the space outside, twisted until it was unrecognizable.

"Obviously, we were successful." Spock no doubt read Kirk's thoughts on the captain's all-too-expressive human face. His own face was impassive, dark eyes flicking over the maelstrom outside as though counting every misplaced star. "The engines imploded."

Unless what we're racing toward is the afterlife. Only minutes before, they'd been screaming through Psi

2000's upper atmosphere, plummeting toward the planet's disintegrating surface with half the ship's crew incapacitated by a neurogenic virus for which they hadn't yet devised a cure. One of those infected crewmen had shut down the ship's main reactor hours before, for reasons known only to his own fevered imaginings. The engines had been left powerless, her matter/antimatter cores too cold to ignite by the time Chief Engineer Scott discovered the full extent of what had been done. If they didn't want to end up just another cloud of detritus amid the planetary rubble, they had to be willing to dare a drastic gamble.

Theory said they could throw matter and antimatter together without the usual quantum physics introductions, so long as there existed a magnetic bottle of such perfect mathematical shape that the resultant explosion could be turned back in upon itself, collapsed into a microsecond's singularity, and all of its raging energy channeled into a reactor ready to cast it back out again in an instantaneous leap to light speed.

"It's never been done," Spock had objected when Kirk explained the plan to him.

As far as Kirk knew, no one had ever pulled a 190,000-ton starship out of a planetary nosedive before, either, but that wouldn't stop him from trying. "We might go up in the biggest ball of fire since the last sun in these parts exploded, but we've got to take that one in ten thousand chance that we'll succeed."

And taking that minuscule chance had flung them here. Wherever "here" was.

"Captain!" Sulu twisted around at the helm, straining

to look at Kirk and his panel all at the same time. His face was still drawn and pale in the aftermath of viral infection. "My velocity gauge is off the scale!"

Kirk leaned forward, hands clenched, and flashed keen eyes across Sulu's console. He couldn't see the numbers, but the play of lights across the panel told their own story.

"Engine power went off the scale, as well," Spock told the captain as the readouts began to fall into some kind of strange sense in Kirk's mind. "We are now traveling faster than is possible for normal space."

Faster than Kirk had dreamed possible, even at warp speeds. Middle-school conundrums inspired by Einstein, Hawking, and Cochrane came rushing back like a badly distorted echo, and he heard himself saying, "Check elapsed time, Mr. Sulu," before his conscious mind even realized why he wanted to know.

Yet, somehow, he wasn't entirely surprised by the shock in his young helmsman's face when Sulu complied. "My chronometer's running...*backwards,* sir..."

Of course it was. Kirk settled back into his command chair with a slow nod. They'd performed the impossible intermix, flooded the engines with nearly infinite power, and roared away from Psi 2000 in full reverse. Back the way they'd come. "A time warp. We're going backward in time." Kirk's agile mind was already racing through the implications, rehearsing how he would word his report to Starfleet Command, worrying about just how much he should tell them, then feeling guilty when his first instinct was to withhold as much of the details of how they accomplished this as he could. Starfleet itself could be trusted with the knowledge, of course, but if anyone else ever found out about it and gained the ability to travel through time, changing the past and destroying the future, there was no telling where the havoc would end.

Kirk dragged himself back to the moment. He wouldn't have to worry about explaining anything to Starfleet if they didn't first shake loose from their accidental time slip. He thought about the trajectory Spock and Scotty had so carefully planned for their slingshot around Psi 2000, and about the surge in engine power *Enterprise* had experienced just following her warp core implosion. "Helm, begin reversing power." Sometimes, the most obvious course of action looked that way for a reason.

Sulu's nimble hands flew across his panel. Kirk understood the basics of the language his pilot used to coax the ship to his bidding, but had never met anyone who employed it so instinctively and well. A dim sense of movement, so ghostly it was almost a sound, slid along the length of the vessel in response to Sulu's commands. The distorted image on the main screen bled a few microns closer to resolution; the moment felt suddenly less attenuated, tasted faintly of metal and ozone. When Kirk felt some unexpected resistance buck through the ship's frame, he startled more sharply than he intended. "Slowly," he reminded Sulu through clenched teeth.

The helmsman had the grace not to glance away from his work. "Helm answering, sir," he reported in his usual steady, professional tone. "Power reversing."

The blurry corona on the forward screen seemed to throb, draw inward like the fiery heart of an event horizon, then folded so swiftly in on itself that its brightness snuffed into black like a candle flame in the fist of a god. With an almost bashful slowness, individual stars blossomed one-by-one across the fresh darkness. Tiny diamonds in red, blue, and yellow, washed over by the familiar gauzy veil of the Milky Way.

Spock had gone back to his science station, and was bending intently over his viewer. Kirk heard McCoy release an unsteady breath from behind him, and wondered how long the doctor had been holding it.

"We're back to normal time, Captain," Spock announced, somewhat unnecessarily.

Kirk nodded absently. The stars were too comforting to turn away from just now. "Engines ahead." He was a little surprised at how relaxed he sounded. As though he accidentally hurled his ship backward in time every day. "Warp one."

"Warp one, sir," Sulu echoed.

And just that simply, they were back to business as usual. Kirk almost thought he *could* take the ship through time every day, and his crew would follow without question as long as their captain said everything would be okay. It was a frightening power to hold over them all, but a reassuring one, as well.

"Mr. Spock…" He finally pulled his gaze away from the viewscreen, knowing that its return to a familiar starscape didn't solve the problem of where—and when—they were.

"Yes, sir."

"The time warp—" Kirk swivelled the command chair to face Spock as the science officer descended the steps from his station. "What did it do to us?"

"We've regressed in time seventy-one hours." Then he elaborated, as though the humans listening to him might not appreciate the full impact of what they'd done. "It is now three days ago, Captain. We have three days to live over again."

Thinking about the mental and physical anguish Scott's engine implosion had only barely wrenched them free of, Kirk had to suppress a sudden urge to laugh. "Not those *last* three days." Why was it that you were never given the opportunity to relive your three best days of shore leave? Was that part of the price Fate extracted for letting humans pull off such outrageous feats as time travel to begin with?

"This does open some intriguing prospects, Captain." Spock's brows knit into what would have been a worried frown for anyone else. "Since the formula worked, we can go back in time. To any planet, any era." Apparently, his own imagination had finally begun to catch up to Kirk's.

"We may risk it some day, Mr. Spock." Kirk hadn't forgotten the misgivings that had swept over him when they first realized what they'd done. "Resume course to our next destination, Mr. Sulu."

"Course laid in, sir."

"Steady as she goes."

Lingering beside Kirk's command chair, Spock stirred. "Captain, if I may..."

"Is there a problem, Mr. Spock?"

Spock seemed to seriously consider his captain's question before answering, even though his hesitation lasted barely a heartbeat. "Potential complications," he finally said. Another brief pause that Kirk suspected no one but he actually noticed. "Given our current situation, continuing on to our next destination may be ill advised."

McCoy gave a little snort from behind Kirk. "You've got something against arriving early?"

Spock lifted his eyebrows in a semblance of Vulcan surprise. "Indeed, Doctor, arriving early is precisely the problem." He turned his attention back toward Kirk, tacitly more concerned with his captain's understanding than with the doctor's. "We are presently at stardate 1704. Again. According to Starfleet—according to history—the *Enterprise*'s next scheduled destination is Psi 2000 for the retrieval of the geological survey team."

"So if we show up three days early for our rendezvous with the *Antares,* there will be questions about why we aren't where we're supposed to be." Just as it had when he first realized what they'd done, Kirk's agile mind immediately leapt through the tangle of implications.

"Questions," Spock stressed, "which would be received—and answered—by two separate *Enterprise*s, the first with no knowledge of the second."

McCoy shrugged, twisting the empty serum vial off the hypospray in his hands. "So we explain the situation, tell Starfleet what happened." He fitted the vial back into the medikit at his hip.

"Except we didn't." Kirk waited while McCoy frowned, then stilled as the doctor began to realize where the conversation was going. "We went to Psi 2000, Bones. We stayed there through the destruction of the planet, and we never once heard from Starfleet. Not about *Enterprise* being out of position, not about anything. Which means either something happens to us now, and we never make the early rendezvous with the *Antares*—"

"Or we never tried to make the early rendezvous in the first place." McCoy rubbed his mouth thoughtfully.

Kirk clapped him on the shoulder in an effort to lighten the mood. "I know which of those two options I'd prefer." But he was serious about his concern, despite his wry smile.

"So we do what?" The doctor looked between Kirk and Spock with a scowl the captain recognized as being worried frustration rather than the irritation it resembled. "Hang out in deep space and hope nobody stumbles across us?" He gave an almost petulant grunt. "Seems like an awful waste of three perfectly good days."

"I don't see why being displaced in time should mean we have to waste any." Kirk stood to lean over the railing between his command chair and Spock's station. "Mr. Spock, we left a planetary survey team back in the Tlaoli system, in sector alpha nineteen."

Spock nodded slowly. "They are scheduled for retrieval immediately after our rendezvous with the *Antares*." Kirk had a feeling his first officer already knew where he was heading.

"I'm sure they'll be delighted to have a little company for the next three days. And limiting ourselves to planetside research on a previously uncharted planet—" Not to mention a little judicious shore leave. "—ought to minimize our potential impact on the timestream. Wouldn't you say?"

Spock crossed his arms in what might have been Vulcan displeasure, but the curious arch of his eyebrows made his expression hard to quantify. "It could be argued that our very existence at this moment in time has already altered history in ways we cannot yet recognize. Therefore, any action we take—even inaction—unavoidably impacts the current timestream."

McCoy made a wry face. "And if a butterfly flaps its wings in Tibet?"

Spock frowned and cocked his head, obviously ready to address the doctor's apparent non sequitur, but Kirk stepped between them to head the discussion off. "Unfortunately, we can't go back and take ourselves out of this timestream," he said to Spock, "so we have to work with what we've got."

"True," his first officer conceded. "Then no doubt sequestering ourselves on Tlaoli 4 is our most...productive option." He said "productive" as though congenitally incapable of understanding the human need for almost constant activity.

Kirk had a feeling he'd have no choice but to get used to it if he planned on staying with Kirk for the next five years. "Mr. Sulu, set course for Tlaoli, warp four."

"Aye, aye, sir."

Kirk settled back into his command chair as the ship beneath him began the purring hum up to warp speed. He could feel something subtly amiss, a deep trembling in her bowels that hadn't been there three days ago...three days from now....Something else for Scott to work on while they bided their time at Tlaoli, and while Kirk assessed the rest of their damage, physical and otherwise.

"I don't see what he's so worried about," McCoy grumbled, coming to lean his elbows on the back of

Kirk's chair as the ship got under way. "How much damage can we possibly do to history in just three days?"

Kirk gave a dark little laugh and rubbed at the knot in his shoulder where the antiviral shot still stung. "I think that's exactly what he's worried about, Bones."

"*Enterprise* to Tlaoli Base One. Come in, Base One."

Only silence answered Uhura's standard hail. She frowned, then got a firm grip on her overactive imagination and reminded herself that they were no longer at Psi 2000. The bridge crew behind her wasn't giggling or ranting or threatening to commit suicide—they had all been inoculated against the alien virus, and the ones most affected, such as Sulu and Riley, had been sent down to sickbay for an in-depth toxin screen and some much-needed rest. Even with second-shift officers such as Stiles and Leslie at navigation and helm, the ship's command center had regained its usual quiet efficiency. And for further reassurance, all Uhura had to do was glance sideways at the viewscreen.

The sunlit planet that the *Enterprise* had just swung into orbit around wasn't silver-blue and quivering with tectonic instability. It was old and brown and done with life, worn down to nothing but dusty grasslands and rocky karst plains and thick rims of saltwater swamp around its drying oceans. It revolved around an ordinary yellow star and was accompanied by an ordinary natural satellite about half the size of Earth's moon. The only thing unusual about Tlaoli 4 was the rose-quartz tinge of its atmosphere, caused by the high load of windblown iron oxides and garnet dust. The planetary assessment team had assured them there was nothing strange or dangerous about that. It just meant that the landing parties would see some spectacular sunsets.

Uhura knew perfectly well that this placid little planet had been given the highest safety rating possible, which was why the *Enterprise* had left its landing teams behind while it had gone on to its rendezvous with Psi 2000. There was no hint of peril in the humming silence of her open communicator channel, either, she told herself bracingly. With only a few scientists assigned to each of the three planetary survey teams—and only a few days available for them to describe and catalog as much as they could of an entire planet—the probability of someone sitting at the main communications panel when she hailed was pretty remote. She closed the first base camp's channel and instead scanned through the frequency distributions of the communicators she'd assigned to the fifteen members of the landing party. She had bracketed the ranges so that each team overlapped only with its own members. That made it a fairly easy task to select multiple communicator addresses for her next hail.

"*Enterprise* to Tlaoli Survey Team One." She watched rainbows of subspace frequencies replicate across her board as the communications computer automatically generated the multiple hail. "Come in, Technician Fisher, Lieutenants Boma, Kulessa, and Kelowitz."

The reply came back so fast that Uhura thought she could still hear the hiss of the hand communicator being snapped open. "Fisher here," said a startled voice. *"Enterprise,* are you in system?"

"Yes, we arrived early. Captain Kirk thought—"

"Is the captain on the bridge?" Fisher cut across her explanation with much more urgency than politeness.

"Affirmative." Uhura swung away from her panel and caught the bright hazel glance that immediately darted her way. In the months she'd served under James T. Kirk, Uhura had come to depend on her captain's attentiveness to his bridge crew so much that she had internalized it into her own actions. A slight turn of her head and shoulder would get her noticed in a moment or two, whenever Kirk finished signing orders or conferring with his line officers. A more complete swing got her a quicker look, and a rapid pivot always got his full, focused attention. "Captain, Geological Technician Fisher of Survey Team One needs to speak with you."

"Put him through," Kirk said, and Uhura toggled the open communicator channel into the main bridge speaker. "Report, Mr. Fisher."

"We've got a problem, Captain." One thing Kirk had successfully pounded into his crew over the past year was to waste no time with regulation greetings in times of crisis. "Actually, we have several problems, sir, but the most urgent one is that we've lost touch with Survey Team Three."

Kirk frowned across the bridge at Spock. "Where was Team Three assigned?"

The Vulcan Science Officer opened his mouth, then clamped it shut again and tapped a query into his science panel. The chaotic frenzy of their visit to Psi 2000 had apparently erased even his supernaturally good memory of what the different Tlaoli landing parties had been sent down to do.

Before he could respond, Fisher answered for him through the com channel. "That was the cave exploration team, Captain. They were originally set down on that big karst plateau in the southern continent, but yesterday we flew them up to chcck on a smaller karst terrain in the northern continent, due west of where the wetland team is stationed."

Kirk's frown deepened. "Why did you reassign Team Three's location, Mr. Fisher? I believe your standing orders were to stay near your base camps until the *Enterprise* returned."

"Yes, sir, I know." There was a pause and a mutter of inaudible conversation in the background behind Fisher, as if his fellow scientists were suggesting things for him to say. Uhura could hear the geologist take a deep breath and plunge back into speech as if speed could somehow make his confession less painful. "Captain, we did disobey our standing orders. But it was because of what we found down here after the *Enterprise* left the system. We were afraid there might be a safety risk, sir, to the ship."

"A safety risk to the research shuttle you took down to the planet's surface, Mr. Fisher?"

"No, sir," the geologist said firmly. "A safety risk to the *Enterprise.*"

Uhura glanced over her shoulder in surprise at the drab brown planet on the viewscreen, but saw nothing more threatening on its ancient and worn surface than she had a few minutes ago. She noticed Captain Kirk gazing up at Tlaoli with a similar look of incomprehension. When he spoke, however, his voice held none of the doubt that was so clearly expressed on his face. A good commander like Kirk never passed premature judgement on his crew's decisions, especially when they were on the surface and he was still on board.

"What made you think the *Enterprise* might be in danger, Mr. Fisher?"

The geologist paused to listen to another advisory murmur of voices behind him. "Sir, we think you and Mr. Spock should see this for yourselves. Request permission to uplink our visual tricorder's data buffer through my communicator to the main viewscreen."

Kirk lifted an eyebrow at Uhura, and she nodded back at him while her fingers danced across the communications panel, widening the bandwidth she'd assigned to Fisher's handheld communicator so it wouldn't choke on the much thicker flow of a visual record. "Permission granted. Spock, make sure we get this in the main computer log."

The Vulcan science officer gave his captain the kind of austere look that said the command had been unnecessary, but all he replied was, "Aye, sir."

There was a pause as the data stream from the planet spooled itself into the viewscreen's buffer, then the dusty little planet abruptly vanished. It was replaced by a much more grainy image of sand dunes rippling into the horizon. The image panned slowly to the right, over a long, pale scar where a lake or sea had dried up into what looked like endless salt flats, then paused a moment before zooming in to focus on an anomalous patch of darkness in the midst of all that white. The tricorder continued to increase its magnification until each pixel of the image covered a hand's width of the viewscreen. Even with that lack of resolution, Uhura could clearly see the intricate lines and curves of something unnatural, some shape that had been constructed rather than deposited or eroded.

"Alien ruins?" Kirk said to Spock.

The science officer lifted an eyebrow at the confusing angles and lines now frozen on the screen, waiting for the next spool of data to be received. "That would not be impossible, Captain, but I admit that it would surprise me. Our initial long-range surveys of Tlaoli indicated that its ecosystems have been incapable of sustaining animal life for several millions of years. Very few structures, whether natural or constructed, can withstand surface erosion for that long."

"So we don't know if the planet was ever occupied?"

"On the contrary," Spock said, with the sidelong look of reproof he saved for what he considered particularly egregious leaps of illogic. "Our preliminary studies detected an anomalous lack of near-surface metal deposits, and absolutely no trace of fossil fuels or enriched nuclear isotopes anywhere in the upper crust. Based on that, we assumed that an alien race did indeed occupy Tlaoli once, millions of years ago, but left when its resources became exhausted and its ecosystems began to collapse."

"Or went extinct," Kirk said wryly. "So what the hell is *that?*"

Uhura glanced over her shoulder again. The still

image on the screen rippled and was replaced by another, sharper image obviously taken at much closer range. She could clearly make out the smooth curves of the main hemispherical structure rising from the salt deposits of the former lake. Whatever it was, it looked to Uhura as if the lake had actually dried up around it, embedding the lower parts completely in its evaporated deposits. The tricorder image scanned a little further along, then paused to focus in on two dark towers rising from the salt flats in the background. It took her a minute to recognize them as the ends of pointed fins that looked unmistakably like shorter and bulkier versions of the *Enterprise*'s warp nacelles.

"Captain, that's a ship!" said Lieutenant Leslie from the helm, startled out of his usual phlegmatic silence.

"And it's not an atmospheric shuttle, either," Kirk agreed grimly. "It looks like a deep space vessel. Spock, can the computer identify its origin based on the design?"

The science officer tapped a quick inquiry into his computer monitor and watched the results flicker across his screen at rates faster than any human could have absorbed. "It appears similar to the starships constructed by ancient civilizations we know from the galactic core, Captain, but it cannot be assigned to any known race or planet."

"Hmm." Kirk watched the image until it flickered and disappeared, replaced once again by the undistinguished brown disk that was Tlaoli 4. "Was that the end of the tricorder transmission, Lieutenant Uhura?"

"Aye, sir." She shrank the communicator's data feed back down to the optimum range for voice transmission.

"Survey Team One should be back on line now, Captain."

"Mr. Fisher," said Kirk crisply. "Where and when did you find that ship?"

"About fifty kilometers from our base camp, sir, two days after you left the system. It *is* a starship, isn't it?"

"We think so," Kirk agreed. "But starships have been known to crash on planets for lots of reasons, Mr. Fisher. It might have been shot down in some kind of war, or been forced to land by a mechanical systems failure. It doesn't necessarily mean the planet it landed on is dangerous."

The geologist's answer came back so readily that Uhura knew he must have anticipated Kirk's remark. "That's what we thought, too, sir, when we first saw it. We didn't even go any closer to look at it, we just marked it on our survey sheets for a later archeological survey to examine. But after we found the other remains, we started to wonder—"

"Other remains?" Kirk demanded. "Of other starships?"

"Yes, sir." Fisher paused, and this time there wasn't so much as a whisper of voices to be heard in the background. The explanation for the Survey Team's violated orders had obviously reached a crucial stage. "We were doing a geophysical survey of the salt flats, Captain, when we first spotted that thing, so we knew what its electromagnetic signature looked like. And for the next two days, we kept seeing what looked like that same signature over and over again, but it was always deep below ground so we couldn't be sure. Then we started surveying the smaller karst plateau on the northern continent, and we could actually see down to where the signature was coming from, at the bottom of a couple sinkholes. A lot of them weren't very well preserved, and none of them looked the same as any of the others, but they were all definitely spaceships." Fisher paused to take a deep breath. "Sir, I know it sounds unbelievable...but including the signatures we detected under the salt deposits, we think at least nineteen different starships have crashed down here on Tlaoli."

Chapter Two

THE BRIDGE OF THE *Enterprise* was never truly silent, with the white background noise of the ship's life-support systems overlain by the clicks and taps of crew members interacting with their various data stations. But there were times, like now, when the bridge crew seemed to take a collective breath in such unison that Kirk felt as if silence had abruptly descended.

Spock was right, he thought, a bit wearily. *We should have hidden out in deep space and just waited for the rest of the universe to catch up to our timeline.* But even as he thought it, he knew that a three-day delay in arriving at Tlaoli wouldn't have helped the situation. If the *Enterprise* had arrived three days from now to find the landing parties so distressed and the cave survey team missing for nearly a week, Kirk would never have forgiven himself for twiddling his thumbs in safety only a few light-years away.

Still, the thought of plunging back into danger only a few hours after their escape from Psi 2000 was more than Kirk had hoped to ask from his crew.

But the *Enterprise* was on a deep-space mission, and everyone on board her had been forced to learn how to weather one crisis after another without losing focus or succumbing to fear. After only a moment of dismayed silence, the bridge crew went back steadfastly to their monitors and station displays. Kirk saw Uhura run what she probably meant to be a discreet safety check on her station, even as she filtered a faint hiss of encroaching static from Fisher's signal.

"Very well, Mr. Fisher." It was the standard acknowledgment to a subordinate's report, but Kirk tried to make it sound no more formal or full of tension than a simple "so far, so good." "I see why you thought there might be a problem. But I still don't understand why you moved Team Three to a new location."

"Our spatial analysis showed an unusual concentration of wrecks in and around the northern karst terrain, Captain." Fisher launched into his explanation with an ease that made Kirk suspect he appreciated his captain's calm reaction to the news. "Lieutenant Boma's wetland survey team had noticed a lot of subspace static interfering with their tricorder readings whenever they got close to that same area, so we suspected that the karst dissolution had allowed some kind of late-stage ore deposit to form there. That could have concentrated enough transperiodic elements like dilithium or trifluorine to generate a natural subspace aperture." The geologist's voice had taken on the slightly pedantic rhythm of a researcher who was already forming his hypothesis into a potential scientific paper. "A natural subspace anomaly like that was found on the dilithium-enriched asteroid that started the prospecting rush in Beta Carinae back in 2204. It's been suggested by several recent studies that the same kinds of deposits might explain places where things have mysteriously disappeared through time, like the Bermuda Triangle back on Earth—"

"We observed no evidence of either transperiodic elements or subspace radiation in our preliminary surveys of this planet, Mr. Fisher." Spock cut across the scientist's theorizing with the relentless cool only Vulcans could manage. "In fact, Tlaoli 4 was determined by the planetary assessment team to be singularly lacking in anything resembling either an ore deposit or a power source."

The pedantry in Fisher's voice vanished, replaced by a more apologetic tone. "I realize that, Mr. Spock. But it was the only thing we could think of to explain how an uninhabited planet could knock a starship out of orbit. According to the Rogers-Kline-Roth hypothesis, a transperiodic ore deposit *could* interfere with sensor readings enough to explain why it often goes undetected."

Spock lifted a disdainful eyebrow, glancing toward Kirk as though assuming the captain shared his assessment of Fisher's hypothesis. "I do not believe that either Professor Rogers-Kline or Professor Roth understands the physics of six-dimensional space sufficiently well to make any prediction about possible sensor interference, much less one that so conveniently explains away their lack of evidence—"

Kirk did his best to smother a tired grin. "Gentlemen." The situation wasn't particularly funny—nothing about the prospect of losing an entire survey team, not to mention his starship, struck Kirk as something to laugh about. Yet he could never help being at least a little amused by the deadly seriousness with which scientists could debate the least important details of any crisis. "I suggest you continue this academic discussion after we've made sure that Survey Team Three is safely accounted for." Spock closed his mouth obediently, no doubt bookmarking the next sentence in his argument for later retrieval. Kirk turned his attention back to the now-silent geologist on the other end of the com channel. "Mr. Fisher, I'm still waiting to hear why you disobeyed orders and moved Team Three."

"Yes, sir." Fisher paused to clear his throat uncertainly. "We did try hailing the *Enterprise* at Psi 2000, Captain, to tell you about what we'd found and to get updated orders, but no one answered. Since we didn't really have a ranking officer on Tlaoli, we got all the lieutenants together by communicator and took a vote on what to do. It was unanimous, sir. We decided to move the six members of the karst team up to the northern continent and have them explore the cave closest to most of the wrecks, to see if they could verify whether there was a large transperiodic ore deposit there."

Kirk glanced over at his science officer, whose narrow Vulcan face had been growing steadily more somber as he listened to the geologist's report. "What's the matter, Spock?"

The Vulcan's eyes snapped back into focus from their pensive stare. "I have been scanning the entire northern karst terrain with long-range sensors since Mr. Fisher first reported that Survey Team Three had been sent there, Captain," he said quietly. "I have not detected any trace of life, either on or beneath the surface."

"That's exactly the problem, Mr. Spock." Fisher spoke a bit more loudly, as though taking the volume of Spock's voice to mean the science officer had moved farther away from the com station. "None of our scanners have been able to see anything under that karst terrain, either, not since about four hours ago."

Kirk nodded, starting to do the math in his head. "Was that when you last made contact with the cave team, Mr. Fisher?"

"Yes, sir. They entered the caves seven hours ago, and were reporting on their progress hourly. The last time we talked to them, they mentioned having some problems with their tricorders, so when we didn't hear from them an hour later we figured maybe they were having communicator problems as well."

"That's something we should be able to verify." Kirk caught up Uhura's gaze with his own. "Lieutenant, try to punch through to Survey Team Three's communicators. With the power of the *Enterprise*'s signal generator and receiver, we might be able to pick up something Mr. Fisher's handheld communicator couldn't."

"I'll try, sir." Uhura turned to skim her fingers over the panel. Kirk watched without interrupting as she opened a second channel, then jacked the narrow-beam power setting up to its fullest. They could have sent a shout all the way to Sigma Draconis at that power.

"*Enterprise* to Tlaoli Survey Team Three. Come in, please." She cocked her head in her slight pause, as though listening to sounds no one else around her could hear. Another slight adjustment to her controls, then, "*Enterprise* to Survey Team Three, please respond."

Still nothing. Uhura looked back over her shoulder at the captain, shaking her head almost apologetically. "Nothing, sir. If I had to guess, I'd say that Survey Team Three's communicators just weren't working."

Which fit with Fisher's earlier assumptions. "So you were right about their communicators not working, Mr. Fisher. What did you do next?"

"We tried to fly over in the research shuttle and scan for them, but as soon as we got close to the cave area, all of our geophysical sensors started to malfunction. And then—" The geologist's voice tightened. "—then the shuttle started to lose power, too, sir, for no apparent reason. We managed to get out of the karst area and back to the wetlands base camp before we had to set down, but now the shuttle doesn't even have enough power to charge the ionization rings on the impulse engines."

"How far away are you from the cave site?"

"Thirty kilometers, sir. Since we didn't know you'd be coming back early, we put a rescue team together and started hiking from the wetlands back into the karst terrain. Best estimate of our arrival time at the cave is—" Fisher paused to exchange murmurs with someone in the background "—sometime tomorrow evening, sir."

"Thirty hours from now?" Kirk frowned up at the image of Tlaoli 4 on the viewscreen, trying to imagine how any part of its worn and ancient surface could be so difficult to travel. "Mr. Fisher, do you know how far Survey Team Three penetrated into that cave system before you lost contact?"

"At least two kilometers, sir. They started in at local sunrise, which would be about six hundred hours ship time."

Kirk twisted a quick look over his shoulder to glance at the chronometer on the arm of his command chair. "It's thirteen hundred hours now." *God, only thirteen hundred?* "If Team Three had turned around and started back out of the cave four hours ago, when we know their equipment began to malfunction, they should have reached the surface about ship's noon." He paced over to the viewscreen again, peering up at the dots on it thoughtfully. "When you brought Team Three up to the northern continent, Mr. Fisher, did you leave their equipment behind?"

"No, sir. Lieutenant Jaeger thought it might take several days to explore the caves thoroughly enough to find the source of the shipwrecks, so we brought all of their supplies and tents up with them."

"Good." That simplified one thing, at least. Kirk swung back to Uhura. "Lieutenant, see if you can make contact with Survey Team Three's base communicator unit."

Uhura addressed her panel again, repeating her formal hail. Despite the lack of response, even Kirk could hear the faint buzzing that burned across the open channel. "That's the sound of an open subspace channel, sir," Uhura told him, correctly reading the intent look on his face. "I think the main communicator at their base camp is operational; there's just no one there to answer it."

Kirk rapped his fingers thoughtfully on the edge of her panel, his thoughts leaping ahead of him now that his suspicion was verified. "No sane geologist would stay inside a cave if their equipment wasn't working, especially if they knew there was some kind of dangerous transperiodic ore deposit down there." He didn't mean to step through his reasoning out loud, but didn't dare stop once he noticed Uhura and the others staring at him. It wouldn't do to have them see he was sometimes caught off guard by his own impulses that way. "The fact that Survey Team Three hasn't left means they probably *can't* leave." He nodded, certain now. "They're trapped down there."

A worried crease furrowed Uhura's brow. "Captain, do you think their lights have malfunctioned in addition to their tricorders and communicators?" She seemed to hesitate before going on to suggest, "It wouldn't be safe for them to move in total darkness, would it?"

"No, it wouldn't." He didn't even like the image of the survey team trying. "They could also be trapped by a roof collapse, or flooded out by a surge in water levels." He frowned a threat up at the planet on the viewscreen. "A lot of things can go wrong in a cave."

"That's what we thought, sir." He'd almost forgotten about Fisher down on the surface. "What do you want us to do?"

Kirk shook off the parade of unpleasant images Uhura's question had set loose in his head. "All I need right now, Mr. Fisher, is the coordinates of the cave where you lost Team Three, and the location of their base camp. From here on in, the cave rescue will be our responsibility. You head back to the wetlands base camp and start packing your samples. We'll evacuate you and the other survey crews by transporter as soon as you're ready." He barely waited for the geologist to acknowledge his orders before nodding at Uhura to cut the channel. "Mr. Spock, we did a preliminary assessment before we sent the landing party down to that planet. Bring up the surface scans—I want to see what that northern karst terrain looks like."

"Aye, sir." A few brisk taps on his science controls overlaid the small brown planet on the viewscreen with a detailed grid depicting its surface. "This is the topographic data gathered by our long-range scans. I had the computer convert it into three dimensions and zoom to a low-elevation viewpoint to better illustrate the terrain."

Kirk moved down to reclaim his command chair as the network of growing lines slowly enlarged on the screen and rotated on the main screen. What had initially looked like a gently rumpled rock plateau resolved on closer inspection into a jagged nightmare of steep monolithic mounds, knife-sharp ridges and jumbled boulder fields pocked with sinkholes so deep that their bases were lost in shadow. "Where the hell is all that vertical relief coming from? I thought this planet was ancient."

"Twelve billion years old," Spock clarified. "Approximately four times the age of Vulcan. Most of Tlaoli's surface is eroded down to a peneplain, Captain, but in the karst areas, the erosion is occurring underground in the form of caves. When those caves collapse, they form this kind of surface landscape."

Kirk could suddenly understand why it would take more than thirty hours to cross less than thirty kilometers. "Do we have those coordinates yet from Fisher? I want to see where that cave is."

No one said anything in acknowledgment, but Kirk heard the gentle sounds of data transfer behind him as Uhura and Spock combined their information. A red dot appeared near the center of the crazy-quilt terrain. "That is the cave Survey Team Three entered, Captain," Spock said. A smaller blue dot appeared a short distance to the north on the barren gray plateau. "And that is the new location of their base camp."

"Which we know still has power, even if the people in the cave don't." Still half-lost in thought, Kirk bounced the side of his hand against the com button on the arm of his command chair. "Bridge to engineering. Mr. Scott, are you down there?"

"Aye, Captain, but I can't give you any warp drive right now." The chief engineer sounded particularly gloomy, and more than just a little harassed. "I've just taken the warp nacelles offline to clean out the thrusters and recalibrate the field angles. It'll take a half hour to get them put back together again, much less up and running."

Kirk smiled at Scott's attempt at clairvoyance. "Thanks for the heads-up, Scotty, but I don't need the warp drive just yet. What I do need is for your engineers to manufacture some equipment for me so I can outfit a landing party for an emergency cave rescue."

"Aye, sir." Kirk could almost picture the way Montgomery Scott's face crinkled doubtfully as he answered; Scotty had quite the knack for acknowledging an order while still managing to convey his complete incomprehension of it at the same time. "And what kind of equipment might you need that's not already in our stores?"

"Primitive equipment. The kind that doesn't depend on dilithium power cells or permanent magnetic batteries." Kirk paused a moment to mentally outfit a cave party in his head, then translate all the necessary equipment into its old-fashioned counterparts. "I'll need chemical batteries that can run our communicators and tricorders, and headlamps that use carbide fuel illumination."

"You want *combustion* lamps?" The chief engineer sounded scandalized, as if he were being asked to equip the *Enterprise* with a hitch for a team of draft horses. "And just how many of these will you be needing, Captain?"

"Five or six, for sure—twice that many if you have time." Kirk glanced around the bridge, his gaze skipping past the tall figures of Spock, Stiles, and Leslie almost without seeing them, until finally coming to rest on Uhura's far more petite form. "Lieutenant Uhura, you're the smallest communications officer aboard, aren't you?"

Her eyes widened in apparent surprise. "Yes, sir."

"Then you'll be coming with me." He angled his voice back down toward the com. "Mr. Scott, I want that equipment within an hour." The plan became more clear by the moment. Kirk already knew what he had to do for every step before leaving the ship, and was already impatient at having to slow down and actually issue the orders. "Yeoman Rand," he summoned, almost before he'd finished switching channels on the com. "I need you to locate our ship's smallest medic, our smallest power supply expert, and our smallest geologist. And the smallest person on board who's had some recent orienteering experience, say within the last four months."

If his assistant was startled by the strange request, nothing in her composed voice gave the emotion away. "Smallest by weight or by height, sir?" was all she asked.

"By height. We may be crawling through some narrow cave passages, so make sure none of them are claustrophobic. I'll give you a list of the equipment they'll each need. Tell them all to meet me in the main transporter room by fourteen hundred."

"Aye-aye, sir. Rand out."

"Spock, you have the conn." Kirk pushed to his feet, energized at the prospect of taking action. "Keep the ship in the highest orbit that's gravitationally stable, just in case that planet really does throw some kind of subspace aperture at us. And make sure Scotty gets those warp nacelles back online as soon as he can. We might need to evacuate quickly." He vaulted up the steps to the turbolift, but couldn't resist pausing at the threshold to toss a grin back at the silent Vulcan. "It's a good thing we opted for coming here instead of meeting the *Antares*. If we'd waited until after our rendezvous, we might have arrived too late."

Spock arched one eyebrow in an eloquent remark Kirk wasn't sure how to interpret. "Indeed, Captain," was all he said, "that is the aspect of our situation that troubles me the most."

"Listen up, all you scuts! You're not going to be doing anything in there that a well-trained monkey couldn't do just as well or better. Unfortunately, we used up our last trained monkey cold-starting the engines, so you guys are all we have left."

Ensign Pavel Chekov lingered just inside the engine room's main doorway, delaying his departure long enough to eavesdrop on First Technician Singh's welcome to the department's new temporary workers. There were three of them this time, their races and genders obscured by bulky radiation suits, clustered together like mutant goslings as they scurried across the huge bay behind Singh.

"In-and-out in fifteen-minute shifts. I don't want you formulating opinions about the new magnetic bottle, trying to figure out how we pulled off such a nifty ignition feat, or analyzing the engines' function. Your job is to scour subspace residue out of the interior thruster compartments. You've got your scrubbers, you've got your rad monitors. If anything blinks or turns red, get out. We'll have a medic outside with a tasty antiradiation cocktail waiting for you. But if you do everything the way you're told, you'll be eating supper tonight instead of a fistful of meds. Any questions?"

A suited arm waggled above the clutter of helmets, only to sink out of sight again when its owner finally realized that Singh's offer had been largely rhetorical. *Get used to it,* Chekov wanted to tell the new arrival. Because no matter who you were back home, or how brilliant you were at the academy, once you got to a starship you were assumed to be about as useful as a Belgian chocolate until you proved yourself otherwise. Here, you were just the latest batch of scuts.

Sighing, Chekov slipped out into the corridor without waiting to see when Singh would deign to acknowledge the nervous faces and waving arms (he always did eventually; he just liked to make sure that the recent arrivals knew they were at his mercy first). At least this temporary work crew got to do something interesting. Chekov had spent three and a half weeks in engineering, and the most exciting thing he'd done had entailed being locked out of the department while a member of the bridge crew powered down the engines and sang very badly for eighteen hours. Now that there was real, hard work to be done beyond calibrating sensors and counting surplus hand tools, he was off to spend fourteen days in astrophysics. While the ship was in orbit around an M-Class planet. While no one needed stellar analyses, pulsar identifications, or even the most simple navigation equations. As if a month in Planetary Sciences while the ship was in deep space hadn't been irony enough.

How all this leaping from department to department was supposed to help him become the perfect starship commander made less sense to Chekov every day. He still couldn't remember the operational tolerances of a theta-class warp shield, could remember only half of the fifty or so points used to determine the environmental class of a planet (although, thank God, retaining the meanings of the various classifications themselves proved anomalously easy), and he had yet to figure out how to tell which deck he was on without stealing surreptitious peeks at the bulkhead markings. I'm *the future commander of a starship?* he would think with something approaching horror while wandering aimlessly in search of a turbolift shaft that wasn't where he remembered. *What was Starfleet thinking?*

It wasn't much consolation to realize there was apparently no one here from his academy class with any hope of a career beyond polishing laboratory glassware or mopping up coolant spills. Or so Singh and all the other noncom supervisors before him had assured Chekov from almost his first day on the job. This was apparently not the most promising collection of new crewmen to have ever graced the *Enterprise*'s hallways.

But I just want to fly the ship, Chekov could have told them. *I want to be on the bridge, and see the planets when we first come into orbit, and watch the stars drift by while everyone from the daylight shift is at home in bed.* He'd figured out, just from what he'd overheard at mealtimes or in the gym, that the *Enterprise* already had a helmsman so good that the man would have to go blind and lose the use of one hand before Kirk would consider replacing him. That meant the chances of Chekov working on the bridge during first shift were so small he couldn't have found them with an electron microscope. *I don't care where we're going, or who's giving the orders, or what we have to do to get there, just please, please, please! don't leave me down in the lower decks!*

He'd already walked several sections too far forward before realizing he'd completely bypassed the proper turboshaft to take him up to crew's quarters. Maintenance teams had apparently begun the chore of removing graffiti from the starship's bulkheads, thus eradicating the obscene line-drawing Chekov had been using to identify his turbolift for the last day or so. He tried again (unsuccessfully, he was certain) to lock some distinctive image from this junction in his memory, then ducked into the car and sent it racing up toward Deck Six. He could just imagine himself explaining to the captain, "No, sir, I cannot find my own quarters, but I can pilot a starship anywhere in the galaxy without getting lost, I promise."

So while he wasn't exactly *expecting* to walk into someone else's cabin while meaning to enter his own, it wasn't as though he hadn't already had nightmares about this very moment that differed only in the details.

The woman standing beside the room's only desk jerked around with a gasp when the door hissed open. Chekov barely had time to register the hand which flew to her mouth and the shocked embarrassment in her blue eyes before he'd jumped backward through the closing hatch and into the corridor again. That was as long as it took him to realize that it was *his* desk she was standing over, *his* books and disks stacked on top of it, and *his* quarters in which she was doing it. All the same, he spared one extra moment to verify the cabin number and the name stenciled on the door before striding boldly back inside to confront her. "Excuse me—"

She seemed to have recovered herself by this time, and interrupted as though their first compromising encounter had never happened. "There you are! You're late."

It wasn't the painfully abashed apology he'd expected. Blinking, he found himself suddenly unable to think past where he'd already started. "Excuse me?"

"Engineering told me you left twenty minutes ago." She had to be someone's yeoman—probably some high-ranking officer's, judging from her elaborate blonde coif and stiffly superior attitude. No yeoman who worked for anyone below a commander would have had the time to maintain such a hairstyle, much less the gall to speak so disdainfully to someone who was technically her superior. "I didn't expect it would take you half the afternoon to get back to your own quarters."

Chekov decided not to comment on that. Before he could inject something different, she swept up a bundle of clothing and equipment from the top of his desk and shoveled it into his arms as though glad to be rid of it.

Before Chekov could protest, she asked brusquely, "You don't have any mental problems, do you?"

"What?"

The blonde yeoman twirled a finger alongside elaborate tresses, as if he needed to be shown where mental problems came from. "You know—fear of heights, paranoia, claustrophobia. Anything like that?"

What about fear of surreal visits from unfamiliar yeomen? "No."

"Then report to Transporter Room 4. They're probably waiting on you, too."

This, at least, he knew how to respond to. "There must be some mistake."

"You're Ensign Pavel Chekov?" When he didn't answer during her nonexistent pause, she planted her fists impatiently on her hips. "Command track cadet? Just released from a temporary tour in engineering services?"

"Yes," he finally blurted. "But I'm scheduled to report to astrophysics at fourteen hundred hours." He'd estimated that he only barely had enough time to clear out of engineering and visit his quarters to collect his reference books before reporting in—and that was before his twenty minute detour and this ridiculous delay. "I can show you my orders if you don't believe me."

If the yeoman was at all impressed with his version of his schedule, she gave no sign. "It doesn't matter what you were told before. You've been called up to assist on a planetary rescue mission."

"What?" He hurried to intercept her as she whisked past him on her way to the door. The bundle in his arms threatened to tumble apart at the sudden movement, and he struggled to tame it so he wouldn't have to gather up the pieces just to give them all back to her. "What possible use can I be to a rescue mission?"

"How am I supposed to know? I'd think you'd be thrilled to get off the ship for a change." She shooed him toward the door with the same prissy fluttering of hands that old women in the Moscow suburbs used to chase sled dogs out of their kitchens. "Now get going! If you think I'm irritable when you're twenty minutes late, wait until you meet Captain Kirk."

Chapter Three

WHY, oh *why,* did it have to be D'Artagnan?

The teasing didn't start right away, of course. Sulu hadn't heard a single comment when he'd reported to the bridge after McCoy's prototype antiviral vaccine had yanked him screaming back to sanity. The urgent need to escape from Psi 2000's death spasms had dominated the first hour of that watch, followed by the sudden shock of finding out that they'd hurled themselves three days into the past. While the other bridge officers were still discussing the ramifications of time travel, Sulu had been called down to Sickbay where Dr. McCoy had ordered another round of detoxification for him and Kevin Riley, "just in case."

It wasn't until Riley accused the doctor of trying to shield them from unkind comments that Sulu started to wonder exactly what it was that he'd done. His last clear memory of their stay at Psi 2000 was trying to keep a despondent Joe Tormolen from doing away with himself. After that came a blur of running, laughing, and fencing, laced through with the indistinct feeling that he'd made a total ass of himself. McCoy had gruffly denied Riley's charge and told them both to rest while the last viral toxins that his prototype antidote had missed were screened out of their blood.

Exhausted from what felt like hours of fencing practice, and still depressed about the loss of Joe Tormolen, Sulu would probably have obeyed the doctor readily enough. But Kevin Riley in the next medical bed over had been more determined and more creative. As soon as McCoy left them alone, Riley squirmed out of his bed long enough to activate their room's link to the ship's main computer. At his request, the computer had shown them the visual logs it had recorded over the past two days, complete with Riley's tuneless serenades from engineering and Sulu's irrational dueling escapades. Sulu had spent the rest of his medical treatment wondering if Uhura would ever speak to him again, while Riley bemoaned his own stupidity and lack of musical taste.

An hour later, Sulu got a glimpse of things to come.

Nurse Christine Chapel began it, when she stopped by to check his blood counts and clear him for return to duty. "So, how is it with this madman?" she asked in her best professional nurse's voice. Sulu shot her a quick look, startled by the not-very-professional question. The nurse's face looked innocent enough, but the dancing glint in her eyes and the finger she had stuck into an antique paper book with worn gilt letters spelling "Dumas," gave her away. Sulu groaned.

"I read it when I was a teenager," he pleaded. "It had a big impact on me...."

The nurse opened her dog-eared book and read aloud, " 'Never fear quarrels, but seek adventures. Fight on all occasions. Fight the more for duels being forbidden, since consequently there is twice as much courage in fighting.' " She waggled her forefinger at him as if it were a fencing foil. "Was that the part that made such a big impact?"

Her voice held a lilting mix of mockery, laughter, and feminine admiration. Sulu felt his cheeks tighten and he hurried to drag his tunic over his head so she couldn't see what color his face had turned. He muttered something about being due on the bridge and bolted for the turbolift, not even waiting for Riley to join him. As the deck lights flashed by, however, Sulu faced the unpleasant fact that he would soon be stepping onto a bridge filled with people who had watched him swing shirtless down out of a hatchway, like a maniacal cross between a French musketeer and Tarzan.

He got a temporary reprieve when the turbolift whistled to a stop a few decks below the bridge to pick up another crewmate, but his sense of relief was very short-lived.

"All for one and one for all," chanted John Russ, the engineering tech who usually worked the morning shift with him. His tone was insufferably cheerful. "The bridge crew has sworn to stick with you, buddy, even if you get arrested by Cardinal Richelieu—I mean Captain Kirk."

Sulu was saved from needing to reply by the hiss of

the turbolift doors. He headed for the pilot's console with the sound of the engineer's laughter chasing him. Fortunately, Mr. Spock had the conn and merely gave Sulu an impassive glance as the pilot seated himself. But because Riley hadn't reported for duty yet, Sulu had to share the helm with Lieutenant Stiles for now. The second-shift navigator gave him a wicked smile.

" 'Why, this fellow must be the devil in person!' " Stiles said to the departing pilot, Ed Leslie. Evidently, Leslie hadn't decided to take part in the shipwide joke, because he merely gave his fellow pilot a sympathetic look and a clap on the shoulder as he left. " 'Don Quixote took windmills for giants, and sheep for armies,' " Stiles continued smoothly. He must have spent the last few hours memorizing passages from the ship's library. " 'D'Artagnan took every smile for an insult, and every look as a provocation.' "

"Then you'd better stop smiling, hadn't you?" Sulu snapped at him.

Stiles's obnoxious grin merely widened. " 'And for the first time in his life D'Artagnan, who had till that day entertained a very good opinion of himself, felt ridiculous.' "

That, unfortunately, was all too true. Sulu gritted his teeth and gazed down at his helm monitors, checking the orbital equations as carefully as if the *Enterprise* had been circling a complex triplicate moon instead of a normal terrestrial planet. He didn't even look up when the bridge doors swished open again, and knew it was Riley only when Lieutenant Stiles started to hum a familiar Irish tune under his breath.

"Stop it," Riley snapped as he came to a stop beside the helm. "I don't ever want to hear that song again!"

Stiles snorted with laughter. "Gee, that's a shame. You were *so* good at singing it—"

Sulu reached out and caught Riley's fist before it could connect with Stiles's jaw. He succeeded, but there was no way he could disguise his movement to make it look like anything other than the interception of a punch. He heard Commander Spock clear his throat meaningfully behind them.

"Gentlemen, some of you may not be aware of it, but we are in the midst of an emergency operation. In a few moments, we will begin beaming down a party to rescue one of the survey teams on Tlaoli. And because of a possible danger to the *Enterprise* itself, we are maintaining a heightened state of alert on the bridge." The tone of the science officer's voice was so cold and steely that it sounded almost—but not quite—like irritation. "All departing shift members should clear the bridge immediately, and all arriving ones should review the ship's logs to acquaint themselves with the situation."

Given that direct order from a senior officer, even a troublemaker like Stiles couldn't find an excuse to linger and torment them further. Sulu sighed in relief when the turbolift doors slid shut behind him.

"Get used to it," he advised Riley quietly as the navigator dropped into the seat beside him. "Neither of us is going to live this down for a while."

Riley shot him a sour look. "Easy for you to say, D'Artagnan. *You're* not the one who almost got the ship blown up the other day."

Sulu gritted his teeth and began reviewing the helm records to find out what had happened while he was gone. If even fellow victims of the Psi 2000 virus couldn't resist teasing him, he knew the next few days weren't going to be fun. Maybe he'd use his spare time on this shift to figure out exactly how they'd managed to slingshot themselves back in time. If he could fling the *Enterprise* even farther into the past, he just might be able to steal every copy of *The Three Musketeers* from the San Francisco public library before a certain impressionable young fencing student ever read one.

Chekov was on deck three of the primary hull, halfway down the corridor to Transporter Room 4, when he finally decided this had to be some kind of elaborate joke. It had taken him that long to verify what combination of turbolifts and corridors would take him to his destination, and it was only just before exiting the last lift car that he'd finally taken a moment to paw through the bundle that had been thrust upon him by the prickly yeoman.

The coverall wasn't all that different from the jumpers they'd sometimes worn in engineering, except this one was gold and it carried the command division star over the left breast instead of the twisted engineering lightning bolt. A lumpy plastic pouch with a loop of black nylon cord contained everything else, and it was dumping out this miscellany that finally convinced him he'd been targeted as just another scut on someone's humor radar.

A manual tape measure and compass. A smaller pouch-within-a-pouch of reflective directional markers.

A bound booklet of blank waterproof plastisheets, a plastic-and-graphite mechanical pencil to go with it. And a metal whistle. It reminded him of the paraphernalia they were issued at the beginning of the Academy's orienteering course. And it was all ridiculously redundant and useless on any kind of planetary mission he could think of. Tricorders and communicators did these jobs now, and did them better than humans. Issuing these sorts of materials to a new crew member could only be some kind of statement on his lack of usefulness, a joking implication that he might be left behind on some planet and have to find his own way home.

Indignation stopped Chekov just outside the transporter room door. He didn't want to go in blushing with anger, but didn't want to walk in as though he was too stupid to have figured out what was happening. Truth be told, he didn't want to go in at all. He just couldn't figure out what was worse—facing and identifying his tormentor, or slinking away to be laughed at behind his back for the rest of his term on this ship.

Of course, there's always the possibility that a landing party really is waiting for you in there.

The thought of walking away from an actual duty summons was more frightening than any of the other prospects. He took a deep breath and straightened. If he were about to become the butt of some junior officer's underdeveloped sense of humor, at least he could console himself with the knowledge that he'd let it happen rather than risk disobeying a direct command.

Lifting his chin, he stepped boldly forward through the sliding doors.

All but one of the six people who turned to look at him were sealed into jumpsuits just like the one he now hugged against his chest. Three women in a rainbow of Services red, Command gold, and Science blue; a stocky man maybe twice Chekov's age wearing a blue jumper that had seen better decades; the indifferent transporter tech in his unremarkable duty uniform; and the only other man in command gold, pale eyes irritable with waiting and a metal whistle bouncing impatiently in one hand.

"Ensign Chekov." It wasn't a question or a guess, even though Chekov knew he'd never met the captain face-to-face before. Kirk's eyes flicked over him. "You're not dressed."

The blush Chekov had tried so hard to leave outside the door roared over him again. "Uh, no, sir. I assumed there must—"

"Let me worry about the assumptions, Ensign. Get dressed."

"Yes, sir." He willed himself not to stammer, but only partially succeeded.

Kirk turned to collect the rest of the room with his gaze while Chekov hastily shook out his jumper and began stepping into it. "All right, everyone, listen up. We'll be beaming down to the survey team's base camp, because we know it hasn't been affected by whatever on this planet drains power and pulls ships out of orbit. That will give us a one-kilometer hike to the cave entrance itself. The terrain is wicked, so I want us to stay close together, both on the surface and once we get inside the cave." His gaze swept across them and, to Chekov's relief, snagged up on the woman in the gold jumper instead of him. "Ensign Martine, I'll want our power supplies kept close to Lieutenant Uhura so we can maintain contact with the ship as we travel."

The pretty, dark-haired woman nodded, reaching back to touch the bulky pack across her shoulders as though to make sure it was still there.

"Lieutenant Wright, I'm going to ask you to stay in the middle of the group until we locate the missing survey team." A surprisingly boyish smile flashed across Kirk's face. "If anyone is going to run into trouble, I'd rather it wasn't our only medic."

"I understand, sir." The blue-clad medic passed a hand through her close-cropped blonde hair. "To tell you the truth, I'd rather it wasn't anyone."

Kirk grinned again. "Point taken." Then he waved forward the last figure in Science Division blue, catching the abbreviated helmet the other man tossed to him. "Equipment orientation now. Mr. Sanner, if you please."

Sanner worked down the line of them, pushing a helmet toward each of them and barely pausing long enough to make sure each one was taken. "I know they're uncomfortable and they look stupid," he said, with that complete lack of formality only research scientists could get away with in Starfleet, "but wear 'em anyway. You'd be amazed what you'll find to bump your head on inside a cave." He thumped a lumpy structure on the top of the helmet he was handing Martine, and it rattled as though filled with small marbles. "Once we get underground, you're going to need to light your carbide lamp. There's water in the reservoir here, carbide rocks down below. This little knob controls the drip. The more water you add to the carbide, the more gas it lets off, which means you can turn up the flow if you need a bright light, but you're gonna be using up your light faster that way. I've got extra carbide with my gear, in case one of you decides he has to go wild and light up an entire chamber." This time he paused in front of Chekov, quickly demonstrated how to start the water drip again, and triggered a small ignitor with his thumb. A neat feather of blue-and-gold flame sprang to life just in front of the lamp's brightly polished reflector. "Don't blow it out," he instructed, "or you'll waste gas. Just turn off the water." Which he did, and the little flame guttered and died.

Turning the helmet over to Chekov, Sanner wandered back toward his place near the base of the transporter. "I've got a rope ladder, if we need it, and plenty of pitons. You've all got whistles—make as much noise as you can if we get separated in the cave, and we'll find you. Otherwise..." Sanner shrugged, seating himself on the transporter's steps. "Don't step anyplace where you can't see the bottom."

Kirk gave a businesslike nod, tucking his own helmet under one arm. "All right, then. Any questions?"

Chekov raised his hand tentatively, more convinced than ever that some horrible mistake had been made. At Kirk's sharp glance of acknowledgment, he admitted, as evenly as possible, "Sir, I don't understand why I'm here."

"You took the orienteering course at Starfleet Academy."

The answer was so close to his earlier thoughts that

Chekov wasn't sure at first what to say. "Yes, sir." It seemed a safe enough option.

To his even greater surprise, Kirk smiled, a little gently. "We're going into an uncharted cave to retrieve a lost survey team, and there's a very good chance we won't be able to use tricorders to map our way in and out. I need someone who can accurately record the route we take into this cave, and read his own map well enough to get us all home again." Kirk clapped a hand to his shoulder. "Can you do that, Ensign?"

The course had, indeed, covered the basics of mapmaking and surveying. But Chekov had always viewed it as an interesting introduction to the science of navigating, not to mention a complementary elective to go with his other mathematics courses. It had never occurred to him that the primitive marriage of compass and measuring stick would have any practical use once he got to outer space.

There was a lot about serving on a starship that he hadn't expected.

"Yes, sir. I can do that, sir."

Kirk gave a satisfied nod. "Then let's head into the abyss."

There was something wrong with the *Enterprise*'s orbit.

Sulu wasn't sure when he first became aware of the problem. Despite McCoy's viral detoxification, he'd spent the morning trying to ignore sporadic attacks of hand tremors and the unpleasant feeling that a layer of cotton wool had been inserted between his brain and his sensory nerves. From the sidelong glimpses he'd caught of Kevin Riley clenching his jaw or pinching at the bridge of his nose, he suspected the navigator was feeling much the same. Fortunately, with the *Enterprise* parked in slow, stable orbit around Tlaoli's Earth-sized mass, Sulu didn't think his muzziness posed too much danger to the ship.

Until he noticed that their orbital altitude had decayed by almost twelve percent.

"Mr. Spock, permission to adjust orbit," he said at once.

Commander Spock glanced down at him from the engineering station, where he was working with Crewman Russ and Commander Scott to finish bringing their warp nacelles into alignment. "Why should our orbit require correction, Mr. Sulu? I do not recall ordering any course changes."

"You didn't, sir." Sulu scanned his monitors with a frown, wondering if his tremors had jerked his hands into doing something his brain had never ordered. But all of his controls insisted that no helm changes had occurred since Stiles and Leslie had first laid in their course several hours ago. Which made their current position even more of a mystery. "According to my logs, sir, we didn't change course. But somehow, we're fifty kilometers closer to the planet now than we were an hour ago."

"Due to a helm malfunction?" Spock crossed the bridge with strides that looked calm and unhurried but still brought him to Sulu's side within seconds. "Run a systems check, Lieutenant."

Sulu programed it in with a quick stab, aware of Riley doing the same thing on his side of the console. In a moment, green monitor lights flashed across both their panels, as one by one the ship's internal systems were checked and verified. None showed anomalies, but the gap between the perfect yellow circle that should have marked their orbit around Tlaoli and the blue spiral that was their actual position continued to widen. Spock lifted an eyebrow when he saw it.

"Correct our heading, Mr. Sulu."

"Aye, sir." Sulu lifted the ship's nose and nudged it gently to starboard. With a kick of impulse acceleration so subtle that he wondered if anyone besides him even noticed it, the *Enterprise* slid back onto the plane of her stable orbit, and the blue and yellow lines merged into a smooth white curve.

"Interesting," Mr. Spock murmured. "As well as disturbing."

From across the bridge, Montgomery Scott made the deep rumbling noise that was his version of clearing his throat. "It didn't look as if the ship had any trouble regaining altitude, Mr. Spock."

"No," the Vulcan agreed. "But given the record of previous starships that have crashed on this planet, Mr. Scott, I fail to find that entirely reassuring. Please continue to observe our position, Lieutenant. If this discrepancy occurs again, I want to—"

"Hail coming in from the captain!"

The loud declaration from the communications station sliced through whatever Spock had been going to say. As a second-shift bridge officer, Lieutenant Palmer was perfectly competent, but she didn't have Lieutenant Uhura's deft ability to announce a hail without disrupting the flow of normal ship business. Sulu could have sworn Spock let out a tiny sigh behind him, but all the

Vulcan first officer said out loud was, "Put it through, Ensign."

A burst of static followed his words, intense enough to make Sulu's teeth hurt. After a moment, it subsided to a low-pitched drone, and he could hear Kirk's voice. It seemed to be haloed in echoes, as if the captain were standing in a large empty room.

"We're about one hundred meters inside the cave system, Mr. Spock." Kirk sounded as calm and composed as if he were seated on his own bridge. "It's really cold in here, and we're already seeing some instability in our tricorder readings, even though we've got it rigged to battery power. Any suggestions for shielding it from whatever disruption we're running into?"

"I believe it may be counterproductive to protect the tricorder's scanners, Captain." Spock's voice held the carefully neutral note that he usually employed to disagree with his captain. "Any shielding device you installed would prevent the tricorder from detecting the source of whatever is affecting it, perhaps leading you into greater danger than if you left it unshielded."

"Good point, Spock." One of the things Sulu liked most about his captain was Kirk's ability to accept criticism and modify his plans accordingly. "Is there anything else we can do?"

"I would suggest, Captain, that you program the tricorder to take an average of several readings and report the error function along with the median value."

"Did you get that, Mr. Sanner?" Kirk's voice faded as if he had turned away from his communicator's voice detection panel.

From farther away in the echoing cave passage, Sulu could hear a muffled male voice saying, "Yeah, but what do we do if the error function is larger than the reading?"

"We'll worry about that when it happens," Kirk told him, then his voice strengthened again. "Spock, I'm going to have Lieutenant Uhura begin reporting in every fifteen minutes as we proceed through the cave. If you stop getting reports, try to lock in on our communicator signals with the transporter and follow us from that point. Is that clear?"

Spock exchanged doubtful glances with Chief Engineer Scott, and his voice dropped into careful neutrality again. "Your instructions are clear, Captain. However, given our previous failure to locate the lost survey team on long-range scanners, I estimate the probability of our being able to carry them out to be less than thirty-five percent."

"Understood," Kirk said calmly. Sulu just hoped the other members of the rescue party shared their leader's love of a challenge. "Do the best you can, Mr. Spock. Kirk out."

Scotty was already closing up the warp control panel on the engineering station. "I'll get down to the main transporter room, Mr. Spock, and start tracking them now, while we still have a good connection to their communicator signals. We can finish the warp alignment later. It's good enough now for anything you'll need to do inside the system."

"Very well, Mr. Scott." Spock returned to the command chair, although, as usual, he stood near it rather than occupy it in Kirk's absence. "Lieutenant Palmer, please inform Mr. Boma's base camp that we are going to interrupt the transport of their rock samples back to the ship. I want the transporter free to evacuate the rescue team on a moment's notice."

"Aye-aye, sir." Palmer relayed the Vulcan's message. A few moments later, she turned from the communications desk again. "Mr. Spock, Geologic Technician Kulessa wants to know if we can beam him and Mr. Fisher over to Team One's original base camp so they can begin packing up the samples there. He says they left some important fossiliferous specimens behind when they went to move Survey Team Three to the northern karst region."

The Vulcan tilted his head to one side as he considered the request. Instead of answering directly, he touched the intraship communicator controls. "Spock to main transporter room. Commander Scott, are you there?"

"Just arrived," said the engineer's dour voice. "Don't tell me you need to beam the captain out already?"

"No, but we have a request for a cross-surface transport. Can you lock onto Mr. Fisher and Mr. Kulessa's communicator signals in the wetlands region and transport them to the coordinates of Base Camp One?"

"That I can," Scotty replied. "Locked on and beaming now."

And that was when it happened. With a deflection so swift and small that it barely escaped the automatic suppression of the inertial dampeners, the *Enterprise* broke out of orbit and began to slowly spiral down toward the planet again. Sulu activated the systems monitor as soon as he felt the change, and a moment later it confirmed what he already knew. He turned around to report his discovery to Spock, but two other voices overrode him.

"Transporter room to bridge," said Montgomery Scott's voice. It sounded even more somber than it had before. "We got those geologists to their destination, Mr. Spock, but just barely. The transporter beam hit some kind of energy field down on that planet, and now our long-range sensors aren't working at all. I can't focus in on the cave party's communicators."

"Neither can I, sir," said Lieutenant Palmer. "There's a burst of subspace static coming from the cave region. I'm barely maintaining contact with Lieutenant Uhura's narrow-beam communicator."

Despite the competing claims on his attention, Spock's keen Vulcan gaze focused directly on Sulu. "Have we experienced another helm change, Lieutenant?"

"Yes, sir. Thirty seconds ago, the *Enterprise* veered two degrees to port and five degrees off vertical." Sulu tightened his grip on his helm controls to still another spasm of tremors. "Permission to correct our course heading, sir."

"Granted." Spock came forward to the helm again, stooping to watch the piloting monitor. "Computer, run the helm log buffer backward for the last ninety seconds."

The monitor obediently flashed an inset miniature of its usual display, one in which the course curves contracted back on themselves instead of extending forward. Sulu glanced from the real-time orbital path which he had just adjusted back to a stable white line, to the data buffer which was replaying the previous ninety seconds of helm control. Two discrepant blue and yellow lines raced each other backward for fifty seconds, then suddenly jogged back into a single white line.

None of the engine or helm displays showed so much as a whisker of movement when they did.

"It's not a ship malfunction, sir," Sulu said.

"No," Spock agreed. "Nor does it resemble the kind of natural subspace aperture Mr. Fisher suspected. Nevertheless, I believe we may be seeing what caused the crash of nineteen other spaceships." His dark gaze lifted to the nondescript, sunlit curve of Tlaoli which filled half the viewscreen. "Some unknown force on that planet is beginning to pull the *Enterprise* down toward it."

Chapter Four

THE LAST TIME Uhura had been inside a cave, she had been twelve, and there had been handrails to help you through passages like these.

She edged her way along a sinuous vertical cavern, the glow of her carbide lamp inching forward with each cautious step. Where the light touched the wet cave walls, it made the translucent flowstone shine like polished marble. Occasional cascades of runoff splattered down to pool on the narrow ledge where she walked before they spilled over into the darkness below. Smaller trickles fell from the travertine draperies and stalagmites that filled the passage above her head. Uhura had learned the hard way to be wary of them. Her sturdy cave helmet protected her from bumps, but it also had an unfortunate tendency to divert trickles of water right down the back of her neck. The nano-woven fabric of her cave jumper wicked away the moisture, but it couldn't protect her from the shiver of cold that came with each unexpected drip.

"You know what I'd like to see?" asked a voice from the darkness ahead of Uhura.

She thought for a moment, then suggested, "A concession stand?"

"Hey, good idea!" The pleasant tenor could have belonged to any of the three men on the rescue team, but only caving expert Zap Sanner could sound so nonchalant after the hours they'd spent threading through this cold, wet maze. Uhura saw the misty glow of his carbide lamp appear around the shoulder of rock in front of her, followed a moment later by his scratched and dented caving helmet. "How about one with a transporter pad built in, for all us wimps who don't want to finish the all-day tour?"

"I'd settle for one with a restroom." Uhura shifted back a step along the ledge, to where the footing was a little flatter and drier. If Sanner was backtracking, that meant he intended to confer with the rest of the rescue team and perhaps make them retrace their steps. Again.

The geologist confirmed her guess by hunkering down on the edge of the bedrock ledge they'd been following, his muddy arms folded across his knees. "I'd settle for a tape measure, to see just how far down this solution fracture goes."

"Why? So you could figure out how long it would take you to fall if you slipped?" The caustic female voice was followed by a third halo of light inching its way forward beneath the overhanging flowstone. Medic

Diana Wright was even shorter than Uhura, but built along sturdier lines. She had to be careful to keep her shoulders parallel to the rock face so as not to overbalance and tip backward into the open chasm, which made the tartness of her voice a little more understandable. "Maybe you could take a tricorder reading while you were going down."

Fortunately, Sanner was as good-natured as he was oblivious to cold and damp. "You'd probably get a better measurement by counting how many seconds it took before you heard me hit the bottom." He gave his geologic tricorder an exasperated look. "Even using Mr. Spock's error-averaging technique, I'm pretty sure I can spit farther than this thing can scan right now."

"Want to try another chemical battery?" Angela Martine came around the curving passage in Wright's wake. Even after two hours of cave exploration, the weapons officer looked barely encumbered by her pack-load of power sources. Uhura felt almost guilty about carrying a light day pack with only rations and water and a narrow-beam communicator inside. She had offered to share Martine's load, and had been politely but firmly turned down. All she could do now was squeeze a little closer to Sanner, to make more room in the curving passage for the arriving members of the team.

"It's not the battery," Sanner was saying. "It's the weird subspace interference that comes out of the rocks down here. It's like it reaches out and grabs whatever power is flowing through the electronic circuits, so no matter how much the battery generates, it's never enough. All my data looks wacky now, even the stuff I collected before when Mr. Spock's averaging program was working." He glanced up at the rest of the team. "Are your instruments working any better?"

Uhura carefully wriggled out of her backpack and slid the narrow-beam communicator out of its waterproof case. The last time she'd used it, it had been able to open a subspace channel to the *Enterprise,* but the internal amplifier hadn't been able to separate words from the fierce crackle of static. She hoped the computers on the ship had been able to process her status report out of the subspace background noise. Whether the source of the problem was a transperiodic ore deposit or not, there was no doubt they were drawing closer to it. When Uhura toggled the communicator this time, the dim glow of the wavelength monitor didn't show a single frequency open for hailing.

"We've got no subspace reception," she reported. "The ship may be able to track our signal with its sensors, but we can't hear them and we can't hail them."

Diana Wright freed her medical tricorder from where she had slung it beneath one arm and bent her carbide light directly on it. The tricorder came to life with a chirp that sounded odd even to Uhura. After a moment, Wright looked up at them with a wry smile.

"Here's how well my instrument is working. According to it, we all have Andorian distemper."

Martine snorted, dropping her pack beside her and hunkering down on her heels to sort through it. "Is that fatal?"

"Only if you're an Andorian camel. Which, apparently, is what we now are." The medic snapped her instrument shut and stowed it back under her arm. "What about your phasers, Martine?"

"Their circuits are working," said the weapons officer, lifting one up to carbide lamp level to run an internal check. "But if you keep them fully charged, they lose power at a ridiculous rate. I have them all drained and disconnected now, so we'll have to snap in new charge units if we need them. And I'm not sure how long they'll hold out."

"Then let's hope we don't need them." James Kirk came through the curve of passage behind them, as sure-footed and secure as if the wet ledge of bedrock were his own bridge deck. He was shadowed by the smaller and stockier figure of the young command-track ensign he'd brought along to carry the rescue gear and map the cave the old-fashioned way, drawing all of its twists and turns in a waterproof plastisheet notebook. Uhura hadn't quite caught the ensign's name when he'd first been introduced, and all she remembered now was that it was something Slavic.

"Do we have a problem, Mr. Sanner?" The glow from Kirk's carbide lamp brightened as he turned up his water drip, then swung around until it faced the cave specialist. Still, it barely made enough of a dent in the darkness around them to reveal the frown on Sanner's mud-streaked face. "Have we lost the trail of Survey Team Three?"

"Not exactly," said the geologist.

"Then what exactly have we done?" Kirk inquired. It was hard to see his expression beneath the glare of the carbide lamp, but Uhura knew that tone well enough to straighten up automatically, even in the darkness.

"We ran out of cave," Sanner said baldly. "This passage ends around the corner."

The silence that followed his remark was the thudding kind Uhura usually associated with stand-offs between groups of armed men. Oddly enough, it was the quiet young ensign who broke it. "So we're on another sidetrack?" he asked stoically, pulling out his notebook and flipping through to find the most recent page.

"No." Sanner took off his helmet and turned it around in his hands, slanting it down along the wall of the vertical fracture. About a meter in front of Uhura, the unmistakable print of a human hand gleamed on the rock face, outlined by diverted runnels of cave water. "Survey Team Three came through here. They left prints on the travertine all the way to the end." He put his helmet back on with a snort. "I thought Jaeger knew better than to let them touch flowstone with their bare hands like that. It poisons the crystal growth faces and kills the formation."

"Maybe they'd lost their lights by the time they got here," Angela Martine said quietly. "Holding onto the wall might have been their only way to keep from falling."

"But if they came this way, where are they now?" Wright asked. "We went down every cave passage that looked like it might be worth following. Every time, we either came to a dead end or saw no evidence that Survey Team Three had gone any farther than we did."

"So they're not behind us," Uhura said. "And if they can't be ahead of us, either—"

"—then there's only one place they can be." The geologist leaned out over the chasm, angling his carbide lamp to catch the narrow ribbons of water that spilled off the ledge, disappearing into glitter and dark. "Which is why I wish I could see how far down this goes."

Kirk leaned over, too, adding his carbide glow to Sanner's. The mist-filled depths stayed obstinately dark. "Why would they have climbed down there?"

"To see if it goes," Sanner said, as if that explained everything. Their silence must have told him that it didn't. "There's lots of times like this when you're exploring caves and it looks like you've come to a dead end. But if you just keep poking around in the little cracks and roof holes and pinches, you can get through to whole new sections of the cave."

"This," said Kirk wryly, "is not what I'd call a little crack."

"No," Sanner admitted. "If there was any other hole that looked more promising, I'd be squirming through it now. But we didn't see any good side passages coming here, and there's no use going up a vertical solution fracture. It always just narrows upward, and it hardly ever leads to another section of the cave." He jerked a thumb at the water cascading from their rock ledge. "The real cave development is always down where that stuff goes. That's where rocks get dissolved the most."

"And you think Lieutenant Jaeger would have known that?" Kirk asked.

"We've gone caving together on at least a dozen planets, sir. I know if I'd gotten to this point and still had my lights, I'd be trying to get a little farther through." Sanner sighed and wriggled out of his backpack. "I hate to throw our one rope ladder down there when we don't know how deep it is or how jagged the rocks are at the bottom, but the damn tricorder can't scan past the end of

63

my arm. We'll have to hope this is close to where those guys went down—"

"Wait, Mr. Sanner." Kirk sounded thoughtful. "You say you've caved with Jaeger. If he had any inkling that his lights and survey instruments were on the verge of losing power, would he have still gone down into this fracture?"

"No, sir," Sanner said emphatically. "No way. The first rule of cave exploration is to head back out at the first sign of anything going wrong."

"So if we're sure Survey Team Three went down this crack, that means they still had full power for their lights." Kirk reached up to tap the lamp on his helmet, making some of the rocks inside rattle and hiss out more of their flammable gas. "Our carbide lamps are probably one-tenth as strong as the photon lanterns the survey team carried. They must have been able to see much further down, maybe even spotted an opening…"

"Possibly, sir," Sanner agreed. "But we can't see what they saw. Our best bet is to go down right here, so we don't miss their trail."

"You're assuming the bottom is accessible everywhere." Kirk glanced along the narrow rock ledge they stood on, then moved to stamp his foot down hard on an out-thrust part of the rim. A large section of rock broke off and plummeted into the crevice below. It vanished into the mist and darkness, but they clearly heard the splash that echoed up after it. It sounded as if had hit fairly deep water. "I'd rather not have to swim once we got down there, Mr. Sanner."

"Me, either." Sanner scrubbed thoughtfully at his chin, leaving mud streaks from his caving gloves.

"Maybe we could lower the rope with someone on it in a couple places, to see how accessible the bottom is."

"I've got a better idea." Kirk held out a hand to Martine and she gave him the phaser she was still holding. "Let's charge up three or four of the weapons and fire some wide-angle sprays at low power into the crevice. They should be able to light the place up so we can see what Survey Team Three saw." He handed the weapon he was holding back to the young ensign. "Lieutenant Uhura, you take one, too. I want you and Mr. Chekov to concentrate your firing on the upper parts of the fracture. Ensign Martine and I will aim for the lower, narrow parts."

"Aye sir." Uhura took the phaser and charge unit Martine had handed to Wright. She started to insert the charge unit into the butt of the weapon, then paused. "Power up now, or on your signal, Captain?"

"On my signal, for maximum illumination," Kirk said. Out of the corner of her eye, Uhura saw the young command-track ensign hurriedly eject his charge unit, then stand with his shoulders a little hunched, as if he expected to be called on his mistake. She wished she had a chance to tell him that on a real landing mission like this, he wasn't being graded on his performance.

Martine handed the captain a phaser, then extracted a fourth one for herself. "We could spread out a little farther, sir, and still overlap our light on wide-spray," she suggested to Kirk.

The captain nodded. "Mr. Chekov, go a few meters back down the passage. Lieutenant Uhura, follow Mr. Sanner a few meters further ahead. Fire on my signal."

Uhura moved along the ledge toward the shoulder of

wet rock at its end, leaving just enough room for Sanner to stand and watch the light show. She turned and adjusted the phaser, then aimed it toward the upper parts of the chasm. "Ready, sir," she said, and heard a Russian-accented voice echo hers from further down the passage.

"On my mark," said Kirk. "Fire."

The wide-spray beam of the phasers dazzled Uhura's sight for a moment. Her eyes quickly adjusted to the brighter light, but all she could see inside the chasm was a chandelier glitter of falling water drops and the mirror-sharp reflection of standing water below. The walls on both sides of the vertical cavern looked as smooth and opaque as poured milk.

"Nothing here, or around the corner," reported Sanner.

"Cease fire," Kirk ordered. It took Uhura's eyes longer to adjust back down to the warm carbide glow of their helmet lamps. She glanced at her phaser's charge readout and could barely believe what it told her.

"Captain, my power unit is nearly drained!"

"Mine, too." Kirk unclipped the power cell from his phaser, frowning. "We must be close to whatever is leaching power out of them. How many more cells do we have, Ensign Martine?"

"Fifteen, sir."

"Then from now on, we'd better fire only two at a time." Kirk turned to retrace their steps. The glow of his carbide lamp sketched a glittering path along the wet walls, then snagged on the motionless figure at the end of the line. "Is something wrong, Mr. Chekov?"

"No, sir." The young man hurriedly turned to go, then

glanced over his shoulder with the tentative look that ensigns often got when they weren't sure they had the right to state their own opinions. "Begging the captain's pardon—is it my imagination, sir, or has it gotten colder in here since we fired the phasers?"

"Colder?" Kirk repeated. "Why would it get colder?"

Uhura paused to let Wright take her time on a particularly wet and treacherous part of the ledge. As soon as she stopped moving, she felt it, too—a chilly bite in the dank air that hadn't been there before. "I think Mr. Chekov's right, Captain," she said, and got a grateful look from the young ensign. "I feel colder, too."

"We might be passing an opening to another cave passage. Sometimes, the first clue is that you feel a draft." Sanner peeled off one of his caving gloves and waved his bare hand through the air as they continued along the ledge. "It does feel like it's getting colder along here. Captain, could we fire the phasers again?"

Kirk took the power cell Martine held out to him, and passed it along to Chekov. "Mr. Chekov, you aim high. Ensign Martine, you'll fire with him. Lieutenant Uhura and I will wait for the next section of cave. Ready?"

"Aye, sir," said Martine and Chekov in unison.

"Fire."

Once again, the brilliant white of phaser light flashed out in the cavern, chasing all the shadows out of the dangling stalactites and turning the blackness below them into a glittering fountain of white falling water. Uhura scanned the rock walls on either side of the cascade, and saw only long spans of travertine laced with occasional balconies of thicker flowstone. She craned her head to see if there was a pool of water in the bottom of this section, too, but before she could even catch a glimpse of mirrored reflection, the phaser light flickered and died.

"The power cells drained faster this time, Captain," Martine reported grimly.

"I noticed. Mr. Sanner, any sign of a passage?"

"No." The geologist motioned them to continue onward. "But there's got to be one around here somewhere, sir. Feel how cold it's getting?"

No one answered him, because no one needed to. The cave air, formerly cool and soft with underground humidity, now held an almost wintry bite. Uhura shivered, chilled for a moment before the temperature-sensing fibers of her cave jumper measured the change and adjusted their insulating capacity upward.

"I know it wasn't this cold the first time we came through here, because I'm not sweating at all this time." Wright glanced down into the chasm beneath their feet and grimaced. "And I'm just as scared now as I was then."

Angela Martine cleared her throat. "Could we be affecting the temperature by firing the phasers? Maybe we're helping to open the cave up further every time we fire."

"Or maybe the phasers are catalyzing some kind of reaction in the transperiodic ore deposit," Sanner suggested. "If it's undergoing some kind of chemical change, that could explain the weird subspace static and power fluxes that we're seeing down here."

"Be that as it may," Kirk said crisply. "It doesn't alter the fact that some of my crewmen are trapped somewhere inside this cave, and we have to find out where they are. We need to keep firing the phasers, even if it does make us a little colder than we were before." They rounded another curving twist in the passage, and the sound of falling water grew fainter below. "This seems like a good spot to check. Lieutenant Uhura, are you ready?"

Uhura slid the new power cell Martine handed her into her phaser, leaving it just short of making contact. "Ready, sir."

"Fire on my mark." Kirk lifted his own phaser, then slapped the power cell into it in one smooth motion. "Fire!"

Uhura tamped the power cell down and triggered the wide-angle phaser spray. Her eyes seemed to adapt faster this time to the white dazzle of light—or was that dazzle a little less white than it had been before? It was certainly shorter. Before Uhura even had time to glance away from the phaser's rapidly falling power indicator, the bright light flickered and faded away. As it did, a distinct arctic chill swept through the cave, accompanied by an almost subliminal crackling. Uhura could feel her cave jumper hum with the effort to tighten its weave even further and maintain her body heat against the sapping cold.

"I think I saw something," Sanner said urgently. He leaned out over the chasm and angled his carbide reflector downward, but the hazy light made no headway against the darkness below. "There's still water down there, but there seemed to be some kind of opening along the side wall, just a little further down the way we came."

"Let's see if we can get one more good look at it." Kirk held out his hand to Martine for another power cell, then fired his phaser in the direction Sanner pointed. The flash was fierce but swift, more like the glare of a bursting photon torpedo than a weapon designed for hours of steady use. In that burst of light, however, even Uhura caught a glimpse of the shadowy arch of something that looked almost like a window set into the travertine walls of the fracture.

"That's it." Sanner's breath misted in the frigid air, frosting immediately into tiny ice crystals. He seemed too excited to care. "I know Jaeger would climb down to look at that, if he still had lots of power."

"Then that's where we're going." Kirk pocketed his phaser, and swung around on the ledge, gesturing Chekov to begin moving again. Their carbide lights seemed to Uhura to spark an unusually bright glitter off the cave walls near them. She froze abruptly, her muscles locking up before her brain had even finished putting together bits and pieces of what she'd glimpsed.

"Careful!" she called out, when she finally realized what she had seen. "The run-off is starting to freeze—"

Her warning came too late. She saw one of Kirk's boots slip out from under him, but the captain's quick reflexes let him grab onto the travertine wall and pull himself back to safety. The young ensign named Chekov wasn't so lucky. Both feet slipped out from under him on the ice-slicked ledge and his grab at the wall caught only air. With a sound more like a gasp than a yell, he went plunging down into darkness.

Kirk crooked his fingers into the wall's irregularities, suspended his breathing, and willed his weight to drift forward over his toes instead of backward into the abyss. He hovered with his cheek not quite touching the slick travertine only because the alignment of muscles and bones had accidentally placed him here. As if to punctuate the delicacy of his position, he heard the fragile shattering of the water's surface somewhere behind him and unknowably far below. He intuited what had happened even though he didn't dare crane his head around to see. "Sanner!"

He didn't have to ask the question outright—the geologist wasted neither words nor time. "The kid's down." The scrape and clatter of boots and equipment belts as Sanner scrambled to some new position. "I can't see his light." Another moment's pause, this time filled with a brisk ripping sound as Sanner tore open his pack. "It'll take me a minute to tie off the ladder—"

Then there was no point spending even longer discussing it. "Do it. Meet us down there as close to Jaeger's exit as you can."

"Captain, I wouldn't—!" One of the woman. Kirk assumed it was Wright. It didn't matter—before she'd finished her warning, he'd let his balance deviate the necessary hair's breadth. He was already so close to falling that the mere thought of doing it made it so.

The moment's free fall rushed past more quickly than Kirk expected. He had time for one instant of surreal panic as the total darkness swallowed his lantern flame in the wind of his fall, then razor-bright cold crashed around him and sucked him into silence.

His whole body seized once, violently, in reaction. He'd clenched his teeth before impact with the water, so was only able to take in an agonizing noseful when his lungs tried to gasp. He thought about Chekov, unprepared for both the drop and the landing, and felt a pulse of adrenaline bring his body back under his control. He tried to remember how long someone could go without breathing while immersed in frigid water—he knew it was longer than under normal circumstances, but the exact figure wasn't the sort of detail he'd thought to memorize in his capacity as a starship commander. His lack of foresight irritated him now.

The smooth irregularity of flowstone bumped against his hip. Twisting to find the solid bottom with one hand, Kirk brought his feet under him and pushed off. But instead of breaking into air, he glided a too-long distance only to fumble headfirst into another expanse of rock. He felt his way in the direction all his instincts said was upward, found himself jammed shoulder-to-shoulder between two equally impenetrable surfaces, surged away from that confinement into limbo again. Why hadn't he anticipated this disorienting darkness? *Too used to waterproof lights.* It hadn't even occurred to him that carbide would be useless underwater. The edge of panic he'd tasted earlier flooded his mouth, threatened to ambush his common sense and leave him flailing. Kirk fought the animal impulse to gasp for air—any air!—and concentrated instead on stilling his thoughts and calming down his pounding heart.

Common sense. He couldn't see, he couldn't hear, he couldn't breathe, but gravity still functioned. Kirk's body and his equipment pack were both heavier than water, which meant they would sink straight down, given half a chance. Expelling the stale air he'd been hoarding, Kirk tried to notice the feel of the bubbles as they rolled past his face, tried to sense toward which direction they were rising. He couldn't. So he slipped his pack off his back and dangled it from one hand, barely maintaining a hold on its strap so that gravity could take it from him and draw it away. If this didn't work, there were no other options. He'd blown away any second chances with his last lungful of air.

Kirk didn't feel the pack try to sink, only a vague tension in his arm in response to its heaviness. He counted his heartbeats to keep from focusing on the deepening burn in his airless lungs. *One. Two. Three.* The pack's weight seemed to abate slightly, his floating body equalizing with its new lack of movement. *Four. Five.* Still gripping its strap in his fist, Kirk carefully brought his feet down to find the stone on either side of the sunken pack. This was bottom. This was *down.* He tipped his head back to face the darkness beyond his head. So this direction could only be *up.* Had to be up, or he and Chekov would drown down here forever and the ship would never recover their bodies.

Sixseveneight!

His heels struck hard into the rock, pistoning him toward air. Kirk thought he felt himself move upward, then jolted painfully as instead the pack was ripped from his grasp and his legs, shoulder, torso tangled sideways into rock that was both there and too rapidly falling away. A rumble like dull thunder, or distant rapids, exploded suddenly into the crash of water onto open stone as frigid air replaced freezing water. Kirk gulped in a breath so cold and desperate it hurt, even as he realized that he was not only free of the water, he was falling.

Then he hit bottom for a second time, this time with all the force of gravitational acceleration. He tried to roll with the landing, but couldn't time himself without being able to see the ground. The rock floor smashed away the breath he'd just taken, cracking against his helmet like a thrown boulder and battering him with a heavy curtain of water. He dragged himself over onto his belly and buried his face against his arms. He still couldn't breathe, but at least he could avoid the irony of drowning while stretched out in the open air.

Faint movement, barely loud enough to hear over the cascading water, caught his attention from what seemed only a short distance away. Kirk pushed up on his elbows and turned to look out of instinct. Nothing. Only the same unyielding black that had enveloped him since his carbide snuffed out on the way down.

But he wasn't underwater anymore. Or, at least, he didn't have to be. Pulling himself up onto hands and knees, he crawled forward, away from the already-weakening torrent. High above him, the birdlike shrilling of whistles danced off the cave walls, punctuated by the occasional bellow of a masculine voice. *As soon as I get my wind back, I'll answer you,* Kirk promised Sanner and the others. Although they sounded impossibly farther away now. Whatever he and Chekov had fallen through—however they had fallen through it—they were now several meters further down in a cave that had already swallowed one landing party.

Nano-weave hugged him more tightly as he finally dragged himself completely free of the waterfall. It sounded like little more than a bathtub faucet turned up to maximum now, still rumbling and threatening, but rapidly losing the ability to damage anything. Or so Kirk hoped. Clawing loose the chin strap, he rolled onto his knees and leveled the helmet across his lap. Cold fingers found the lumpy outlines of his carbide lantern, traced it until he found the round reflector and its attached striking mechanism. A quick sniff verified that the distinctively acid smell of acetylene still hissed from the pilot hole, but he had to thumb the striking wheel five or six times before the waterlogged apparatus finally rewarded him with a spark. Light shattered the darkness with a tiny *puff!*, and a flame no longer than the end of Kirk's thumb pirouetted in front of the shiny reflector like a vain ballerina. The illumination was so welcome, he didn't even resent the pain it drove through his dark-adapted eyes.

After long moments of darkness, the tiny shred of fire might have been a supernova. Kirk spotted Chekov immediately, barely raised up on his elbows not far from where a steady rivulet of water still drizzled from the ceiling. At least he was breathing, Kirk thought with almost dizzying relief. At least he didn't have to write a letter home to the boy's poor mother, explaining how he'd dragged her son halfway across the galaxy just to drown him on the very first planet he visited.

"Mr. Chekov?" Kirk didn't really expect a reply. The boy was busy coughing out all the water he'd taken in, and was having trouble enough breathing between spasms to try and make conversation. But Kirk wanted him to know he wasn't down here alone. "Sorry if dropping us from a great height wasn't very graceful. I'm a little rusty on my lifeguard technique."

Chekov, still coughing, nodded as though his captain had offered the most reasonable explanation in the world. It occurred to Kirk that Chekov was either too busy trying to breathe to pay him much attention, or the boy didn't have a sense of humor. The latter possibility reminded Kirk of Spock, and made him smile a little. He tried to hide the expression by turning away to blow a quick blast on his whistle. Up above, Sanner's whistle answered in frantic staccato, then fell silent.

"Well, let's have a look at where we are." Pushing to his feet, Kirk dialed the flame on his helmet light to maximum before holding it out at arm's length and turning in a slow circle. The tunnel surrounding them was maybe twice as wide as one of the *Enterprise*'s corridors, and taller again by half. A surprisingly regular hole—and the clutter of rocks beneath it—marked where Kirk had kicked through the smooth, domed ceiling in an effort to find the water's surface. So the roof of the tunnel was the bottom of the lake. Or what used to be the lake—icicles were already accreting around the edges of the hole as the last of the trapped water dribbled down to join the stream now slithering off away from them across the floor. But it wasn't the water, or the rapidly crystalizing ice, that riveted Kirk's attention near where the dark, corrugated walls met the ceiling. He took a slow step closer, lifting the helmet light higher over his head to illuminate the uppermost corners.

"I don't understand...." He heard Chekov climb shakily to his feet, following a few steps behind. His voice still sounded thick with inhaled water. "How did we get here? Where are the others?"

"On their way down to join us, no doubt." A strip of what might have been wainscoting ribbonned the upper wall, obviously a refined metal for all that time and water had frosted it as dark as tarnished silver. Rusty streaks wept down its rippled surface, neatly tracing the spidery-thin etchings that decorated its surface like scattered grains of rice. "I have a feeling this isn't flowstone."

Chekov moved up next to him, just into his line of sight, and squinted upward toward where Kirk aimed the light. The blue chill to his lips worried Kirk a little, but he was reassured by the keen intensity with which the boy studied the rows of alien markings. "It's writing," Chekov said at last, with a sort of dull certainty that caught Kirk by surprise.

The captain nodded slowly. "Possibly. It's certainly not anything natural." Then he smiled down at this new member of his crew as the thought suddenly occurred to him. "Congratulations, Ensign Chekov. You've just discovered your first alien artifact."

Chapter Five

"WATCH THE LAST FEW STEPS," Sanner yelled up through the rush and pour of falling water. "They're icy!"

Great, Uhura thought, tightening her grip on the rungs of the rope ladder. *It's not bad enough that I'm climbing down through a waterfall. It has to be a freezing waterfall.*

She wished she could take a deep breath to ease the tightness in her chest, but at the moment there was too much water splashing around her to make that safe. The chasm above her drained itself in fits and starts into this new lower level of the cave system. When she had started down the ladder, the rush of water had been a mere trickle, but another section of ponded cave runoff must have broken through and was now pouring itself down this new drain. The icy water had drenched her so thoroughly that her carbide lamp had gone out and the

78

wicking fibers of her jumper had expanded like foam in a vain effort to keep her dry. Uhura ducked her head below one shielding arm to take a breath, and still got enough water mixed with her air to make her cough as she took another step down the ladder.

There was no time to stop and clear her throat. Uhura felt the polymer strands jerk and twist as Martine swung onto the rope ladder from the cave ledge above her. The fear of getting her hands stepped on sent her down the next few rungs a little faster than she'd intended. When she hit the strand of rope that was slick with ice, her boot sole skidded off so violently that it took her other foothold with it. Uhura was left dangling from gloved hands, swinging her feet through buffeting water as she tried to find ladder rungs she couldn't see.

"You're almost down!" Sanner's voice barely cut through the clatter of water hitting the jagged edges of travertine through which Kirk and Chekov had fallen. "You can slide from there!"

Uhura tried to cast a glance down to make sure he was right, but all she could make out were watery shadows silhouetted against a dim carbide glow. She swung her gloved hands around to the outside of the rope ladder and tightened her grip as much as she could, then deliberately let herself drop. It wasn't until after she began sliding that she felt the icy slickness of the rope ladder's sides as well as its rungs. Her pace downward quickened alarmingly, despite her fierce grip.

"Got you," said a calm tenor voice, and Uhura felt herself plucked from the ladder and swung out of the rush of water in one smooth movement.

"Thanks—I think!" Uhura swiped the water from her face and scowled upward, intending to give Sanner a piece of her mind about his advice to slide. To her surprise, the face that gazed down at her was youthful, and lit with amused hazel eyes.

"Yes, Lieutenant?" Kirk asked blandly.

"Nothing, sir."

He smiled and turned away, ducking back out under the icy waterfall to join Sanner at the base of the rope ladder. The light went with him, and Uhura hurriedly took off her helmet to fumble with its extinguished carbide light. It ignited on the second try, its glow reaching out until it touched the rounded surfaces of a conduit ten feet in diameter and as smooth as the inside of a pipe. The passage sloped slightly, making a gradient that pulled the cave runoff down into darkness on the far side of its new plunge pool. Thin veils of mist shredded off the waterfall as it slowed back to a trickle again, making Uhura wish she'd waited just a few minutes more before she'd made her descent. The mist turned instantly to ice in the frigid air, some of it clinging like hoarfrost to the shards of rusty metal and shattered travertine that littered the conduit floor. The rest swirled in the drafty breeze, forming a fog of tiny ice crystals that made breathing unpleasant and visibility poor.

Uhura picked her way carefully up the sloping conduit, heading for a vague clot of lamplight she could see through the murk. Her movement sent water trickling down her cave jumper in thick runnels as its nanofibers wrung themselves dry, wicking off the water she'd absorbed on her way down the waterfall. Unfortunately, since her hair wasn't made of microscopically engineered polymers, it remained completely sodden. Uhura just hoped it wouldn't freeze to her helmet. The cave air felt even more glacial down here than it had in the vertical chasm above.

As she came closer to the carbide light, she could see Diana Wright crouched near the huddled figure of Ensign Chekov. The young Russian was shivering despite his cave jumper's insulation, and breathing so harshly that at times it almost sounded as if he were strangling.

"Hang on, kid." Wright loaded medicine from a vial into the tube of her hypospray, then pressed it to Chekov's throat above the collar of his cave jumper. "That should help you breathe a little better. Can you stand up and move around? You need to generate some kinetic energy so your jumper can pump all that absorbed water out. That's why you feel so cold."

"I don't—" Chekov broke off with a grimace, pushing himself halfway to his feet. Uhura hurried forward and helped Wright haul him the rest of the way up and then push him gently into motion. He walked between them obediently enough, his breath easing to a rasp as the medication took hold, but shivers still racked his body. A wet sheen began to coat his jumper as the polymer expelled its absorbed water.

"I'm not sure how I got here," the young man blurted after a moment, as if it were a shameful confession he had to make. "I told the captain, but he didn't say anything."

Uhura and Wright exchanged speculative looks behind his back. "You don't remember falling into the cave?" the medic asked. She began to examine his skull under his hair, dark and slick as a seal's coat with the water it had absorbed. "You might have gotten a concussion after you lost your helmet. Does your head hurt anywhere?"

"No," Chekov said. "And I do remember falling. There was ice on the ledge, right after we fired the phasers." He shivered again, strongly enough that Uhura almost lost her grip on his shoulder. "It just seems like that was a long while ago. Didn't something else happen after that?"

"Captain Kirk jumped in after you," Uhura told him. "You broke through the bottom of the cave into this level, and then he whistled so we knew you were here. Maybe that's what you're remembering."

"It must be." Despite his words, the young man didn't sound entirely convinced. He glanced at the conduit around them as they moved further up its gentle slope. The double glow of Uhura's and Wright's carbide lamps clearly showed its artificial curvature, unbroken here by jagged rents or waterfalls. "The first thing I remember clearly is lying on my back and coughing while the captain lit his carbide light. Then he found some kind of alien artifact…"

"You can take the credit for that discovery, Mr. Chekov." Captain Kirk materialized out of the chilly mist as if he'd just transported in. Sanner and Martine followed him, their cave jumpers and backpacks glistening with extruded water in the gathered light. "We never would have seen it if you hadn't fallen in where you did. It's on the wall over here." He stepped past Chekov and Wright, crossing the conduit until his carbide light finally drove the darkness back from the far side. "Any idea what it might be, Lieutenant Uhura?"

Chekov seemed a little steadier on his feet now that his cave jumper had drained out most of its water. Uhura released him and went to add her light to the captain's. Several rows of rice-like markings jumped into high relief under the double illumination. It looked as if they'd been engraved into the rust-streaked metal of the passage wall, rather than being painted on it. Perhaps that was why they'd survived as long as the cave itself.

"It's definitely an alien script, Captain. The breaks and repetitions make it look like a series of phonemes, but I've never seen any alphabet quite like it before." Uhura glanced over her shoulder at Sanner. "I don't suppose we can take a visual recording?"

"With this thing?" The cave specialist hefted his tricorder with a snort. "Only if you draw on the screen with a real sharp rock."

"You could make a copy by hand, in Mr. Chekov's map book," Martine suggested. She was peering at the writing and didn't see the effect of her words, but Uhura was still looking back at the rest of the group. She saw the young ensign slide his hand automatically into the chest pocket of his cave jumper, then jerk in dismay when it came out empty.

"Captain, the map—" Chekov stopped and swallowed when Kirk turned to face him. The light of the captain's carbide lamp showed them all the young ensign's stricken expression. "Sir, I don't have it anymore."

* * *

"Commander Spock, I'm adjusting orbit again."

Sulu didn't wait for a response from the first officer. This was the third time he'd had to correct the ship's heading in the past hour, and the procedure had become almost routine. Almost. Despite Spock's intensive use of the ship's scanners and sensors, they still had no idea where these inexplicable losses of altitude were coming from. That uncertainty bothered Sulu more than he cared to admit.

It was true that whatever force Tlaoli was exerting on them was trivial compared to the power of the *Enterprise*'s warp drive. Even their sublight impulse engines barely needed to be pulsed in order to bump the ship back up into stable orbit. Chief Engineer Scott thought they were encountering a subspace anomaly in Tlaoli's gravity well, and had suggested programming an automatic correction into the impulse engines. But something in Sulu balked at the idea of not knowing exactly when and how the orbital changes were occurring. He had an uncomfortable image of all the ships now rotting on the planet's surface having made just such an automatic adjustment right before they fell out of the sky. Besides, whatever was affecting the ship didn't feel like gravity fluctuations to Sulu; they felt like the tug of a more purposeful force. And the only clues to what that force might be were the timing and magnitude of the shifts themselves.

"Was the adjustment within the usual parameters?" Spock inquired without looking up from the communications station. He had temporarily evicted Lieutenant Palmer from her post in an attempt to augment the ship's signal discrimination amplifiers. Tantalizing flashes of contact had been coming in from the surface of Tlaoli, brief bursts of unusual subspace static from the vicinity of the caves. Only the timing of the bursts, received at precise fifteen-minute intervals, marked them as attempts at communication. No actual message could be filtered out of the snarl of subspace noise.

Sulu checked the helm records to verify his manual adjustment. "Yes, sir. Six percent decay, initiated thirteen minutes after the previous shift."

The science officer made a noise that was almost, but not quite, a sigh of frustration. "Unfortunately, I do not believe the addition of that data point will allow the computer to identify the origin of these anomalies. Until we see a shift large enough to extrapolate a vector of interaction, we will remain ignorant of the root cause of these diversions."

"Spock, why don't you just come out and say that you don't know what the hell is going on?" Leonard McCoy had come up onto the bridge half an hour ago, ostensibly to check on Sulu's and Kevin Riley's vital signs, but more likely to keep a watchful eye on their efforts to contact the captain's rescue team. Sulu wasn't sure if McCoy actually doubted the first officer's leadership, or if he just didn't trust the junior bridge officers to ask the kind of blunt and probing questions he did. "Anyway, isn't our real problem that we can't contact the rescue team?"

"No, Doctor," Spock said evenly. "That is our *immediate* problem. Given the evidence of the previous starships which have crashed on this planet, I suspect the real problem is something much larger and more fundamental, which is causing both our loss of altitude and the captain's loss of contact."

McCoy groaned. "Please don't tell me we've got another planet getting ready to blow up on us. I don't think I could deal with that."

Spock lifted an unsympathetic eyebrow. "Your emotional condition is irrelevant to the discussion, Doctor. At the moment, all the evidence suggests that Tlaoli is stable but generating some kind of anomalous force whose interactions with us cannot be predicted. Whether or not that force derives from a natural transperiodic ore deposit—which seems doubtful—it certainly does appear to coincide with the region of caves Survey Team Three was exploring. If we could determine the nature of that anomaly, we might be able to neutralize it sufficiently to keep the *Enterprise* safe, and to rescue the lost survey team and the captain's party."

"And if we can't determine its nature?" McCoy demanded.

The Vulcan lowered his voice, but Sulu was still close enough to the command console to hear his grave reply. "Then, Doctor, there is a statistically significant chance that we will become the twentieth starship to crash on this planet."

There was a moment of tense silence inside the fog-shrouded darkness of the alien cave. Then Captain James T. Kirk did the kind of thing that made his crewmen willing to follow him into Hell. He didn't swear, exclaim in surprise, or even ask young Ensign Chekov how he could have possibly lost the only map of their escape route. Instead, Kirk said matter-of-factly, "After the dunking you got, Mr. Chekov, that's no surprise. We'll just have to reconstruct it as we go along."

He made the missing map sound like a minor inconvenience, a problem they could rectify with just a little hard work. And Captain Kirk's gift for command, Uhura thought, was that he brought out so much of the best in his crew that he really could turn catastrophes like this into minor inconveniences. She saw the young ensign's shoulders straighten with fierce determination. "Aye-aye, sir." He reached into his backpack for his spare notebook. "I'll start on it right away."

"Good." Kirk swung around and eyed the dark length of passage that ran uphill, away from the trickling waterfall and their dangling rope ladder. "We'll explore this side of the passage first. That should give the cave runoff enough time to finish draining before we go down the other way."

"Let's just hope the survey team isn't down where the water's draining to," Wright said. Uhura flinched, and wished the medic hadn't put that particular fear into words. It was all too easy for her to visualize the landing party trapped without lights in the underground darkness, hearing the rush and spill of oncoming water but unable to get out of its way—

Wright's comment must have had the same effect on the rest of the rescue team. An appalled hush fell over them, made even more intense by the quiet trickle of the plunge pool in the background. Uhura could see Kirk frown and glance back in the direction of the waning waterfall, as if he was reconsidering his decision. Before he could break the silence, however, Angela Martine spoke in an urgent whisper.

"Voices! I hear voices!"

Sanner frowned and opened his mouth, but Kirk gestured him back into silence. "Women hear better than men," he reminded the cave expert, in an almost soundless whisper. "Everyone quiet."

Uhura stiffened, trying to calm her own breathing enough to let her hear past it. At first, all she could sense was the soft drip and splash of water behind them, then above that came an almost inaudible murmur, the distorted and wordless slush that words turned into when they echoed down long stretches of empty space. "I hear them, too," she said. "They're coming from uphill."

Kirk's breath misted out in a small but intense sound of relief. "Start walking—and whistling." He set off at a brisk pace with his own whistle clenched between his teeth. He blew a loud clarion blast, then paused to see if there was a response before he blew again. One by one, all of them joined in until the conduit echoed with the pulse of whistle blast and pause. All except Chekov, that is. The young ensign was intent on sketching a memorized version of his cave map into his plastisheet notebook as they walked, using the borrowed light of Diana Wright's carbide.

The murmur of echoed voices grew to a distant clamor as their conduit joined up with another. They had to pause for a moment to make sure which branch the echo sounded loudest in, but both Uhura and Martine agreed on the steeper of the two paths. After that, the response to their whistles had slowly resolved into a muffled chorus of male and female voices, while the passage curved up into a distinctly engineered spiral. As soon as the word "Help!" resolved from the din, Kirk dropped his whistle and ordered the rest of them to do the same. "This is Captain Kirk, and we're coming to get you," he shouted back. "One person keep shouting, to make sure we don't lose the way."

"Captain!" That was a strong male voice, suddenly sounding energized despite its hoarseness. "We weren't expecting a rescue team from the ship! What are you doing back at Tlaoli so soon?"

"We—" Kirk paused, then apparently decided it would be better not to try and explain the events of the last few days. "We got a little ahead of schedule at Psi 2000."

"That's great!" The voice grew more faint, as if its owner had turned to shout in a different direction. "Hey, guys! It's Captain Kirk!"

There was a pause, then a distant burst of laughter from the lost survey team. "Very funny, Mr. Tomlinson!" This was a different male voice, a little lower-pitched and a lot more exhausted. "So which survey team finally found us, hm? Mr. Fisher's or Mr. Boma's?"

"I'm telling you, it's the captain, with a team from the *Enterprise!*"

"Of course it is. And I am telling you that you don't want to admit you have lost our bet. That would mean that it's Mr. Fisher. Hello, Edward!"

The voices grew clearer as they hiked up the last steep curve of the spiral. "We've got to be getting awfully close to the surface, Captain," Sanner commented. He peeled off one glove and licked his finger, then held it up above his head. "I can feel a draft of warmer air coming through here. We may not need to backtrack all the way through the cave to get out."

Kirk glanced over his shoulder at Chekov, still sketching furiously in his notebook. "Let's not make any assumptions until we know what's going on," he said quietly, then raised his voice. "Survey Team Three, you still there?"

"Nowhere much else to go, Captain," said the first hoarse voice, at surprisingly close range. The conduit suddenly straightened again, and the glow of Kirk's carbide light caught on a mud-sodden figure in a gold jumper standing at the end of it. The young man blinked furiously at what must have seemed to him like a fierce glare of light, but he managed to smile despite that. "With the captain's permission, sir, allow me to say that you are a sight for sore eyes. Er, literally."

"It's good to see you, too, Lieutenant Tomlinson." Kirk was already reaching up to adjust the water flow on his carbide lamp, dampening the rush of acetylene gas. The glow around them dimmed to a softer gold halo as Uhura and the others did the same. "What's the status of your party?"

"Holding up pretty well, sir, after four hours of digging in the dark," said the young weapons officer. He waited for them to reach him, then turned to walk beside Kirk as they climbed up another tight spiral of conduit. "We were pretty sure one of the other survey teams would come looking for us after a few hours. In the meantime we've been trying to clear a path through a pile of cave breakdown that Mr. Jaeger thinks is blocking a natural exit from this upper cavern. Crewman

Davis, our surveyor, got hit by some falling rock and has a pretty bad concussion. We've been taking turns watching to make sure she doesn't lose consciousness. Lieutenant Jaeger has done most of the crawling through the rubble pile, and he's a little banged up. The rest of us are okay."

"You have blood on your hands," Martine noted softly.

Tomlinson glanced over at his fellow weapons officer, and his smile warmed a little at the look of concern he saw on her face. "Yeah, well...caving gloves only last so long when you're trying to dig through rock with your fingers. We were almost getting ready to give up when we heard your whistles, way off in the distance."

"For that you can thank Ensign Chekov—" Kirk's voice broke off abruptly as Tomlinson led them around a final curve of conduit and, without warning, into a space that looked like an underground cathedral. Huge columns of travertine ran from floor to arching ceiling, frosted and laced with flowstone until they looked like tall, thin wedding cakes. A giant rubble pile spilled down the back of the space, and hanging draperies of travertine above it showed where the mineral-laden cave runoff had come from to decorate this space. Above the rubble, the room's smooth, constructed roof had cracked and split upward into a darkness so high that their dimmed carbide lights couldn't chase away all its shadows.

"Wow." Tomlinson paused to regard the jagged spill of boulders. "That looks a lot worse than I remembered from when our lights went out. No wonder we were having so much trouble getting to the top."

"I'd think getting down again would be even worse." Kirk followed the young weapons officer out into the echoing space of the chamber, to where four other survey team members waited around a jumble of packs that had been heaped up to make a bed for the fifth member of the party. They were all blinking like owls at the approach of light, although not as painfully as Tomlinson had done. Their eyes must have had a chance to get accustomed more gradually as the carbide glow of the rescue party spilled through into their cavern.

"Is it really the captain?" asked the woman on the bed, turning to squint in their direction.

"Yes, it is." Kirk headed over to the injured crewman, with Diana Wright nearly treading on his heels. "How are you feeling, Davis?"

"Like someone fired a photon torpedo through my head, sir." The dark-haired woman began to sit up, but Wright was already beside her and had lowered her back down before she could do more than grimace in pain. The medic began unwinding the clumsy blood-stained bandage on the surveyor's head. "Sorry, sir. I really can stand up and walk, if you need me to."

"With any luck, we won't." Kirk glanced around at the other members of the survey team, all mud-stained and exhausted but beaming with the unexpected relief of being rescued by the man they trusted more than anyone else aboard the *Enterprise*. One of them, a stocky young Asian woman in security red, had as many bloody scrapes on her hands as Tomlinson did, although it didn't affect her cheerfully crooked smile. Another, a middle-aged man whom Uhura vaguely remembered from a previous landing party, had a badly swollen eye and a reddish gray bruise spilling down one cheek to meet a fresh cut on the edge of his mouth. His blue cave jumper had long gashes across the shoulders despite its toughly woven nanofibers. Although his facial injuries kept him from smiling, the look he threw at Sanner was definitely amused.

"Carbide lamps, eh, Zap?" The slight trace of a German accent told Uhura this must be Karl Jaeger, the survey team's cave specialist. "Wait until the Society of Interstellar Speleologists hears about that."

Sanner scrubbed at his chin, looking embarrassed. "It was Captain Kirk's idea. When Fisher told us about the power problems you guys were having down here, the captain figured you might have lost your lights. He decided to use something that didn't run on electricity."

"Mr. Fisher had power problems, too?" Jaeger exchanged worried glances with Tomlinson. "He didn't try to bring the research shuttle here to look for us, then, did he?"

"Yes, he did," Kirk said. "And nearly crashed when it lost power, although he didn't say that in quite so many words. But he made it back to the wetland base camp. In fact, he's probably been beamed back aboard ship by now." He glanced around at the members of the lost survey team, clearly noticing the exhaustion on their faces now that the initial excitement of being rescued had faded. "When did you start losing your power?"

"Not for a long while into the trip," said one of the blue-clad women in the party. She lifted a surveying tricorder from the ground beside him and gave it an exasperated look. "Crewman Davis says she got the whole upper level and most of the lower level of the cave mapped into her tricorder before it crashed and lost all the data. That took us almost three hours, didn't it, Lieutenant D'Amato?"

The other male scientist, as muddy and tired as Jaeger, nodded. "But I noticed the first fluctuations in my tricorder when I started to analyze the rocks around the ice cave. That was about half an hour earlier."

"Ice cave?" Kirk demanded.

"A large chamber similar to this one, but at the lower end of the conduit system," Jaeger explained. "It was much colder than the rest of the cave when we first entered it. I initially thought it might be the location of the natural transperiodic ore deposit we were looking for, but that was before we realized this whole structure was an alien installation." He glanced up at his darker-haired colleague. "Lieutenant D'Amato still thinks the power drain is coming from somewhere near that chamber, which was another reason we decided to stay at this end of the caves. We didn't want the other survey teams to run into the same problem we did."

"We thought maybe they would hear us digging and help clear the cave exit from the surface," said Tomlinson. "That way, we could just climb out here instead of retracing the whole trip in."

"With any luck, we won't need to do either of those things now." Kirk glanced around until his gaze found and snagged on Uhura. "Lieutenant, I think it's time to contact the ship."

She blinked, then pulled her narrow-beam communicator out of her pack, seeing from its lack of monitor lights that its chemical battery had died since the last time she'd used it. Martine was already extracting another battery from her backpack. "I can try to hail them, sir." Uhura attached the new power supply, although she left in the inert spacer that kept the chemicals separate until electrical power was required to flow. "But there's so much subspace static on the channel that I'm not sure they can hear anything I'm saying."

"Can they detect that we're hailing them?"

"Yes, sir. As long as Lieutenant Palmer keeps this frequency centered on her receivers, she'll know when it's active. She probably gets a burst of static whenever I call."

"Well, that should work," said Kirk. It was hard to see his expression in the dimmed glow of their lamps, but Uhura thought he was gazing at her impatiently. "Shouldn't it, Lieutenant?"

Uhura felt a small burst of sympathy for Chekov, who must have spent much of his time on this planet feeling as unsure and bewildered as she did now. "Work for what, sir?"

"For sending a message up to the ship." Kirk reached up to tap on his helmet. At first, Uhura thought he was rattling his carbide rocks to make them burn brighter. Then she heard the rhythm he was making, and her eyes widened in comprehension. "We're going to do it just like we're doing everything else on this rescue mission, Lieutenant. The old-fashioned way."

"Commander Spock!" Lieutenant Palmer swung around from the communications panel, her voice loud and excited enough to cut through all the other conversations on the bridge. "I'm getting a signal from the planet!"

Spock's eyebrows lifted abruptly, the closest he ever came to showing surprise. "Put it through, Lieutenant."

"Aye, sir." Palmer swung back to her panel and punched a control there. Sulu grimaced as a burst of static assaulted the bridge of the *Enterprise,* followed by a few seconds of silence, then by an even longer salvo of static. Another silence, another short burst—

"It's Starfleet code!" Palmer said. "Lieutenant Uhura must have guessed that we weren't able to deconvolve her signal, so she's turning her communicator off and on to contact us."

"N," recited Spock, as he listened to the static. "S, P."

"That's not the beginning of the message, sir." Palmer bent over her communications panel, scrolling back the buffer to the beginning of Uhura's coded communication. "It started with T, R and A."

"Transport," Sulu said softly.

He saw Spock nod confirmation as the long-short-long code for the letter "O" crackled through the bridge, followed by the two short bursts that were "R". The static paused for an unusually long time after the final "T", then began the pattern all over again. "She's just repeating that word, sir," Palmer said unnecessarily.

"Then we shall presume that Captain Kirk wishes to be transported back to the ship." Spock leaned over the arm of the command console and activated the ship's intercom. "Bridge to Mr. Scott."

"Scott here."

"Commander, how wide an area can we encompass with the ship's cargo transporter?"

"Depends on how careful you need to be with the cargo," the chief engineer responded. "If you want it beamed in molecule for molecule, then I'd say about four cubic meters."

"Spock!" McCoy took a step closer to where the Vulcan first officer stood near the empty command chair. The doctor's forehead rumpled with the intensity of his scowl. "You're not going to beam up the captain and his team like a pile of packing boxes, are you?"

"I have no choice, Doctor," said Spock patiently. "None of our long-range sensors can focus on the karst terrain, and the landing party's communicators no longer appear to function. Our only solid connection is through Lieutenant Uhura's narrow-beam communicator, and that gives us only a single point coordinate."

"Which is *exactly* why you shouldn't be transporting anyone based on that," McCoy snapped. "If the edge of the transporter beam happens to land halfway through someone's skull, you're going to kill them by beaming them up!"

"I am aware of that, Doctor." Spock templed his fingers and rested his chin against them, a pose that usually meant he was sorting through a complex sequence of logical deductions. "We can presume that the captain is aware of it, too, since he knows we cannot lock on to their communicator signals. If he still wants to be transported out of the cave system, then either he has managed to gather his team into a tight group around Lieutenant Uhura's communicator or—"

He fell silent, as if he didn't think the doctor would appreciate where his logic had led. McCoy's frown deepened, and after a moment he jabbed a finger toward the Vulcan, although Sulu noticed that he didn't quite poke him. "Or *what,* Spock?"

"Or the captain is in such dire straits that the risks of an incomplete transport are outweighed by their need to escape." The Vulcan turned away without waiting for McCoy's response. "Lieutenant Palmer, transfer the frequency of Lieutenant Uhura's narrow-beam signal down to the main cargo transporter, so that Mr. Scott can use it to center the beam."

"Sir, he'd better hurry," said the junior communications officer urgently. "The signal's fading fast."

"I'm on it," said Scotty's voice from the open intraship channel. "I've already got the cargo controls linked through to my console here, and as soon as we get that frequency—aah, there it is. I've got the beam centered, Mr. Spock. On your orders."

Sulu glanced up at the haggard brown crescent that hung in their mostly dark viewscreen. Tlaoli's day side was slowly withering as the system's pale yellow sun swung out of view, in what looked like the most pedestrian of sunsets. What was going on under the surface of that seemingly innocuous planet? he wondered. Had the captain found the survey team in need of immediate evacuation, or was the rescue team itself in such danger that they were willing to risk an unlocked transport?

"Spock," McCoy warned. "Think about what you're going to do here."

"I always do, Doctor." Like Sulu, Spock gazed up at

the viewscreen as if he could somehow see the effects of his decision there. "Proceed with transport, Mr. Scott."

"Transport initiated—no, shut down, shut down *now!*"

Sulu had less than a second to wonder what the chief engineer's outburst meant. An eerie shudder ran through the bridge, so strong and deep that he knew it must have shaken the entire ship. He shot a glance down at his helm controls and saw their smooth white orbital curve spiral off into multicolored chaos as the ship slewed into an insane and unplotted deceleration curve. The unknown force that had previously flirted with them, gently tugging them toward the surface, had in the space of an instant become a full-fledged roaring pull, like a tractor beam operating on a monstrous and inhuman scale.

Sulu reached for the impulse controls before he was even aware of conscious thought, jamming them to full starboard thrust to compensate for the ship's sudden curl toward the planet. For an instant, he felt the sublight engines hurl themselves into the effort to turn the ship, then their power indicators abruptly fell to zero on his screens. An instant later, the screens themselves went dead, the lights on the bridge snuffed out, and Sulu heard the eerie silence as the life support systems stopped functioning. He grabbed onto the helm as hard as he could, knowing what was coming next. But the ship was wheeling too sharply to port. When the inertial dampeners gave way, the centrifugal force they'd been holding back slammed across the bridge like a tidal wave.

Chapter Six

THERE SHOULD HAVE BEEN SIRENS, Sulu thought dazedly. He reached out for something to hang onto, trying to brace himself against the persistent pull of centrifugal force. His hand slid helplessly across a smooth surface that could only be the main viewscreen. *Where are the sirens and flashing red lights? If this isn't an emergency, I don't know what is.*

But the bridge of the *Enterprise* remained eerily silent, and the only light came from the fluorescent glow of the evacuation lights, triggered by the dark and lack of power. Sulu glanced around and saw fallen figures everywhere. Only Spock was still on his feet, fighting the ship's dizzying spin with that superhuman resilience Vulcans could summon in emergencies. The first officer had just finished lifting Dr. McCoy into the command chair, and was flipping open his personal communicator. Sulu spared a moment to admire Spock's quick thinking. With no power, the ship's internal communications system would be as useless as its inertial dampeners.

"Spock to engineering. We need auxiliary power on the bridge."

Sulu levered himself up to hands and knees, and took advantage of an aft plunge to slide toward the helm. He caught it just as the ship rolled to starboard, and cursed as his own chair banged him smartly in the back. At least he was now close enough to grab onto it and pull himself up into his seat. He hit the emergency belt release, hoping it would still work. Fortunately, the ship's designers must have made it internally powered, and it sprang out to encircle his waist with a reassuring click. He saw other members of the bridge crew doing the same thing, one by one struggling back into position. Unfortunately, their stations remained dark and lifeless, so there was nothing any of them could do once they got there except wait.

Except for Spock. He headed over to join John Russ at the engineering panel, somehow managing to keep his balance despite the ship's severe roll and pitch. He looked like a man walking through an invisible windstorm. "Commander Scott, can you hear me? We need auxiliary power on the bridge."

"I hear you, Mr. Spock." The chief engineer sounded as close to frantic as Sulu had ever heard him. "But I'm stuck here in the transporter room with none of the turbolifts working. I've got my crew down in engineering working on the auxiliary generators, but we lost every shred of backup power we had stored in our batteries. It'll take us a minute or two just to prime them. As soon as I've got any power at all, I'll be routing it up to you. I'll warn you, though, that it won't be enough to run all the bridge stations."

Spock was already hauling panels out of the engineering station. From somewhere in his engineer's tool kit, Russ had found a stronger emergency light and was slanting it down onto the intricate boards. Sulu could see the Vulcan's slender fingers flash across the controls, rearranging the flow of nonexistent power. "I am giving priority to helm controls and sensors," Spock said into the communicator that he had given Russ to hold. "Send the rest to the impulse engines, Mr. Scott."

"Can't we fire the impulse engines manually?" Sulu asked. Without a working viewscreen or helm monitor, he couldn't be sure where the *Enterprise* was heading, but his pilot's instincts told him that it was down toward the planet again. "If we continued on the heading we had just before we lost power, we've got to be deep into the gravity well by now."

"A distinct possibility," admitted Spock. "But without enough power to charge the ionization rings, there is no way to activate or aim the impulse engines."

"How about the warp drive?" Russ asked.

"Bollixed." Even heard secondhand and distantly through Spock's communicator, Scott's voice sounded very grim. "That was the first place the power drain headed for after it knocked out the main transporter. I had to cut every circuit between the core and the drive nacelles or the electromagnetic surge would have blasted our dilithium crystals to smithereens. I think I managed to save the core, but it's not connected to anything now."

"Did you let the rest of our power just get drained?" McCoy demanded.

"Aye, Doctor," said Scotty. "I don't know what kind of energy field that transporter beam activated, but it overrode every safety switch I threw. There was no stopping it without destroying all the power circuits in the ship, like I did in the warp core. I thought it would be better to just let it run its course and power the ship back up when it was gone."

"A logical prediction, Mr. Scott," said Spock. A dim flicker of light appeared on the main viewscreen, but Sulu ignored it to focus on his piloting monitor instead. Light began to pulse on the helm as it got a wash of power from the auxiliary generators. Sulu hurriedly punched through the helm's initial start-up sequence, canceling most of its safety checks and tests in order to get it up and running sooner. "Let us hope that the *Enterprise* manages to stay aloft long enough for it to come true."

Sulu glanced up from his coalescing orbital curves just in time to see the night-dark surface of Tlaoli rising toward them on the viewscreen.

A wave of frigid air rolled across the underground chamber, cleaving itself on the narrow flowstone columns until it seemed to come at them from all directions with hurricane force. Kirk ducked his head to avoid the bite of blowing ice, realized even as he did that the gesture was pointless. There was no wind. The flames on the rescue team's carbide lamps never so much as flickered, and Chekov—still engrossed in his map reconstruction—made no subconscious move to protect his thin plastisheet pages from fluttering about. It was just another temperature drop, Kirk realized. As sudden and profound as all the rest.

An eerie hiss filled the chamber as a new skin of ice adhered to the travertine walls. Kirk had clustered both parties into a single tight group as far from any nonliving structure as he could, offering as clean a lift as possible on the assumption Scott would opt to pick them up with the cargo transporter. He'd placed Uhura with her open communicator channel at the center of the group, letting the others fit in where they would. Right now, he was just relieved that no one was touching the flowstone during this latest quick freeze.

"This is getting ridiculous." Sanner bumped shoulders with Kirk as he batted fresh frost off the front of his jumper. "Does anybody know the minimum temperature these cave suits are rated for?"

No one did.

"I would give my eye teeth to know what is causing this effect." Jaeger, close on Kirk's other side, heaved a frustrated sigh that materialized in front of his face as a tattered curtain of steam. He looked across Kirk toward Sanner, one frustrated scientist appealing to another. "I don't care what Fisher says, there's no way this can be due to transperiodic ore deposits. They generate heat and create energy, not the other way around! This negative gradient that we're seeing in both power and heat... that energy has to be going somewhere."

"Into the latent heat of crystallization," his fellow geologist said cryptically.

"But that wouldn't be enough to explain…" Jaeger's unswollen eye narrowed in a way that gave him a slightly piratical look. "Not unless there was some trace contaminant in the cave runoff that inhibited freezing and allowed the crystals to absorb far more than the usual amount of energy."

"Something like dilithium?" Kirk inquired wryly.

"We analyzed for dissolved dilithium, Captain, back when we first entered the cave." That was the third and quietest geologist, D'Amato. "The levels were always below detection limits."

"Then maybe there's some other element or compound here, something we don't even know about yet," Sanner said excitedly. "I've seen papers proposing the existence of ultra-transperiodic quadra-hydrogen—"

"And I've seen papers that say Zephram Cochrane had outside help in designing the first warp drive," retorted Jaeger. "That doesn't make it true! It's more likely we're seeing an exaggerated version of evaporative cooling due to subsurface airflow through the caves."

Sanner let out an explosive snort. "Yeah, that would be reasonable—if the air in here were moving at about a thousand kilometers an hour!"

"Do you think the cold is why the aliens built this place?" Tomlinson asked from the other side of their huddle. He stood just behind Ensign Martine, a little closer than Kirk suspected was strictly necessary for transporting purposes. Tomlinson's fellow weapons officer did not appear to mind the proximity. "To take advantage of the refrigerating effect?"

Jaeger was busy scowling at Sanner and merely made a curt, dismissive gesture with his hand. It was the other geologist, D'Amato, who answered. "The structure we're inside—" He motioned vaguely at the huge chamber around them, "—the conduits, these larger chambers—those are all millions of years older than the cave system above us. I'm not even sure this structure was originally underground when the aliens built it." His hands played restlessly with the cover on his tricorder, as though wishing he could snap it open and access the information trapped inside. "The limestone was probably deposited over the structure, then began dissolving millions of years later, probably because the original conduits and rooms provided large, natural permeability contrasts. The only reason we see flowstone decorations inside the man-made—well, alien-made— parts is because of cracks that formed in the ceiling a few millennia ago, like the break at the back of this room."

"You're assuming this travertine formed the same way it would in a natural cave," Sanner objected. "But what if it was the cold that made it precipitate out in the first place?"

Jaeger heaved an exaggerated sigh. "Zap, please recall that most carbonate minerals have retrograde solubility—"

Kirk restrained his own sigh, all too aware how obvious even the most quiet expression of frustration would be right now. While in one regard he appreciated the way scientists could generate a speculative debate out of anything, right now it was the conspicuous absence of the transporter beam, rather than the presence of the cold or the relative age of caverns versus ruins, that bothered him the most. He caught Uhura's eye while Sanner and Jaeger began to vigorously debate the pros and cons of freeze-drying versus evaporation as an explanation for the various travertine formations they had seen. "Anything yet?" he asked quietly.

The communications officer looked as though she'd been waiting for his question. "I'm sorry, Captain. I signaled until I ran out of power, and I didn't get any indication that the ship was attempting to respond."

"But you're sure the signal got through?"

She shrugged a little. "As sure as I can be, sir." Half-turning, she reached toward Martine for another chemical battery. "Would you like me to try again?"

Kirk shook his head and waved Martine to stop digging about in her pack. "No, Lieutenant, thank you." He caught himself sighing anyway. "Either the *Enterprise* wasn't able to receive our message, or they weren't able to comply. In any case, wasting another battery isn't going to get us out of here any faster." He noticed abruptly that the rest of the group had fallen silent, listening to his conversation with Uhura while at the same time trying to seem as though they weren't technically eavesdropping. "At ease, everyone," he ordered, a little brusquely.

The team broke obediently apart, heading to different quarters of the chamber in groups of two and three in what was no doubt their effort to give Kirk some privacy to sort out where they'd go from here. He wasn't sure whether or not he fully appreciated the gesture. Only Ensign Chekov stayed within an arm's length of his commander—he simply sat down where he stood and continued working on his map. Uhura stooped to quietly leave her helmet on the ground next to him before following Martine and Tomlinson. Kirk wasn't certain the boy had consciously heard the dismissal, much less noticed the lieutenant's simple kindness. *He's either very good at concentrating, or just old-fashioned anal.* Both of which traits had their uses.

Kirk waited until Wright had finished settling Davis back on her makeshift futon of packs with D'Amato and Palamas sitting on either side to keep her warm, then summoned the medic over with a flick of his hand. He met her halfway, letting her fall in beside him as they walked a little distance away from the others. "I need a report on Chekov and Davis," he said quietly. "Are they able to walk out of here?"

Wright tossed a look back over her shoulder, taking in both patients with that single quick glance. "Ensign Chekov's fine," she said, turning back to Kirk. "His breathing's clear now, he's alert. I'm not so sure about Davis. She's in a lot of pain, and while she hasn't suffered a loss of consciousness, I'm not convinced she's entirely stable."

Kirk nodded his understanding. "But can she walk?"

"If she can't, I'll carry her." At first, Kirk thought she'd meant the remark as a joke. Then he saw the serious crease between her dark blue eyes. "Captain, until I can do a proper medical scan, I can't tell how badly she's injured. That bump on her head could just mean a killer headache, or it could mean she's bleeding into her brain. It's important that we get her out of here as soon as possible."

It's important to get us all out of here. No matter what kind of temperatures their cave jumpers were designed to withstand, Kirk knew that none of them would survive the night if the cold continued to deepen. He thanked Wright, trying to seem calm and confident about their chances, and started back across the chamber to check on the other two parts of his plan.

Chekov still sat where Kirk had left him, cross-legged with his compass and map notebook balanced in his lap. Kirk paused just behind him to steal a look at what might be their only roadmap home. "I'm impressed."

Chekov jerked in surprise, instinctively clapping one hand down on top of his notebook as though hiding illicit notes from a prowling teacher. But not before Kirk glimpsed a nearly complete rendering of the cave system's upper level, with remembered measurements appended to the main passage and many of the dead ends and side tunnels simply not filled in.

The captain tried on a fatherly smile; he hadn't intended to startle the boy, and now felt slightly guilty for appearing to sneak up on him. "You have a good memory, Ensign. That map's going to help us a lot."

"Thank you, sir...." Chekov looked back down at his work, then glanced abruptly at the helmet next to him as though equally startled to find it there. Kirk couldn't tell for sure in the dark, but he thought the boy was blushing. "I'm sure it's only because we were over the territory so many times, sir."

Not that many. But maybe it felt like more when you were the one who had to first walk it, then measure it, then draw it and walk it again. "Put your finishing touches on," Kirk warned him. "We're going to be heading out soon."

"Aye-aye, sir."

Which left only one element of their escape still open to question. "Mr. Sanner—How confident are you that you can climb back up that crack we all came down half an hour ago?"

Sanner paused to balance himself halfway up the pile of rubble Jaeger's team had tried to clear a way through. "With the ladder all frozen to the walls?" He gave a crooked grin and hopped a few levels closer to the floor. "Do I have to promise not to fall?"

Kirk wasn't in the mood for the geologist's humor. "That would be preferred, yes."

Picking up on his captain's tone, Sanner finished his climb to the floor. "I can do it if I have to, sir," he said, more seriously. Then he tossed a concerned look toward Davis on her makeshift infirmary. "But even if we make it up the ladder, I'm not sure everybody else is going to be able to walk that ledge back to the cave entrance. Not with all the ice that's going to be there. I don't have enough crampons for all of us."

And trying to pass one or two pairs back and forth down a line of inexperienced cavers was a disaster just waiting to happen.

"Captain..." Jaeger sat on one of the larger travertine

boulders, collecting samples of stone and ice into slides and tiny jars. "Am I correct in assuming that we won't be transporting out of here?"

"It's beginning to look that way, Mr. Jaeger."

"Then might I suggest an alternative?" He answered Kirk's nod with one of his own, then carefully snapped shut the last of his little jars. "There is another cavern similar to this one at the other end of the conduit system."

"I remember," Kirk said. "You called it 'the ice cave.' "

"Because that was where we first noticed the chilling anomaly, yes." Jaeger made a little face, as though he regretted that particular misnomer now that every surface in the cave system was covered in ice. "According to our tricorders, that chamber was only a few dozen meters below the natural cave's main entrance. There were breaks in the ceiling's integrity that I think correspond to a cluster of vertical pipes just inside the mouth of the cave." His hands outlined what he was trying to describe, and Sanner nodded enthusiastically.

"I remember those! I wanted to drop a light down to see how far they went, but we didn't have time." He turned to Kirk with renewed intensity. "Even if I have to rock climb up those pipes, I'm pretty sure I could get back up there and drop a rope for the rest of you."

With any three of the men up above, they could simply tie the rope around Davis and haul her up manually if she couldn't make the climb on her own. A fist of dread that Kirk hadn't even fully acknowledged began to loosen its grip on his heart, but a thought occurred to him that made it vise-tight again.

"Didn't you say that was where you thought the transperiodic ore deposit was?" Kirk jerked his head back toward D'Amato, tinkering with his tricorder even as he wedged himself tighter up against a shivering Davis. "Where Lieutenant D'Amato thought the power drain was coming from?"

"True," Jaeger admitted. "But a lot of that was based on the unusual chilliness we noticed in that room. Now that the cold has spread through the entire cavern system, I'm not sure that going through the ice cave would necessarily be any more—or any less—dangerous than any other route we could take."

"And if those solution pipes lead us straight up to the cave entrance," Sanner pointed out, "we can get out of here a hell of a lot faster than if we went back along the ledge through that vertical chasm."

If for no other reason than that, Kirk was willing to investigate this alternate route. No matter what strange phenomenon was causing the increasing cold in these caves, so far all it had done was get progressively worse. It would be worth taking a calculated risk as long as it paid off in a quicker escape.

"All right, gentlemen, we'll try your way first." He helped Sanner collect up the rest of Jaeger's gear. "Maybe while we're hiking, the *Enterprise* will have a chance to fix whatever problems she's having topside and we can try hailing her again."

"That would be an even better solution," Jaeger agreed. He sounded weary with the cold and the long hours spent waiting in the dark. "It seems almost unbelievable that the ship should be having mechanical problems right at the moment when we needed her to retrieve us."

Kirk considered the events of the past few days and found an unexpected smile tugging at his mouth. He hoped it didn't look as sardonic as it felt. "Not really, Lieutenant. Not if you knew what the ship's been through since we left you here."

"Well, there is one thing we know for sure." Sanner swung a pack over his shoulder and straightened his carbide light on his head. "Whatever's going on up there, it can't possibly be as bad as what's going on down here."

Sulu had a hard time tearing his gaze away from the ominous planetary shadow that was Tlaoli. He knew that staring at its looming bulk wouldn't do anything but deepen the icy spike of adrenaline in his bloodstream, but there was something hypnotic, almost majestic, about the way the planet swirled closer and closer on their visual scanners. It might almost have been beautiful if he hadn't been sickly aware that it was actually the *Enterprise* doing the spinning as she was dragged down the curve of Tlaoli's gravity well by the strange forces emanating from this malevolent alien planet.

"Helm, report!" Spock said sharply.

Sulu glanced down at his monitors and discovered that his hands had somehow punched in the appropriate course analysis commands while his brain was transfixed with the unexpected beauty of disaster. "Five minutes to terminal atmospheric impact," he said. "We need full thrust from the auxiliary engines in two minutes or less, sir, or we won't be able to change course in time to avoid it."

"Mr. Scott, did you hear that?" Spock asked through his personal communicator. He had handed it to McCoy to hold for him now, and the doctor had thoughtfully dialed its amplifier to maximum levels. Right now, that only made it easier to hear the bleakness of the chief engineer's voice.

"I can't give you impulse power that fast, Mr. Spock. The ionization rings have just started charging. Three minutes is the soonest I can give you even partial thrust."

Sulu punched the estimate into his projected course curves. "That will put us through the thermosphere and several kilometers into the mesosphere before we change course," he warned. "Without shields, the ship could burn up or break apart completely."

"And we cannot power the shields without creating further delay in the ignition of the impulse engines. Hmmm." Spock's tone was deliberative rather than despairing, as if he'd just been given a complicated intellectual puzzle to solve. Sulu heard an indignant snort from McCoy, still strapped into the command chair.

"Don't just stand there thinking about how ironic it all is, Spock. Do something!"

The Vulcan turned, swaying just a little as the ship plummeted into another series of spins. "Do you have a suggestion, Doctor?"

McCoy glared at him. "No. But if the captain were here, I know he wouldn't just be standing around thinking! He'd be—hell, I don't know—throwing rocks out the hatches to lighten the load or something!"

Spock's voice turned very dry. "Dr. McCoy, we are not a hot air balloon."

"But we could throw out photon torpedoes!" said Sulu. "If we could manage to get the shields up in time—"

At first, he wasn't sure Spock understood what he meant. Before he could open his mouth to explain further, however, the Vulcan first officer swung around so abruptly that for the first time, he lost his balance and slid across the plunging bridge. McCoy shot out his free hand to steady him, but instead of grabbing hold, Spock simply plucked the communicator out of the doctor's hand and let his momentum carry him across to the unmanned weapons station. "Mr. Scott! Stop charging the impulse engines and divert that power to shields and torpedo bays. I repeat, divert impulse power to shields and torpedo bays!" He glanced over his shoulder at the engineering station. "Mr. Russ, reroute the power circuits from helm to weapons control—"

"I can do it quicker from here, Commander." Sulu punched in a command he had only ever used in battle simulations, usually ones in which the ship ended up being destroyed. It was designed to shunt all helm power temporarily to weapons, so the ship could fire one last-ditch salvo at an overwhelming enemy. An ordinary planetary gravity well probably wasn't the sort of enemy the ship's designers had foreseen when they built in that emergency override, but otherwise this was exactly the kind of desperate situation it was designed for. Sulu just hoped the final outcome would be better.

His helm panel abruptly went dark, and Sulu glanced

over in time to see a flicker of lights spring up on the weapons panel instead. "Torpedo bays at full power!" said Scotty's tense voice. Sulu wondered if he, like Spock, had understood the plan without being told, or if he was loyally obeying orders that must have seemed suicidal on their face. "It's going to take a few minutes for the shields to reach full strength—"

"We don't have a few minutes." Sulu had glanced at the countdown clock on his monitor, just before the screen went black again. The neon shriek of auroral discharge across the viewscreen confirmed his memory of where the orbital curves intersected the planet's atmospheric layers. "We're already into the thermosphere. If we don't change the ship's course in the next thirty seconds, we won't be able to avoid terminal impact."

"Launching torpedoes now," was the first officer's terse reply.

There was a brief pause, just long enough for the silence on the bridge to become almost suffocating in its intensity. In that hush, Sulu could hear the hissing of Tlaoli's uppermost atmosphere across the *Enterprise*'s unprotected hull. Then a streak of silver knifed across the spinning night sky, the glow of gases scorched to phosphorescence by the force of an unseen object tearing through them at tremendous speed. In another minute, that same glow would envelop the *Enterprise* and all hope of avoiding destruction would be gone. "Torpedo detonation in five seconds," Spock said calmly. "Four, three, two, one—"

Photon torpedoes made impressive light displays when they exploded in deep space. In the plasmalike thermosphere of a terrestrial planet, however, they were nothing short of spectacular. The initial burst of light was only a little larger than normal, but its afterglow seemed to expand and brighten rather than fade. It flared from white to blue, from blue to nearly ultraviolet. For a moment the glow almost vanished, but then it burst out again as a series of auroras that streamed and rippled and dripped down the sky like liquid ribbons.

The atmospheric shock wave hit the ship three seconds later, slamming it so fiercely back toward empty space that sparks flew out from the weapons station and Mr. Spock finally staggered and fell. Sulu felt more than heard the deep groaning thunder of the ship's tough duranium hull as it absorbed the force of the impact through the incomplete shields, and heard the distant shriek of hull breach alarms. After a moment, he realized they were coming from Spock's open communicator, which had fetched up against the helm console.

"Rerouting power to helm control," Sulu said, although he wasn't sure if anyone was listening to him. He reversed the emergency override and ran through another abbreviated start-up sequence, then waited impatiently for the helm's internal gyroscopes to detect the speed and direction of the ship's unpowered motion. His instinct told him the *Enterprise* had reversed her course, but she was now surging in an unknown direction, helpless as flotsam carried on the expanding tide of the torpedo blast. He waited while the helm curves built up on his screen, and was relieved to see that although they were an unstable pulsing green, they were at least no longer spinning in multicolored chaos.

"We've been thrown out of planetary orbit and are headed for the outer edge of the solar system on vector nine-one-seven, speed seventeen hundred kilometers per second and stable." He glanced over his shoulder, searching for Spock's tall figure. It was nowhere to be seen, and the empty command chair told him that McCoy must have gone in search of the fallen Vulcan. "Commander Spock?"

"Helm report acknowledged," said a tight Vulcan voice. Sulu heard a grunt from McCoy, then saw the doctor lever Spock carefully to his feet near the viewscreen. The Vulcan stood with one shoulder hunched so awkwardly that the joint must have been knocked out of place. "Are any planets or asteroids known to intersect this heading, Lieutenant?"

"Nothing closer than the system's cometary cloud, sir," Riley reported as his own navigation boards came to life. Despite the continuing wail of alarms from the fallen communicator, power was starting to flow back into all of the bridge stations. Sulu could hear the life-support ventilators reactivate, filling the bridge with their familiar white noise. "And we should have several hours to adjust our course before we get there."

"Very good, Mr. Riley." Spock shrugged off McCoy's supporting arm and walked up the inertially generated tilt of the bridge deck toward the command chair. For once, the Vulcan actually sat down in it, releasing his breath with a small hiss although no expression of pain touched his narrow face. His intraship communicator whistled to life and he began to reach toward it, but froze in midmotion. "Doctor, if you would—" he said between his teeth.

McCoy snorted and came over to depress the button for him. "That's what you get for disobeying safety protocols, Mr. Spock. The regs clearly state that when inertial dampeners aren't working—"

"All sectors, damage reports," Spock said into the intercom, effectively cutting off the physician's lecture.

"Scott here," said the main intercom. Behind the sound of the chief engineer's voice, Sulu could hear purposeful shouting and the sound of running feet as the lower decks crew scrambled to cope with the breach in the *Enterprise*'s hull. "Since the ship isn't tearing herself entirely to pieces, Mr. Spock, I'm assuming we managed to blast ourselves back out of the planet's gravity well."

"You are correct, Commander. How much damage did we sustain in the explosion?"

"Enough to keep me busy for the rest of our three-day visit here," Montgomery Scott said. "We didn't lose anyone in the hull breach, thank God, but it did wipe out our entire sensor array. If you want to do anything that involves scanning, beaming, or even communicating with that planet down there, Mr. Spock, you'll have to wait at least six hours to do it."

"That is—unfortunate," Spock said after a moment. His voice held a deepening timbre that might, in a human, have signified either sadness or regret. Sulu glanced over his shoulder in surprise, and saw Dr. McCoy giving the Vulcan an even more astonished look. Spock gazed back at them with a hint of reproach in his eyes, as if he found it hard to believe that the recent crisis could have erased their memories of what had taken place just before it. "I assume you recall our previous discussion, gentlemen, about why the captain might have called for immediate transport back to the ship. If any of our inferences were correct, six hours may be far too long a time for the cave rescue team to survive."

Chapter Seven

THERE WAS A STRANGE kind of time dilation that occurred during times of crisis, Sulu had noticed. The rush of adrenaline triggered when your life hung in the balance stretched each individual second out like a bead of molten glass, drawn and twisted to an unbearably fragile thread. Once the instant had been endured, however, it melted back into transparency and was gone, leaving no trace of its passage in your mind. More than once when he'd piloted the *Enterprise* during long frantic chases or escapes, Sulu had glanced down at his helm chronometer and been astounded to see just how long he'd actually been on duty.

But time also took its revenge. The stretch of duty that followed right after a serious crisis moved as slowly and ponderously as geologic time, each minute weighted with the leaden aftermath of too much adrenaline and too much stress. It made some officers talk more than usual and others fall silent; some reluctant to leave their posts even when their shifts had ended and others anxious for release. In Sulu's case, the aftermath of tension always left him restless and bored and itching for more work. He could usually quench his unrest with a fierce session at the gym and a good night's sleep, but he did occasionally wonder if it meant he found the rush of making life-and-death decisions addictive. He wasn't sure that was a good trait to have when you were climbing Starfleet's command ladder...although he privately suspected that it was a trait he shared with James Kirk.

"Stop fidgeting!" Riley grumbled at him from down the helm. The navigator was usually one of those crewmen who got light-hearted and garrulous after a crisis, but Sulu suspected he was restraining his natural reaction so as not to remind anyone about his recent antics back at Psi 2000. "You're driving me and the computer both nuts."

Sulu glanced down at the stylus he had been tapping absently against his helm monitor, and was abashed to see that he had left a trail of thousands of little points dotted along their new orbital curves, as the computer obediently recorded each of his mindless marks. "Sorry," he said, erasing the electronic litter with a brush of his hand across the screen. "I was thinking."

"About changing the orbit again?" Riley asked. "Sir," he added as a hasty afterthought. With Spock currently down in sickbay to have his shoulder put back in place, and Scotty deeply absorbed in trying to repair the damaged sections of the ship, command of the *Enterprise* had unexpectedly defaulted to Sulu. He hadn't bothered to call Rhada or Hansen to the bridge to replace him at the helm, since he knew Spock wouldn't let McCoy keep him out of commission for very long. But Sulu had never missed fourth-in-command Uhura more than right now.

"I think the orbit's fine just the way Mr. Spock approved it," Sulu told his navigator, and wished he could believe that as firmly as he could say it. When they had first gotten impulse power back and swung the *Enterprise* away from her unplanned trip to the cometary cloud, he and Riley had laid in a course that kept them safely distant from Tlaoli and its starship-snagging power surges. It wasn't common for a ship to maintain a cruising level that far away from the planet, because when gravity could no longer be balanced against the ship's momentum to create a stable orbit, constant monitoring was required of the ship's pilot and navigator. But since Tlaoli's gravity well was no longer safe to orbit in, and neither the ship's scanners nor her transporters needed to be in range of the planet's surface until they had been repaired, Sulu hadn't expected any objections when he'd asked the ship's commanding officer to approve the course change.

But to his surprise, Commander Spock had vetoed the new course that had been presented to him. Instead, he'd ordered Sulu to resume cruising at their previous orbital level, at the far end of gravitational stability but well inside the planet's gravitational field. The Vulcan's rationale was, as usual, chillingly logical: To study the forces generated by this seemingly mundane planet, they had to activate it by staying within its reach. Of course, as Riley had sourly pointed out after Spock had left the bridge, the counterargument to that was pretty much the exact same statement.

"So what *were* you thinking about?" Riley inquired, and once again only tacked on the obligatory "Sir?" afterward.

"Warp cores," said Sulu absently, then took in a deep breath as he realized what he'd said. The restlessness plaguing him had been so bone deep that his surface thoughts had seemed trivial in comparison, idle speculations on the various salvage operations going on around the ship at that moment. *I should tell the commanding officer about what I just realized,* Sulu thought, then remembered that the commanding officer right now was himself. He sat indecisive for a moment, before it occurred to him to consider what Captain Kirk would do if he'd been the one to think of this. That made it easy.

"Riley, take the helm." The simple act of leaving his seat released so much of Sulu's restlessness that he suddenly understand why the captain tended to roam the bridge whenever things got tense. "I'm going to go check on something. Rhada will be coming on duty soon. Call her to the bridge early if anything strange starts happening."

"But you can't—" Riley closed his mouth on that protest, apparently realizing that, as the ship's current commanding officer, Sulu could in fact do anything he wanted. Even though he was technically Sulu's subordinate at this moment, however, they were still junior officers together, and junior officers looked after each other. "You sure you know what you're doing here, D'Artagnan?" the navigator asked in an undertone of real concern.

"Yes," Sulu said. And then, in a burst of honesty, "Pretty sure."

Riley snorted. "Well, get going, then. I'll try to remember the difference between forward and reverse while you're gone."

He was joking, of course. Like all starship navigators, Kevin Riley had trained as an emergency pilot and was perfectly capable of watching over the *Enterprise* as she orbited Tlaoli's modest disk. Unless the planet began tugging them down toward it again. That thought didn't stop Sulu, but it did lend some extra speed to his leap up the bridge steps and into the turbolift.

The lift seemed sluggish, and it jerked rather than slid through the transfer to the secondary hull. The auxiliary power generators were strong enough to run the ship's essential systems, but that didn't mean they all ran as smoothly as usual. Sulu caught himself drumming his fingers impatiently on the side of the lift chamber and forced himself to wrap them into fists instead. The trip to the main shuttlebay always took longer than he thought it should, he reminded himself. For all its deceptive nimbleness in battle, the *Enterprise* was an immense ship of the line, after all.

The turbolift finally slowed to a halt, its final jerk strong enough to make Sulu sway on his feet. The door didn't even try to slide open, however, and after a moment it occurred to Sulu that the force of the photon shock wave might also have breached the shuttle bay. A slow, underpowered hiss built up in the lift chamber and, with another little jerk, the doors grudgingly slid open on the vast coldness of the main shuttle bay.

It was entirely dark.

It was a good thing, Sulu thought in exasperation, that he was fifth in line of command among the primary bridge crew. Of course the shuttle bay would be dark. Hadn't he just been thinking about how only the ship's essential systems would be powered up to minimize the strain on the auxiliary generators? If he had been Captain Kirk, he'd have already thought of that and brought along a portable light for his inspection. As it was, he either had to face a long turbolift ride back up to the bridge—and possibly an interrogation from Mr. Spock once he got there—or take his chances bumping around in the dark looking for shuttles.

This time, Sulu's moment of indecision paid off. The longer he stood in the open doorway, the more his eyes adjusted to the dark, until eventually he could see the vague firefly glow that marked the cockpit windows of each shuttle nose. All the controls inside were alight and flashing, ready as usual for instant deployment should the need arise. The refracted glimmer of multicolored lights not only reassured Sulu that he could locate the shuttles in the darkness, it also told him that his original speculation about them had been correct.

He strode out into the shuttle bay with confidence, not even faltering when the turbolift door hissed shut and made the immense dark space even darker. He ducked under the first shuttle's landing gear with only the slightest brush of his head against the hull, and fumbled along the side until he found the touch panel that activated its hatch. It folded itself open with the powerful hum of a vessel whose warp core was functioning and fully connected. Brightness cascaded down around him as the internal lights sprang on in the shuttle's hold.

"Yes!" breathed Sulu in satisfaction. He vaulted into the hold and hurried forward to the cockpit. The shuttle's communicator was as alive and glowing as the rest of it, and he tuned it easily to the internal *Enterprise* frequency.

"Lieutenant Sulu to Commander Spock."

There was a pause, as if the ship's communications systems were having a little trouble with the automatic channel connection back to this unexpected source. Then he heard an imperturbable voice reply, "Spock here." From the background roar and shriek of ventilators and welding torches, Sulu guessed the first officer had already left the confines of Sickbay and was supervising the repairs to the hull and sensor array.

"Commander Spock, I'm down in the main shuttle-bay—"

"And who has the conn, Lieutenant?"

Sulu swallowed. It had not occurred to him that he had to delegate command of anything but the ship's helm when he'd left the bridge, and none of the other junior officers there had thought to remind him. "Umm—Lieutenant Riley, sir."

"May the saints preserve us all." That was Montgomery Scott's distant but heartfelt voice through the din. Sulu winced, remembering that only twenty-four hours ago, the young man he'd just left in charge of the ship had been holed up in the engine room, blithely consigning them all to total destruction.

"Yes, well—it occurred to me, Mr. Spock, that the shuttles weren't connected to any of the *Enterprise*'s power circuits when the transporter beam hit that energy field. I came down to see if their internal warp cores were still functioning. And they are, sir."

"You're a remarkably bright lad, Mr. Sulu." Scott's voice held nothing but admiration now. Even alone in the darkened shuttle bay, Sulu felt his cheeks tighten a little with embarrassment. "We can hook one or two of those little warp cores into the main circuits and punch ourselves back up to full power before you can say whist."

"I actually wasn't thinking of that, sir," Sulu admitted. "I was thinking that we could take a shuttle down to the planet right now, without waiting for the transporters to be fixed."

For a while, there was only forbidding silence on the other end of the communicator channel. "An interesting suggestion, Lieutenant," Spock said at last. "But allow me to point out that the research shuttle originally sent down to the planet lost its power when it flew over the caves where Captain Kirk is now trapped. What makes you think that any other shuttle would be safe to fly?"

"Nothing, sir. But if I stayed away from the cave region, I could at least evacuate the members of the landing party that didn't get transported back to the ship." Sulu took a deep breath, gazing down at the reassuring lights that flashed up from the piloting boards. "And after that...you were the one, Mr. Spock, who said we needed to activate Tlaoli's energy field again in order to study it."

"Indeed," Spock said. "However, it would be preferable, Lieutenant, not to be in danger of falling out of the sky when you did so."

"If you don't mind me interrupting, Mr. Spock," said Montgomery Scott's voice in the background. "Now that I've seen how well our warp core's magnetic shielding stood up to that planet's power drain, I'm thinking that I could manage to install a similar shield around the shuttle's core and engines together, so they couldn't be made to lose power. Mr. Sulu might lose his communicator and his sensors, but if he can fly by sight he at least won't fall out of the sky."

"I can fly by sight," Sulu assured them both. "During the day for certain, and maybe even at night once I've found my way around the area once or twice."

"There should be several hours of daylight remaining on the side of Tlaoli where the remaining survey crews are." Spock's voice had lost its repressive edge and now sounded merely thoughtful. "How soon will you be able to divert a crew of engineers to the task of shielding one of the shuttles, Mr. Scott?"

"If it means getting the captain back and evicting that young idiot Riley from the conn?" Sulu could practically feel the gust of the Chief Engineer's snort. "Immediately!"

"You've got ice in your hair."

Chekov combed a hand back through his hair without actually looking up from the map he had wedged against the conduit wall. Bits of half-frozen water spattered the surface of his notebook, deflating on impact into regular liquid drops, only to begin freezing again almost immediately. He'd given up being irritated by them. Swiping them off his workspace with the side of his hand, he then had to pull his glove off with his teeth to keep from smearing wet nano-weave all over the map. At least he knew the glove would dry. It had managed to do so the dozen other times he'd paused with it suspended in his mouth while he finished updating his measurements.

By now the ice was everywhere. It had coated the travertine flowstone like poured polyurethane, sharpening the delicate oranges, greens and reds of the original mineral salts into a crystalline riot of color. The omnipresent shush and drip of water that had accompanied their descent into the caves was now silenced. In its place, expanding ice ticked an irregular rhythm, sometimes firing off a deep-voiced cannon shot to catch everyone by surprise and make them jump. It reminded Chekov of how the lake at the heart of Gorky Park grudgingly gave itself over to autumn's advance every year. You could hear the battle raging several blocks away for weeks at a time, until winter finally swept in one long bitter night and put an end to all of it. The next morning, the lake lay still and silent, as smooth and tame as if it had been paved over by glass.

Tlaoli's caves were not so simple a matter. Chekov had long ago given up trying to represent the true shape of their passages on his map. Ice had reduced them all to narrowed, glass tubes, with less floor exposed every meter they traveled, and only faint hints of the surfaces beneath. If the landing party somehow passed from these artificially straight and regular conduits into more wild and undirected natural cave at this point, Chekov almost doubted any of them would be able to tell until they caught themselves straddling another abyss. Which made the compass readings and measurements he recorded on this new map even more important than the ones he'd had to recall from his memory of the trip in. At least up top they would have the fallback of the spot markers they'd left propped on little ledges and piles of stones, pointing back the way they'd come in. Down here, they had only Jaeger's memory and Chekov's maps to tell them where they stood in relation to the surface world. A discrepancy of five or ten meters could mean the difference between finding the topside entrance, or wandering about down here until their carbide ran out.

A little laugh from the other end of his old-fashioned tape measure brought part of his attention back to the security guard Kirk had assigned to assist him. "I don't know how you can work in this cold without gloves." Crewman Yuki Smith switched the metal roll from one hand to the other, careful not to move it from the spot where Chekov had instructed her to hold it, but obviously eager to alternate her gloved hands in her pockets in an effort to keep herself warm. "They're gonna have to cut off half my fingers by the time we get home."

Chekov flexed his own fingers, noted that they were pink with cold but only a little stiff. He shrugged and went back to writing. "It's not so bad."

Smith fidgeted foot-to-foot for another long moment, then guessed, "You're Russian, aren't you?"

The question, so apparently unrelated to anything else they were doing, surprised him almost to the point of embarrassment. He looked up for the first time, and found Smith's round Asian face split by a delighted smile.

"I thought you might be," she explained cheerfully. "I could kind of tell by your name, and your accent. But mostly it was just by how the cold doesn't seem to bother you while I'm *dying!*" Then, when it seemed to occur to her that even further explanation might be required, "I lived in Moscow for four years." She sounded quite proud of this feat. "My dad's a history professor— he had a temporary position at the University of Moscow when I was six." Just as quickly, she colored self-consciously and dipped an awkward little shrug. "Everybody at the University knew English, though, so I never did learn how to speak Russian."

As near as Chekov had been able to tell, no one else on board the ship knew how to speak Russian, either. "You pronounce *Moscow* correctly," he told her. Partly because it was true, and partly because it seemed like the sort of thing she would be glad to know.

He was right. Her smile exploded into full brightness again, as though he's just paid her the most wonderful compliment. "I do?"

"You do." He released his end of the tape measure and let it go skittering back toward her across the icy floor.

Smith caught the slithering tape in a smooth, athletic gesture, arcing the metal holding reel over to her other hand as she again switched pockets. "You must be really good at this." It seemed an odd compliment to pay someone who was only doing what he'd been told, but became odder still when she continued, "You haven't had to ask me even once for the measurement. I can never estimate distances like that."

Ice as cold and killing as anything the cave had yet produced curdled inside his stomach. "Of course I've asked. I must have asked!" Every passage they'd traversed had its length marked in meters on his map, every minute angle or turn they'd made had its own compass reading carefully noted alongside. And yet even as he protested, he realized that he couldn't specifically remember asking Smith to read off any values. Ever. Not even when they first left the big column-crowded upper chamber where Smith's party had waited for so long. Chekov tried to swallow with a throat suddenly clogged with panic. "What was the last measurement?" he asked, as evenly as he could manage.

Even though she'd already dropped the reel back into one pocket, she came up with the number quickly enough. "Seven point nine meters."

Which was exactly what he had written within that narrow stretch of tunnel. He hadn't thought he was that good at visually measuring anything, not even a nearly straight line. But at the same time, he hadn't thought he could reconstruct his original map in the kind of detail he'd finally managed. Once he'd gotten started, though, it had all seemed very straightforward and obvious—as though he were sketching streets that he knew well, even if he'd never drawn them before.

While anyone else might have given himself credit for simply discovering skills he hadn't known he possessed, Chekov found himself struggling with the urge to retrace their entire route through these lower tunnels, checking each value he'd already committed to his map but apparently never measured. It was bad enough that he'd had to make the reconstruction at all—he didn't want to find out how Captain Kirk would react to finding out that the new maps they had might be completely untrustworthy.

"We should catch up with the others." He tried to mask his unease by hastily gathering up the rest of the gear. Chiseling a little shelf in the ice for one of the spot markers, he arranged it extra carefully, as if that could make up for everything else he'd done wrong today.

They measured the next two segments—both of them straight and purely line-of-sight—with maximum care and minimum conversation. Chekov made a point of verifying each compass reading before writing it down, and of asking Smith (sometimes twice) for each linear value before letting her roll up the tape measure. In every case, he knew what the answer would be as soon as he thought to look for it. Even so, the thought of backtracking gnawed at him as they approached the entrance to the final chamber. *What kind of an officer am I?* he thought angrily. *If I'm not sure about the accuracy of my work, I should say something!* Yet another part of him *was* sure. He knew without being able to defend his conviction that the numbers as they stood were correct—that backtracking would only waste time without supplying them with the slightest bit of useful information. His certainty about that scared him a little.

It seems like you're scared of everything. And he realized that fear was what lay at the heart of his frantic need to be right about this. Not just fear of being wrong, or fear of being reprimanded. Fear in general, and the fact that it churned in his belly like an out of control fire while being apparently absent in everyone else.

Chekov caught himself slowing as they reached the archway leading into Jaeger's "ice cave." Human voices floated out to meet them on the soft glow of a half-dozen carbide lamps. Sanner had produced a few extra of the primitive devices, although the earlier landing party's helmets had no place to mount them. Chekov and Smith had one of the unmounted lamps, dangling from a piece of rope in the security guard's hand when it wasn't waiting equidistant between them while they measured out some distance for the map. Chekov used adjusting the flame on the clunky device as an excuse to pause while they were still out in the ice-bound conduit.

"Crewman Smith—"

"You can call me Yuki."

He nodded absently, not wanting to lose his momentum now that he'd gotten started. "Yuki...When you're down on planetary missions, do you..." He looked squarely at her, committed himself to the question. "Are you ever afraid?"

She lifted her eyebrows in surprise, as though the thought had never occurred to her. "Nah. Why should I be?"

Why indeed. Although she wasn't quite as tall as Chekov, she was powerfully built and possessed of the reflexes and easy coordination that Chekov had always envied in natural athletes. In addition, she was a security specialist. Unlike the command cadets, who were expected to know a little bit about almost everything, trained security personnel focused only on the skills required to protect a starship and her crew from every imaginable danger. If someone like Smith didn't feel one hundred percent capable and safe while doing her job, who on board could?

He nodded slowly, handing back the unmounted lamp and holding out his hand for the tape measure in return. He realized now that he should have expected as much from an experienced crewman. He should have known when he first came to, vomiting up what felt like ten liters of water after tripping stupidly on an icy rock ledge, to find Captain Kirk kneeling beside him and joking about their predicament. Joking. They'd gone down the same chasm, nearly drowned in the same freezing water, and Chekov had been so scared he felt like crying. More than ever, he found it very hard to believe that there was anything resembling command potential hiding anywhere inside him.

Smith caught his elbow when he turned to escape into the final chamber. "Hey, wait a sec...."

He stopped, but couldn't bring himself to turn and face her. *Cowardice has many forms.*

"I lied a little." She said it very quietly. Chekov couldn't tell whose dignity she was hoping to preserve, his or her own. "The first time I went down—maybe the first two or three—I was really scared." Her hand fell away, and she moved around in front of him to sit on a boulder just outside the entrance arch. "I know that probably sounds stupid. But I've been out of Security Academy for almost a year, and it seems like we lose somebody from the division every month. There are so many guys that I helped pack up to go down...only to have them not come back. When Chief Giotto first told me I was going on a landing party, I almost called in sick." She tried on a little smile that came nowhere near its earlier brightness.

"But you don't get scared anymore?"

She shrugged, seemed to reconsider giving him another too-easy answer. "Just nervous now, I guess. I mean, I still feel something, but so far this is the first excitement I've ever seen on a planet, and it hasn't been so bad." She aimed a playful punch at his shoulder. "And I got to meet you, didn't I?"

Right now, Chekov wasn't sure how much value she ought to place on that.

"Don't worry—you'll get used to it. After you've been down two or three times, you'll get so psyched about seeing all the new stuff and learning all the new things, you won't even think about being scared. I promise."

Somehow, that completely sincere assertion charmed him most of all. He smiled. "Two or three," he echoed, trying for a touch of humor. "I'll start keeping count, then, so I don't miss the one where it gets easy."

She laughed, a full-bodied, brazen peal that echoed marvelously off the frozen walls. Chekov was beginning to suspect that Smith did very few things by half-measures.

"Do me a favor—" She bumped close to him as they passed through the entrance, grabbing his arm again to whisper in his ear. "—don't tell anybody what we talked about. Security guards aren't supposed to get scared, you know."

Neither were future commanders. He gave her hand a single solemn shake. "You have my word as an officer."

Her return grip was a good deal stronger than he expected. "I'm not an officer, so all I can do is promise."

"That's good enough for me."

The ice chamber seemed to swarm into existence from the darkness as they made their way inside. Flows and curtains of ice, as intricate as any travertine, glowed as their light swept across them, and Chekov could just pick out the positions of the other party members by the auroras haloing their helmet lamps. The ceiling overhead soared higher than the reach of the dim carbides, but its surface twinkled like the stars outside where ice had clustered in the crevices. Mist swirled in gentle eddies, tiny frostlike crystals coalesced out of the chamber's ambient humidity. Chekov had no idea if this chamber was any colder than the one they'd left behind, but the twisted columns of ice staggered across its expanse leant a unique sense of chill to its murky air.

"Stop here." He pushed the tape measure back into Smith's hand, and backed away from her toward the nearest column. She clapped her end to the edge of the doorway without having to ask what he was doing.

Already their cave jumpers had dulled to a soft pastel, furred over with frost as though they were grains of sand in an oyster's maw. It occurred to Chekov that these pillars of ice must have formed in the same way the flowstone structures had in the previous chamber—built up by dripping water leaking in from overhead. While their spacing wasn't strictly regular, they occurred often enough across the expanse of room that Chekov suspected they corresponded to the breaches in the ceiling Jaeger had described earlier. That meant matching them precisely to the details of the upstairs map would go a long way toward guaranteeing their safe exit from this place.

Apparently, he wasn't the only one to have considered that possibility.

"Heads up, Rand McNally!" Sanner appeared as if out of nowhere, sliding down the pillar behind Chekov in a shower of dislodged frost. He pushed himself neatly off the column just in time to hit the frozen floor flat-footed. "Sorry about that—" The geologist tousled Chekov's hair in a gesture the young ensign assumed was meant to be friendly. New bits of ice went flying everywhere. "I didn't want you to end up with a crampon in your head."

"I appreciate your dedication to team safety, Mr. Sanner." Kirk's voice preceded the captain out of the darkness. He'd apparently left his helmet and its attached light with one of the other groups, and joined them now bareheaded in the circle of Sanner's carbide. "How do our chances of making the top look?" the captain asked Sanner. Chekov started to excuse himself, but stopped when Kirk lifted a stilling hand.

Sanner grinned as he picked ice off of one boot. "Good! This one doesn't go through, but I'm sure a lot of these must." He twisted loose a piton with some effort. "Once we locate the right one, I shouldn't have any trouble getting up there and securing a rope."

"Then our only question is how to locate the right one." Kirk turned to Chekov. "Have you got those maps handy, Ensign?"

"Yes, sir." Chekov handed Kirk the notebook without thinking, then realized the captain might not immediately follow how he'd tried to overlay the various pages of mapping one on top the other. Feeling his face heat up with discomfort, he moved awkwardly alongside Kirk to flip through several of the sheets. "I didn't map all of the holes in the floor when we passed them inside the first entrance, sir," he explained, hurrying to find that sheet to illustrate his explanation. "But as long as we know for certain *where* this room is below that entrance—" He flipped back several pages to the newest maps. "—we should be able to identify which of these columns corresponds to the holes I did record."

Kirk studied the maps for a moment, turning back and forth through the pages himself as if committing them to memory. "All right, then, Mr. Chekov—which pillar is your first choice?"

Chekov opened his mouth to stammer an answer, then shut it again abruptly. *This is when you should tell him! This is when you should admit that you don't know how you made this map!* But he couldn't. Everything inside him insisted the map was correct—as correct as he could make it—and he couldn't pretend it wasn't just because fear made him insecure. He waved Smith over, took the lamp from her hand and positioned her with the tape measure against the side of the frozen column. Then, consulting the earliest of the maps he had redrawn, he said to her, "Tell me when I've gone almost seventy-five meters."

He flipped open the compass, rotated it carefully to place himself just a few degrees shy of Tlaoli's magnetic south, and began pacing off the distance to the closest hole he was sure of. Behind him, he could hear

Kirk's steady footsteps, and the arrhythmic *clank, clank* of Sanner wrestling the last of his pitons out of the pillar before following a few meters farther back. *Please, let this be right,* Chekov prayed. He didn't think he could stand to fail Kirk another time.

He didn't know how far they'd gone—he had his end of the tape held near his hip, and Smith had the end with the readings that counted. But he knew they must be almost to the pass-through he was looking for when Kirk's hand suddenly seized on his shoulder. "Do you hear that?" the captain asked with frightening urgency.

Chekov tried to listen, tried to turn and face his commander before asking what he was supposed to be listening for. Instead, his feet seemed to drop out from under him, and the cold crashed in with a force so powerful, he felt his whole body go numb with shock and terror. Then water flooded into his lungs and he was drowning. And he had no idea or memory of how he came to be here.

Chapter Eight

LATER, what Uhura would remember about that moment wasn't the shock of the event itself or the sudden awareness of danger that prickled in the cavern's frigid air. It was her own sickening plummet from hope to unexpected horror. She had let herself be lulled into premature confidence, watching Sanner clamber so easily up the icy staircase that could be their ladder out of darkness. She'd even smiled a little, hearing Tomlinson tease Martine about finally giving up the responsibility of her pack full of power supplies. There had been a warmth in the young weapons officer's voice that implied a little more than camaraderie, although not yet quite affection. Uhura was just romantic enough to appreciate that delicate transition in a man's voice, and just old enough not to wish she had been its recipient. So she had smiled and remained discreetly silent, listening to Martine gently refuse to ever surrender her burden to a man who'd spent ten hours trying to dig his way out of a cave with his bare hands. There would be small notes and flowers appearing on the weapons deck as soon as they were back on the ship, Uhura thought in amusement. And it was then, in that moment of relaxation, that instant of certainty that there *would* be a "back-on-the-ship" in the very near future, that she had heard Sanner's fierce bellow of alarm.

"They're *gone!*"

The cave geologist stood frozen in the circle of his own carbide glow, particles of frost kicked up into a swirl around him from his sudden plunging stop. Beyond him, where Uhura's subconscious mind had a moment before recorded an impression of light and activity and human presence, there was now only darkness.

"What happened? Did someone fall into a crevasse?" The other cave specialist, Jaeger, swung around and began to cross from the far side of the ice-filled chamber. The urgency of Sanner's outflung arm stopped him in his tracks. "A hidden one, covered with a crust of ice?"

"No, nothing like that!" Sanner turned to face them with an exaggerated care that revealed even more so than his strained voice just how apprehensive he was. "They were standing on solid rock, I could see it sticking out through the ice. There was some kind of funny rushing noise, almost like a vacuum chamber opening. And now the rock's still there, but they're gone!" His voice rose as if it needed to cut through something besides the appalled silence. Perhaps it was their stunned disbelief he was trying to pierce. "The captain and Ensign Chekov just disappeared into thin air!"

That was it. In that moment, Uhura felt her easy end-of-mission confidence crash down into something that might almost have been despair. Her first instinct was one of pure denial—Sanner couldn't possibly be right, his story was just too ludicrous to believe. She opened her mouth, but before she could speak, Tomlinson voiced the thought for her.

"Are you sure of that, Sanner?"

"No, Lieutenant, he's right." Yuki Smith's voice held such an unhappy mixture of shock and sadness that Uhura's doubts were shriveling even before the security guard went on to explain. "I was watching Ensign Chekov the whole time he walked the tape out. At sixty meters, he and the captain stopped for a moment, and then they just vanished. The light went away with them—blown out, just like a candle flame."

"You're sure of that?" Jaeger demanded. "They didn't take a step forward or fall down—they were standing absolutely still when it happened?"

"Yes, sir."

Sanner craned his head around, and the appalled look on his face told Uhura he had already come to the same conclusion she had. The mysterious force that had once brought ancient starships crashing down on Tlaoli had just proved that it was still in existence...and that it could make individual people vanish completely. Uhura opened her mouth, unsure of what she meant to say until it emerged.

"Mr. Sanner, I want you to back away very slowly from where you're standing."

He blinked at her, looking a little startled by the sternness of her order. Uhura gulped in an ice-cold breath, feeling a little startled herself. If anyone had asked her a moment ago who among this group was Kirk's second-in-command, she would have been hard pressed to remember that it was her. But now that Kirk was gone and a crisis had engulfed them, the realization that she was in charge and responsible for the safety of this small, stranded group unexpectedly steadied her topsy-turvy emotions and gave her voice an edge it usually lacked.

"How do I know where it's safe to step?" Sanner demanded. Uhura lost a little more of her own hopelessness as she heard the need for reassurance in his voice. She glanced around the ice cave in search of justification for him.

"The tape measure that Ensign Chekov dropped is lying on the ground behind you. If you follow it straight back, you won't hit whatever—whatever took them away." Uhura wasn't really sure about that, but she *was* sure that Sanner needed to move. Whatever alien force had swallowed Kirk and Chekov had swept over them while they were standing still. That implied it could sweep over other members of the party, and Sanner was in the most dangerous spot, only a few meters away from the point where the other two had vanished.

"Move, Mr. Sanner. *Now!*" Uhura put all the force she could muster into that final command, and to her surprise it came out sounding remarkably like something Kirk would say. Sanner gulped, but inched three careful backward steps along the tape measure before turning and covering the rest of the distance in an undignified rush.

"Now, I want everyone else to make their way back here toward the entrance, one at a time. Mr. Jaeger, you're the closest to that side of the cave. Please move first."

The older geologist nodded and came toward her at a less hurried pace. He looked more baffled than worried, and kept peering down at the ground as if he was still sure that a natural cave phenomenon could explain what had just happened. "D'Amato next," said Uhura and watched the other geologist cross back safely from the ice column he'd been examining. Something in Uhura wanted to relax and let them all come back at once, now that three had made it across the ice-sheathed room safely, but she remembered all too clearly her recent brush with overconfidence.

"Palamas next," she ordered, ignoring the impatient way Sanner shifted from boot to boot in the entranceway. Since Yuki Smith had never left the threshold, and Davis and Wright were standing right next to it, the number of carbide lights in the chamber had dwindled down to two by now, and the primeval darkness they had chased out of the ice cave was starting to surge back in from its corners. Since Tomlinson wore no light, his shadow stretched out away from Uhura and Martine to join the darkness at the cave edges, like a stream going back to the sea. It wavered a little, either from the carbide flicker or the weapons officer's own weariness. Or maybe—

"Tomlinson next," Uhura said, but before the young man could move, Martine screamed and threw out a hand to stop him.

"There's something there, right beside you—Robbie, hold still!"

"What is it?" Sanner was almost leaping up and down in the threshold in an attempt to get a better view inside the darkened cave. "I can't see anything!"

"I saw something waver in the air," Martine said, her voice tense. "It almost looked like heat shimmers, like the afterglow you get right after a torpedo goes out the bay. It's just to Lieutenant Tomlinson's right."

"I see it." Tomlinson craned his head across one shoulder. He took a sideways step toward Martine, then froze abruptly. "Is it following me? I think I saw it move, and I don't want—"

"Lieutenant Uhura." That was Yuki Smith's diffident voice from the entrance. "We might be able to see it better if it were darker in here."

Uhura took a breath that was a little too fast and deep. She paid the price when cold air burned down the inside of her throat, but right now that was the least of her worries. "Everyone adjust your lights down," she ordered, but that wasn't the hard part. The hard part was what came next. "Martine, you and I will shut our lights off entirely."

"Aye, sir," said the female weapons officer, as if it was a perfectly normal command to be given when you were inside a cave with a completely unknown hazard on the loose. She reached up to her helmet quickly enough to make Uhura a little ashamed about her own hesitation, and her light was the first to wink out. Uhura's went a second later, then the glow from the threshold dimmed to orange-gold. The darkness inside the ice cave congealed down to a nearly solid black. Uhura closed her eyes and counted to twenty to help them adjust, then opened them again.

A veil of phosphorescence, the clear burning blue of a flame's heart, hung in the air about ten meters away from her. It rippled and swirled and billowed, sometimes drifting a little further away, sometimes curling a little closer. There didn't seem to be any particular purpose in its movement, but it was eddying perilously close to the darker shadows that were the two weapons officers.

"Crewmen, fall back to your left!" Uhura didn't wait to watch them obey. She could see that she was blocking their only safe line of retreat, and she scrambled to clear it without even looking behind her. A jagged block of ice caught at her heels and nearly spun her to the ground, but Uhura felt a gloved hand catch her and steady her back to balance before she could fall. She glanced up and saw Sanner's face peering down at her worriedly.

"Thanks, Zap." It didn't seem like the right moment to chastise him for leaving the safety of the threshold. "Did Martine and Tomlinson get away safely?"

"Yes, sir." Their joined voices came from so nearly the same place in the darkness beside her that Uhura suspected they were clutching at each other's hands.

"Good." She kept her gaze fixed on the fire-colored phosphorescence that hung across the room from them. "It didn't follow us, did it?"

"No, but it's not exactly staying put, either," Sanner

said frankly. "I'd feel a lot better, Lieutenant, if we were as far away from that thing as we could possibly get."

"Me, too." Uhura reached up to reignite her carbide lamp and brightened it to a fierce white glow that made the ominous phosphorescent curtain disappear. Then she headed back to the entrance of the ice cave, thinking out her orders as she went. "We're going to head back down the conduits. Jaeger and Sanner, you're in the lead. Smith, follow them and make sure you find the spot markers Mr. Chekov left along the way. Wright, you go next with Palamas and D'Amato to help you—" She had been about to say, "carry Davis," but that determined young woman was already making her way unsteadily toward the exit. "—with anything," Uhura finished lamely, but Wright gave her a somber nod before she turned to go, as if she'd heard the thought that had been left unspoken.

That left her with Martine and Tomlinson. Uhura turned to face them, wondering if the two young weapons officers were up to the task she was about to assign. The glare of her carbide light showed her two tired but steadfast faces, as well as a pair of unabashedly clasped hands.

"We're going to be the rear guard," she told them quietly. "That means one of us has to wait in the dark while the rest of the team goes on, to make sure that blue glow isn't coming after us."

Tomlinson reached up ruefully to touch the useless photon lamp on his caving helmet. "I guess that would be me."

"That helmet's not glued to your head," Angela Martine told him tartly. "And neither is mine. We can take turns."

"We'll all three take turns," Uhura said. "Staring at

nothing for too long makes you start to think you're seeing things whether they're there or not." She pulled out her whistle and swung it between her fingers. "We'll leave one lookout on guard for five minutes, then whistle them up the right path to join us and leave a new one behind. Understood, gentlemen?"

"Aye, sir!" said Tomlinson, but it was Martine who asked, "What should we do if we see the blue glow coming behind us?"

"Whistle the Starfleet emergency signal," Uhura said. "Three short, three long, three short."

"Then run like hell," Tomlinson added grimly. "Before you find out the hard way where the captain and Mr. Chekov went."

She had started to measure the trip in watches, Uhura realized. Two more until she had to be the one left behind, then one more, then the ice-cold moment when Martine and Tomlinson tramped away after the rest of the cave party and left her standing alone with her helmet in her hands, watching the twirl of fire die in front of the reflector as a final drip of water sizzled on the reactive carbide rocks inside. By the time her eyes adjusted enough to see the departing glow of Martine's helmet, it was nearly gone. The sound of Tomlinson's voice lingered a little longer, rising once to a crack of laughter at something Martine said. Then the noise faded under the ubiquitous pop and crack of ice crystallizing inside the alien conduits, and Uhura was truly alone in the darkness.

It had gotten even colder than when they first tramped

down this way, cold enough that the engineered fibers of her cave jumper couldn't tighten enough to insulate her body against it anymore. While she'd been walking, Uhura barely noticed the minute heat loss, but as soon as she began standing watch, she could feel a slow, inexorable chill seeping through to her skin. Her first instinct was to start pacing and generate more heat, but the ice-slicked surface beneath her feet quashed that idea. Uhura tried isometric exercises instead, but they didn't seem to keep her much warmer. She finally fell back on swinging her arms back and forth as rapidly as she could. That at least gave her the advantage of counting how many times she had clapped her hands together rather than the ridiculously slow passage of her five allotted minutes.

At clap 173, Uhura thought she saw her hands leave a filmy blue path through the darkness as she swung them in front of her.

Fear propelled her into an unbalanced backward scrabble. She'd forgotten about the icy footing, and when her boots hit a ledge she hadn't been expecting, they skidded out from under her completely. Uhura got her hands down in time to catch her weight and avoid the worst of the jolt, but she was left sprawled and unable to tell which way she had been facing before. She stared fiercely out into the darkness, trying to ignore the melting optical illusions that floated across your vision when you tried too hard to see in the dark. Maybe what she had glimpsed had just been another of those phantom traces of light, coincidentally moving in the same direction as her hands.

"And maybe you're just going nuts," Uhura told herself bracingly. But as soon as she spoke she realized she could see the filigree edges of her misted breath turn blue in the darkness. Her hands shot up, the one with the whistle to her lips, the other to the lumpy carbide light on her helmet. But with her teeth clamped on the small whistle and her fingers poised on the igniter lever, Uhura paused. Now that she had made the decision that would soon bless her with light, she ironically found her nerves steady enough to tolerate another few moments of darkness. And there was something different about this blue light, something she wanted to make sure of before she sparked the carbide's fierce glare and drove it completely out of sight.

Uhura swung her head back and forth, trying to use the more light-sensitive corners of her vision. As soon as she did that, she realized what she was seeing. The bluish glow wasn't hanging in the air—it came through the ice crust that covered the walls of the conduit. Beneath the ice, Uhura could just glimpse a dim and deeper blue-violet radiation shining from the ancient alien walls. It refracted into brighter shafts of blue inside the wall's icy coatings wherever internal cracks and fractures caught and focused it, then sent it slanting out into the cold air. It had been one of those natural crystal mirrors that had illuminated Uhura's hands and breath. If she hadn't been standing in exactly that spot, Uhura realized, she might never have seen the light at all.

She scrambled to her feet, wondering if the sides of this conduit had been glowing all along. If the ice back along their path had been thicker or milkier, neither she nor the two weapons officers might have noticed that near-ultraviolet glimmer. But now that she had seen it, there could be no further doubt. The light was rising off the engraved alien metal that lined this alien passage, and where it was focused into a stronger shaft, it looked exactly the same as the blue phosphorescence that had rippled through the ice cave an hour ago.

That answered two of the questions that had been haunting Uhura while she alternately walked and waited in the dark. Now she knew the force that had swept away Captain Kirk and Ensign Chekov hadn't been an accident, hadn't sprung unplanned from any natural deposit of transperiodic ore minerals. It was a product of some unknown alien technology, still alive and working in this cave despite the millions of years that must have passed since its makers had left or gone extinct. And worse than that—Uhura also knew that their departure from the ice cave hadn't delivered them from the dangers of this ancient alien installation. It had merely put some space between them and the most dangerous part of whatever offensive or defensive force had sprung to life here in the dark.

Far off down the conduit, a whistle blew once, then fell silent. After a pause, it blew again. Martine or Tomlinson, Uhura realized, summoning her up the trail to join them.

Had it really been five minutes that she had sat there, watching the glow of alien light and mulling over all its implications? Uhura shook her head in disbelief and felt ice slide down her neck from the hoarfrost that had settled on her hair. She reignited her carbide lamp, tucked her whistle back into her pocket, then headed up the slippery ice-floored conduit. The back of her neck was prickling, and she knew it wasn't just because of the ice crystals melting their way down to her jumper's collar. Now that she knew these conduits were intrinsically connected to the alien force that had been activated in this underground structure, she couldn't rid herself of the feeling that the darkness she passed through was somehow watching her.

"Lieutenant Uhura?" Martine's carbide glow came partway down the conduit to meet her, not normal for a shift change. "Be careful, the ice is really thick up here. We're back to where the waterfall used to be."

Uhura took a step up toward the other woman and found herself sliding back down the steep, icy slope rather than advancing up it. She accepted Martine's outstretched hand to pull her over the crest of the former plunge pool, which now looked more like an ice-filled fountain permanently frozen in mid-splash.

"Did Mr. Jaeger find the blowhole Survey Team Three used to come down here?"

"He found where he thinks it used to be," Martine said, grimly. "It's completely covered with ice."

Uhura followed her around the frozen torrent of thickly clustered icicles that had once been a waterfall. "Could we break through?"

"Wrong question," said Sanner's voice from somewhere far above her. There was a crunch of metal digging into ice, and a flurry of crushed ice crystals floated down over Uhura's upturned face. Her carbide glow reached up to meet another, ten meters higher and obscured by the jagged edges of the broken conduit ceiling. "The real question is, do we *want* to break through?"

"Zap?" Uhura took a step back, trying to angle her head so she could see the geologist clinging to the icy wall of the fracture. He had set a rope on pitons as he went up that wall, but he was unwinding it just as carefully now that he was on the way down. She watched him rappel down another half meter, his carbide glow swinging wildly as he turned in mid-air to approach the ice at a different angle. "What's the matter? Is it too slippery for us to climb out?"

"Probably." Sanner kicked up a second shower of ice shavings as he dug his crampons into the ice. His voice sounded unusually flat, especially considering the rush of his rapid descent. "But trust me, Lieutenant, you wouldn't want to come this way, not even if I carved you a spiral staircase out of that waterfall."

Uhura frowned, remembering the dim violet-blue glow of the conduit she had just left behind. "The force field, or whatever it is that we saw in the ice cave," she said. "You saw it on the upper level of the cave?"

"In living color." Sanner unwound the last loop of his rope, levered out the piton it had been lashed to, and did an unbraked slide down the rest of the way to the bottom. Shaved ice clung to his helmet, and glittered on his jumper like diamond dust, an incongruous contrast to his somber dark eyes. "Not just tendrils of it, either— the same kind of solid sheet we saw below. It must go right up through the rock like it wasn't there. Hell, for all I know, it keeps going right up to the surface!"

"How close did you get?" That was Jaeger's slight German accent, echoing from the far side of the frozen plunge pool. Uhura glanced across and saw that the rest of the party had gathered there, making a tight knot for warmth while they waited for Sanner. She couldn't see Davis in the huddle, and assumed Wright had placed the injured crewman in the middle for protection. With the cold this intense and their cave jumpers leaking heat, hypothermia was a danger for everyone, but especially for the disabled members of the party. Uhura glanced at Jaeger as well, and wasn't reassured by the way his bruised cheek and cut lip stood out against a too-pale face.

"Not even a hundred meters," Sanner said. "I had my carbide turned way down, so I could see it from far away. And when I saw it, I just turned right around and headed back. We spent enough hours poking around up there to know that there was only one way in."

"One way at that end of the system," Jaeger agreed. He paused to grit his teeth against a chatter. "But there's still the warm draft we felt through the rubble pile in the upper chamber. One of those cracks must lead to the surface."

"Yeah...one of those hundreds of tiny cracks." Despite his words, however, Uhura could see a spark rekindle in Sanner's tired face. Clearly, the thought of squirming through hundreds of tiny cracks appealed to him. "I didn't think you guys would want to go back and start digging there all over again."

"What other choice do we have?" Palamas inquired, sounding almost as dispassionately logical as a Vulcan. Uhura wondered if she did a lot of work with Mr. Spock on the Science Deck. "If we can't go out through either the upper or lower level at this end, and we can't use the transporter, then we have to try the rubble pile again."

"And we'll have lights this time, so it'll be easier to see what we're doing," Yuki Smith said cheerfully. "And a lot harder to fall off."

Uhura nodded. "It's decided, then. We'll go back up to the breakdown cave where we found Team Three, and start digging our way out. Let's head out, same order as before."

Sanner coiled up the last of his rope and stuffed it in his backpack, then headed over to Jaeger. "Come on, Karl," he said, with surprising gentleness. "Let me give you a hand, just over this slippery part here."

The older geologist grunted and let Sanner haul him to his feet. His teeth were definitely chattering now. "Just because you were right about the light going through to the upper level doesn't mean you know everything about this cave system," Uhura heard him grumble to his fellow scientist. "For instance, those weren't vadose passages back there."

"Oh, yeah? Then what the hell were they?"

"Tension cracks, from the deroofing stress created by the conduit—"

Their voices dwindled up the tunnel, and the other members of the original survey team and the rescue team trailed after them. Uhura watched Wright lift Davis to her feet and gesture the quiet D'Amato to help support her on the other side. The surveyor was barely hanging on to consciousness now, her eyes narrowed down to pained slits as if even their carbide lights were too strong for her. Uhura gave Wright a questioning look and got a shake of the head in response that told her wordlessly what she needed to know. Davis wasn't going to be able to take much more of this cold and constant movement. If they didn't manage to break through that rubble pile and get the injured surveyor some proper medical attention soon, they would run the risk of losing her entirely.

Tomlinson and Martine waited with Uhura until the last of the other team members had left the frozen waterfall. "Which of us gets to play rear guard first?" Tomlinson asked. He might have been trying to sound playful, but the words came out just plain weary.

"None of us." Uhura met his surprised gaze with a look she hoped was stern enough to cut off questions. "We know that curtain is still back near the entrance—"

"Not really," said Martine. "Zap said he saw it a hundred meters away, but we don't know exactly where he was when he saw it. We walked a long way from the entrance to that section where Mr. Chekov fell through."

Uhura sighed. She'd been hoping she was the only one to have that disconcerting thought. She could see from the two worried young faces in front of her, though, that the implications had sunk in on both Tomlinson and Martine. She chose her words carefully, trying to think about how Captain Kirk had inspired Chekov to reconstruct his map. "If that force field is moving, we'll just have to deal with it when it arrives," she said, although she didn't have the least idea what she meant by "deal with it." "In the meantime, the important thing is to dig our way out of the rubble pile quickly."

"And we'll be most effective at doing that if we're not panicking about when the force field might arrive," Tomlinson guessed, nodding. "That's a good thought, Lieutenant. We'll keep our mouths shut about it."

"Thanks," Uhura said. "I wasn't sure you'd understand."

Tomlinson glanced down at Martine, then both of them smiled unexpectedly. "When you work in the weapons banks, Lieutenant Uhura, the first thing you learn is not to listen to the battle reports about what might be coming your way," Martine informed her. "You already know you're the part of the ship that the other guy is aiming at. If you waste all your time worrying about when you're going to blow up, then you probably *will* blow up."

"And you won't have any fun in the meantime." Tomlinson touched the small of Martine's back to urge her up the conduit, and kept his hand there as they began walking. Uhura lifted an eyebrow, then saw that he was surreptitiously helping to support the weight of her heavy pack under the guise of flirtation. She wasn't sure what Kirk would have said about that, but decided that she wasn't going to make an issue of it.

The spiraling path up to the large column-filled upper chamber seemed much harder to climb now than when they'd first walked it. Uhura intellectually knew that was because she was far more tired and downcast than she'd been the first time through, but she couldn't help feeling a little nervous as the conduits twisted, then straightened, then twisted again. Had they lost their way without the benefit of Chekov's map? Had Jaeger in his weariness led Sanner and Smith down the wrong side of those branches they'd gone through? Could they be walking into another ice cave, with another curtain of rippling force waiting for them?

A waft of distinctly warmer air against her cold-chapped face proved that the last of her worries, at least, was unfounded. Uhura glanced up from trudging last along their track, in the place she thought the commander ought to have. Ahead of her, she could see only a sharp turn in the passage, but she could already hear the way the other crew members' voices echoed through a large, hollow space. And the warmth of the air flowing out of that upper chamber wasn't an illusion. When Uhura stepped inside, she could actually feel her cave jumper relax its tight, insulating grip on her as it adjusted to a more reasonable temperature gradient. That must be the draft of surface air Jaeger kept talking about.

The sound of voices seemed unusually loud, even given the echo effect Uhura remembered from their first entrance into this cathedral-like space full of travertine columns. She glanced around, seeing Wright and D'Amato carefully lower Davis back to the makeshift bed they had left here, while Palamas began to pile silver emergency blankets on top of her. Jaeger sat in another huddle of blankets nearby, his hands wrapped around the minuscule warmth of an unmounted carbide light. That wasn't where all the noise was coming from.

Uhura's glance swung around to the giant rubble pile at the back of the cave, where Sanner and Smith had already gone to begin their assault. Tomlinson and Martine were joining them, and all four voices were raised in what sounded more like exhilaration than anything else. Uhura blinked, becoming slowly aware of her own tiredness and resultant stupidity. She couldn't see anything worth getting that excited about over there—no sudden breaks in the roof of the cave, or shafts of sunlight slanting in through the boulders. So what on Earth—?

The knot of crew members split apart, and turned to cross back to Uhura. She blinked again, and scrubbed at her eyes to make sure she wasn't mistaken. Four members of the team had headed across to the rubble pile, but five members were walking away from it now. And the small, dark-haired man in the center, walking slowly but steadily back toward Uhura, was none other than Ensign Chekov.

Chapter Nine

AT LEAST THE FIRST question Lieutenant Uhura asked him was the easiest one to answer. "Are you all right?"

Chekov nodded stiffly. "Yes, sir." Then he felt compelled to add, "I think so, sir," because he was cold, and confused, and his stomach felt as though it had collapsed into water inside him, and it occurred to him that he might not be the best judge at the moment of whether or not he was functional.

Apparently agreeing with him, Uhura turned to motion Diana Wright forward out of what had become a surprisingly large group of people. The medic took his elbow and led him back through the little crowd, to where another woman in a gold cave suit already lay stretched out with her hand over her eyes. Chekov felt weirdly inappropriate seating himself on a pack near her feet, as if he was impinging on a stranger's bench space in a public spaceport.

It was weirder still to have the others follow him and Wright with such confident familiarity, crowding around the makeshift bed and staring at him expectantly. He stole looks over Wright's shoulder as she examined his skull and shone her light into his eyes, trying to pick out someone he recognized in the jumble of unknown faces.

His eyes found Sanner standing with an older man in science blue who looked like he'd been on the losing end of a fistfight. Suddenly aware of Chekov's attention, Sanner blurted out, "Where's the captain?" as though he'd been holding his breath around the question ever since they'd stumbled upon Chekov.

"I…" Of all the comments which could have been on the tip of Sanner's tongue, this was not one Chekov had expected. He blinked, unsure how to respond to such an obviously serious and yet ridiculous question. "I thought he was up with you," he finally managed, feeling utterly stupid. "The last time I saw him, sir, he was still with the rest of you."

"You both disappeared together." That was Uhura, visible again at the front of the group now that she had pushed her way between a tall blonde woman in blue and a short, stout, smiling woman in security red.

It was their syntax, Chekov realized abruptly, the English language's damned capacity for inaccuracy and misunderstanding. If he could figure out how to clarify what he was saying, they'd realize there was no way he could know where the captain had gone once he himself had hit the water. "I didn't disappear," he said very carefully, trying to speak clearly and choose the right verbs. "I fell."

Uhura's eyes widened in what could only have been surprise, but the scientist at Sanner's elbow shot his hand into the air with a triumphant smile. "Ah ha! I *knew* it!"

Sanner pinned his companion with a curmudgeonly scowl. "Where? I'm telling you, the floor there was completely intact rock." It wasn't clear if he directed those comments at Chekov or the other man, who must have also been a cave geologist.

Before Chekov could figure out how to answer, the taller woman near Uhura asked, "Ensign, how did you end up back here?"

Who are *you?* he wanted to exclaim. Out of all this weirdness, that was the part that alarmed him the most— the fact that six people whose faces meant nothing to him had apparently joined their party in the brief span of time when he must have been unconscious. Somehow they all seemed to know him and care about the details of his mishap, and he couldn't recall even the most basic introductions. He understood that they must be the members of Survey Team Three, lost in the cave several hours ahead of the landing party. But when had they become part of the rescue party and no longer just the rescuees?

"I don't know, sir." He directed that initial answer to the scientist who'd specifically asked him, then turned away from Wright's examination to face Uhura squarely. "I mean, I fell when the ledge became icy after we fired our phasers. Sir, I don't know where *this*—" He gestured vaguely around him. "—I don't know where we are now. I...I thought there was water below us where I fell, but…" But he was obviously dry and undrowned, and the thin skim of hoarfrost that covered the flowstone columns here came nowhere near explaining the icy plunge that was his last coherent memory.

"We're talking about what happened after that." Uhura came a few steps closer, calm despite his growing panic. "A long time after that, Mr. Chekov, when we went into Mr. Jaeger's ice cave—did you fall again there?"

"There *was* nothing after that." He wished he didn't sound so frightened, so desperate. "I'm sorry, sir, but I don't know anyone named Mr. Jaeger, or anything about an ice cave. I only know that I fell down the crevasse we were walking along, and then…" Then came the horrible chill of being swallowed by near-freezing water, the darkness, the realization that he was standing all alone in a vast empty chamber with a carbide lamp too wet to relight and no whistle around his neck. He'd called out once or twice only to have his voice bounce back to him in grotesquely attenuated echoes. It had actually crossed his mind that he was dead, that this was all there was. "And then I was here," he finished lamely.

The *tock-tock* of water dripping and freezing on the cavern's flowstone floor was what had finally saved him. Unless Hell was vastly more damp than predicted (or Heaven vastly more unpleasant), he had realized that he was still inside the caves of Tlaoli 4 somewhere, which meant the others would find him eventually. Chekov had unscrewed his useless lamp from the top of his helmet then, and had used the helmet itself as an uncomfortable perch on which to sit and wait. In the small eternity that had crept by since then, he hadn't even tried to imagine an explanation for how a fall into an underground cave pond had washed him up here. He realized now that this was because he'd known even then that no good explanation existed.

Diana Wright was the first to break the silence. "It could be shock." She shrugged when the others all looked at her. "He doesn't show any signs of having a concussion, or any other physical damage for that matter. But we don't know exactly what that force field did to him."

Chekov twisted around to stare at her, convinced she must be joking. "Force field?" But the medic, unsmiling, only glanced a further question toward Lieutenant Uhura.

"Ensign, I want you to listen to me." Uhura squatted down in front of him, catching him by the arms and making him look her in the eye. Her smooth dark face was remarkably calm and serene, considering how insane she must think he was. "After you fell down the crevasse, Captain Kirk jumped into the water after you and you both broke through a rock ceiling into a lower set of cave passages. That's where we are now. We located Survey Team Three—" She motioned toward the unfamiliar people surrounding them. "—that's Lieutenant Jaeger and his people." The older scientist by Sanner—Jaeger, Chekov realized—sketched a short, polite nod. "They led us to the other end of the cave system, to a chamber a lot like this one, where Mr. Jaeger thought we might be able to find a faster way back to the surface."

"You mapped the whole way," the burly female security guard added. "I helped you." She held up his tape measure as if this somehow proved her claim. Her warm smile made Chekov feel oddly guilty that he couldn't even recall her name.

"Once we got there," Uhura continued, "you and Captain Kirk walked out into the middle of the room..." She trailed off into a shrug, the way people do when the only thing they can think to say is something embarrassing or unpleasant.

Sanner, on the other hand, never seemed at a loss for words. "And you vanished. Poof. Into thin air."

Chekov looked back and forth between them for what seemed a very long time, not even sure how he felt about all this new information, much less how he was supposed to react to it.

"You don't remember anything?" Uhura finally asked.

Chekov shook his head miserably. "I'm sorry, sir."

"What about the captain?" The woman on the pile of supply packs barely moved, her hand still across her eyes and her lips still drawn down into a tense line. Her words sounded thick and blurry. "If that force field sent Ensign Chekov here, maybe it sent the captain here, too."

The other members of the combined parties stirred restlessly. Even Chekov caught himself squinting out into the darkness as though expecting to catch some glimpse of something no one else could see.

"If he's here," Sanner asked, "then why haven't we found him?"

Uhura pushed to her feet. "Maybe he's lost his memory, too. Maybe he doesn't even remember who we are." She turned to the slim young man holding Angela Martine's hand. "Tomlinson, Martine, start searching that side of the cavern. Smith—" This was apparently the broad-shouldered security guard. "—you'll come with me. Mr. D'Amato, I want you to stay just outside the entrance and watch in case that alien field gets any closer."

The quiet male scientist at the back of the group nodded and pulled together his gear. "I'll keep my lamp turned off."

As D'Amato started off, Sanner volunteered, "And I'll start trying to clear out that alternate exit."

"Keep Mr. Jaeger on the ground!" Uhura obviously meant it as a warning, and didn't move her gaze from Sanner until he'd sighed and given her his promise. Then she said to Wright, "Stay with Davis and Chekov."

"Lieutenant!" Chekov only meant to stop Uhura with his call, but Sanner and Jaeger also paused and looked back at him. He reminded himself to be more specific when he addressed his commanders in the future. "Lieutenant Uhura, sir, I want to help." He came forward a step, hands extended, when he saw her open her mouth to contradict him. "I know I don't remember everything, sir, but I feel fine. And I want to do my part. Please, sir."

Uhura glanced a question at Wright. The medic shrugged. "I can't find anything obvious wrong with him."

The lieutenant hesitated only a moment longer, then sighed as though sure she was going to regret her leniency. "All right. But if you start to feel sick or dizzy or—"

Chekov tried to smile reassuringly. "I promise I won't fall down any more cliffs."

From close by in the near darkness, Sanner made a

little noise that was half laugh, half snort. "You're about five hours too late on that one, mister."

"Drake. Hailing. *Enterprise."* Sulu clipped each word into its own distinct sentence, knowing they would arrive in a barrage of subspace static. Beneath Tlaoli's drab and timeworn surface, some monstrous force was stirring to life. The planet was spitting out subspace noise on every possible communications frequency now, and interfering with most of the shuttle's sensors as well. Even the *Drake's* most basic altitude-finding instruments had error readings high into the red. Sulu had learned the hard way not to trust them when he'd nearly plunged the unwieldy cargo shuttle into a saltwater swamp on his first trip down to the surface. On his second trip he'd flown strictly by sight rules, even through the garnet-colored glow of sunset.

"Enterprise..." After that one word, Lieutenant Palmer's voice disintegrated into another blast of static. Sulu forced himself to wait, his fingers tapping impatiently on the transmit button. If it had been Uhura, he would have replied right away, secure in the knowledge that she wouldn't say more than she needed to on such a static-clogged channel. But just as he'd expected, the junior communications officer was continuing to send unnecessary instructions through the snarl of background noise. *"Drake,* please report in."

"I'm trying to," Sulu growled, but he was careful not to depress the transmission switch until after he said it. From the narrow passageway that led to the passenger compartment, he heard a stifled snort from one of the geologists. *"Drake* is returning to *Enterprise.* Estimated docking time, twenty forty-five."

"Acknowledge. Commander Spock..." Whatever else Palmer said was lost in another tidal swell of static.

"Everything okay now?" Geologic Technician Fisher poked his head through the passage in an oddly tentative manner. Although he was technically second-in-command, and therefore had the right to occupy the copilot's seat, Sulu had summarily evicted him during the launch. He'd told Fisher it was for safety reasons, which wasn't entirely untrue. Scotty's magnetic shielding had kept his engines powered up, but they hadn't protected the *Drake* from the sudden and unexplained changes in course heading that he'd felt back on the *Enterprise.* In the much smaller mass of the shuttle, they felt like buffeting blows of invisible wind rather than gentle diversions of orbit. Sulu had needed all of his concentration and considerable skill as a pilot just to guide the shuttle up through Tlaoli's treacherous gravity well.

"We're past the worst of it." Sulu could see the *Enterprise* emerging around the curve of Tlaoli 4, a shining silver beacon against the utter blackness of deep space. Like a small second moon, the ship was catching sunlight from a star that Sulu could no longer see. Tlaoli's sun had set just as he had loaded the two remaining geologists from the survey team and their precious fossiliferous samples. Below him, the crimson and orange remnants of a glorious dust-filtered sunset made the planet's western horizon look as if it were on fire.

Fisher took another tentative step into the cockpit. He

wasn't looking at the *Enterprise* or, to Sulu's relief, at the alarming displays of red light that flashed across the pilot's console. All of his attention was focused on the darkening planet they had just left behind.

"I wonder what the hell is going on down there?" the geologist muttered, sinking into the copilot's seat with a frown. "God, I hope we didn't send Jaeger and his team into some kind of subspace window or wormhole…"

"You couldn't know that it was going to be that dangerous," Sulu told him. "Tlaoli got the highest safety rating a frontier planet can have."

"That was before we found nineteen wrecked starships down here," Fisher said gloomily. "We should have known there might still be something dangerous around. But all we could think of was that we might have found a natural transperiodic ore deposit, and that wouldn't be dangerous to people, only to starships with warp cores…"

"You never found any alien ruins in your survey?"

"No," Fisher admitted. "But Tlaoli's deeply eroded. Anything that was built on the surface has turned to dust or deep-sea mud by now." He craned his head to catch the last glimpse of the planet's dried-blood twilight. "But maybe the aliens who used to live here built something underground for protection, some kind of planetary defensive system that could explain what happened to the *Enterprise*."

"It still wouldn't necessarily threaten people who went near it." Sulu swung the *Drake* around to line her up with the orbital plane of the *Enterprise*.

"No." Fisher heaved a worried sigh. "Unless maybe it thought they were there to attack and disarm it."

As the *Enterprise* approached, Sulu could see the shuttle bay doors roll open along her secondary hull. On his previous trips, the doors had to be manually wrenched open and closed, taking four engineers in spacesuits several minutes to achieve what normally would have taken a few seconds. But Commander Scott must have finally restored full power to the bay, allowing the shuttle to swoop in without even needing to brake. The doors rolled shut behind them and Sulu felt the usual turbulence shiver through the shuttle as air flooded back around it. He held the *Drake* steady until it was done, then dropped onto its landing pad, where empty grav-sleds and full pallets of medical equipment waited side by side.

"Go back and help Kulessa get your samples ready to offload. I want the shuttle emptied as quickly as possible," he told Fisher.

The geologist rose from his seat obediently enough, but paused in the cockpit door to give him a quizzical look. "You're not making another trip back down tonight?"

Sulu forced himself to look back at Fisher without a giveaway glance at the red warning lights on his console. "Why not? The cave team could be out on the surface now."

"But landing on that karst surface, in the dark—" Fisher broke off, shaking his head. "Better you than me, buddy."

Sulu waited until he'd gone, then leaned forward to reboot the shuttle's instrument buffers. They blinked and went dark, then began coming back on one at a time. Some of the gauges still flashed red, warning that even at this distance Tlaoli's subspace racket was inter-

172

fering with their ability to function, but most came back a solid, reassuring green. The pilot grunted in satisfaction and began running the shuttle through a preflight mechanical safety check. In the background, he could hear the thump and whir of grav-sleds being maneuvered out of the hatch, a straggle of conversation cut short by Fisher's voice, then silence. A few moments later, as he'd expected, a single set of footsteps echoed up the hatch and through the empty passenger compartment.

"Lieutenant Sulu."

Sulu glanced over his shoulder, startled. He'd expected to see Chief Engineer Montgomery Scott, intent on making sure that his makeshift magnetic shielding was still strong enough to protect the shuttle's warp core and engines from Tlaoli's mysterious power fluxes. But the wiry figure in the doorway wore science blue rather than the red of ship's services.

"Dr. McCoy." Sulu glanced from the physician's intent face to the old-fashioned black bag he had slung across one shoulder. "Here to give me another antiviral booster shot?"

"Nope." The doctor came forward to sit in the copilot's chair, dropping his bag beside him. "Although I probably should. Scotty says only a lunatic would think about making a flight down to that damned planet after dark."

Sulu tried to make his face as impassive as possible. "It's not that crazy. I've been down there twice already and I know what to expect..."

McCoy waved him to a stop. "I'm not arguing with you, son. The sooner we get down there, the better I'll like it."

"We?" Sulu said, startled again. Before his first trip to Tlaoli, he and Commander Spock had agreed that it made no sense to risk a second life in a shuttle that had a statistically significant probability of crashing. The probability was now much more than just statistical, but if he pointed that fact out to McCoy, he would risk getting the trip itself cancelled. Sulu searched around for another reason to reject the doctor's company. "Sir, this cargo shuttle is only rated for twelve passengers plus pilot. And there are already twelve people down at that cave site."

"Some of whom may be very badly injured," McCoy reminded him gruffly. "What's the good of getting down there and finding someone too hurt to fly out again?"

"But the shuttle's weight limit—"

"—won't be exceeded, provided we leave all their gear and samples behind." McCoy pulled a data padd out of his bag and punched a file up on it. "Captain Kirk deliberately selected the smallest crewmen he could find for his cave rescue team, and the two of us aren't much bigger than they were. If you add in the survey team—well, Tomlinson's pretty hefty and I'm always amazed by how much Yuki Smith weighs for her size, but those other cave experts are all lightweights, too." He turned the padd to show Sulu his final calculation, and the pilot winced. There was no question that it was several percent less than the shuttle's weight allowance, even taking into account Scott's new magnetic shielding.

"I still think you should stay here, sir," Sulu said. It

was one thing to risk his own neck, but he couldn't let another member of the crew come along trusting in a safety margin that wasn't there. He saw McCoy's stubborn headshake and took a deep breath. "Doctor, what I'm trying to tell you is—"

"That if you left now, it would be on a suicide mission," said a deep and completely unexpected voice from behind them.

"*Spock!*" McCoy swung around in his seat, glaring at the Vulcan who stood in the shadows of the cockpit door. "Don't you know better than to sneak up on people when they think they're the only ones on board? You could have given us both a heart attack!"

"As first officer, I have examined the quarterly medical reports for both Lieutenant Sulu and yourself, Doctor." Spock's voice retained the impassive tone that he usually used when verbally sparring with McCoy. "Neither record suggests a susceptibility to myocardial infarction."

"That's not what I meant!"

"Then I fail to understand why you said it." Spock ducked through the cramped passageway to the passenger hold and straightened to his full height in the cockpit. Sulu suppressed an urge to lay his hand across his red-flashing instrument panel as a keen Vulcan gaze swept across it. The motion would have been just as damning as the telltale gauges, and he had the distinct feeling that it didn't matter anyway.

He was right. "Mr. Sulu, may I see the instrument log from your last flight segment?" Spock asked blandly.

"I've already zeroed it out, sir," Sulu confessed. There

was no point in continuing to prevaricate when a superior officer had obviously guessed what you were up to. "It was mostly error readings anyway."

"Yes, I know." Spock flickered an eyebrow at Sulu's startled look. "You should have known that Chief Engineer Scott would never install a brand-new device on a shuttle without adding a monitoring circuit to report on how it was functioning, Mr. Sulu. The subspace interference prevented us from making real-time observations during most of the flight, but as soon as the *Drake* came back into secure transmission range, all of her data banks were copied to engineering. Mr. Scott called me when he saw the size of the error readings."

"Well, what about 'em?" McCoy demanded. "You wouldn't expect subspace instruments to work right down on that power-sucking planet, would you?"

"No," Spock agreed. "But when sudden vertical displacements in the shuttle's altitude exceed the error margin of her proximity alarms by a factor of ten to one, it is clearly unsafe to fly at night. Especially in a terrain such as the Tlaoli karstland, where the elevation can change by thousands of meters from one second of flying to the next."

Sulu met the chief medical officer's astounded look with a wry smile. "I tried to tell you that you didn't want to come," he said. "Would you like to give me that antiviral booster now?"

McCoy scowled. "What I'd *like* is to get down to that damned planet as quickly as possible! For all we know, people are dying down there—" He swung around to glare at Spock as if that were somehow the Vulcan's fault. "—and you're telling me we can't even leave until the sun comes back up?"

This time, to Sulu's surprise and delight, Spock's lifted eyebrow had a distinctly ironic slant. "I do not recall making that statement, Doctor."

McCoy looked even more frustrated by that reply, but Sulu had already guessed what the science officer's response meant. "Moonlight!" he said. "Mr. Spock, when does Tlaoli's moon rise? And how full will it be?"

"Gibbous." Spock said it so calmly that Sulu knew he must have weighed this option long before he'd ever arrived in the *Drake*'s cockpit. "It will rise over the horizon of the karst plateau four hours from now." He gave Sulu a considering glance. "At that time, Lieutenant, and no sooner, you will receive my permission to take the *Drake* down to Survey Team Three's relocated base camp. *Not* to the cave itself."

"Aye-aye, sir," said Sulu.

"Huh." McCoy was less intimidated by the severe tone Spock adopted when he was functioning as ship's commander. "And what if something awful happens to them in the meantime?"

Spock let out a slow and measured breath. "There is no higher probability of 'something awful' happening in the next four hours, Doctor, than of it having already happened in the past ten."

"I know," McCoy said, a little grumpily. "That's what I'm worried about."

"Bring me up another marker!"

Sanner shouted his request back to Chekov in the

same way he had at all the previous stops—as though he fully expected Chekov to trot up to join him, hand outstretched, a variety of reflective spot markers to choose from. In reality, the passage's fifty-centimeter head clearance made it hard for Chekov to even dig the markers out of his jumper pockets, much less crawl within and arm's length of anything but Sanner's feet.

"Here—" He thumped his hand awkwardly on the sole of Sanner's boot, then tossed two or three markers past the geologist's hip in the hopes one would land within reach. "Sir, perhaps it would be better if you carried the markers."

"Are you nuts? I've barely got room to carry the stuff I've got." Light swung at apparent random across the floor, the low ceiling, into Chekov eyes as Sanner twisted to grope for the markers in the mud. "Don't worry—I'm getting a really strong breeze up here. We've got to be close to the exit by now."

"I hope you're right, sir." Chekov raised himself up as high as he could on his elbows to stuff the remaining markers deeply enough into his pocket that they wouldn't work themselves out again. Ironically, he banged his helmet against some outcrop or other not in lifting up but on the way back down again. "I'm not sure how we're going to get the others even this far."

He felt Sanner stiffen, almost as though a physical chill had blown through their dark crawlspace. "We're not leaving anybody down here." Sanner's voice was uncharacteristically quiet and grim.

"Of course not, sir." Chekov hadn't meant to imply that they would. But he couldn't help thinking about how pale and silent Davis had been when he last checked back with the party in the big chamber. Or about how Jaeger, despite his stubborn good humor, had the softness of a scientist about him, and hardly looked capable of making such a cold, arduous crawl even when he hadn't first toppled down a breakdown pile. Chekov knew with every fiber of his heart that they couldn't abandon anyone to this frozen underground. He just honestly had no idea how they were going to avoid it.

Not for the first time, he wished Kirk were still here.

"Come on," Sanner grumbled abruptly, "let's keep moving."

Chekov waited until Sanner had dragged himself a few meters further down the passage, then took a deep breath to steel himself, and started after.

When they'd first dug past the last rubble of the breakdown pile in the big chamber and found the narrow vertical shaft that led up to this level, Sanner and Jaeger had both assured Chekov that the force of the breeze that greeted them meant that a substantial passageway existed beyond the restricted opening. Once or twice along the crawl, it had even looked like that might eventually be true. But every time the passageway seemed as though it might trend toward a little taller, a little wider, a little less muddy or crowded or crooked, it cinched back down again a few meters later and stretched further into what seemed like infinity.

More than once, Chekov had wanted to ask Sanner at what point they gave up. When did a caver admit that a passage went nowhere? That they were just crawling farther and farther away from knowing where they were? The tunnel around them barely looked like a cave anymore. Mud slicked the floor like engine lubricant, and tree roots dangled in irregular clusters from the low ceiling like woody stalactites. During one fifteen-minute delay while Sanner sawed through a particularly thick obstruction with a completely inadequate utility knife (which at least the geologist had thought to bring with him, thank God), Chekov had pushed himself backward out the way they'd come in to reassure the waiting party members that he and Sanner were all right, they hadn't gotten lost in the claustrophobic maze. As it turned out, that thought hadn't even crossed anyone's mind. While they'd been waiting patiently for a report, it had only been less than an hour, nowhere near long enough to worry. It only felt like longer when you were on the inside.

Now, another half-hour further along, he found himself growing numb to the pain in his arms and shoulders, and to the passage of time. There was nothing to look at, nothing to talk about. Even Sanner had run out of appropriate wisecracks what felt like miles ago. Whenever Chekov let himself think about anything besides dragging himself forward, one arm's length at a time, his mind invariably circled back to Kirk, like a ship dragged into an event horizon, unable to tear itself away. Kirk, who was more powerfully built than any of them, even Yuki Smith. Kirk, who was nowhere to be found in the cathedral-like space of the upper chamber, but who could not possibly have passed the party unnoticed on their way back from the "ice cave." Kirk, who could only have exited that upper chamber by squeezing out through this same tiny passage that Chekov and Sanner had been clawing their way through for the past two hours, and who simply could not have done so. *Could* not. Not by any stretch of anyone's imagination.

If Chekov didn't dare suggest that their injured party members couldn't make this crawl, there was no point in drawing anyone's attention to the impossibility of a completely healthy Kirk having done so.

"And thar she blows!"

Ahead of him, Sanner's feet suddenly slithered forward and rolled off to one side. Chekov restrained the first surge of hope that tried to swell up in him—he was too tired to survive another disappointment. But by the time he'd managed to drag himself alongside Sanner, the gentle brightening of the air around them had become more apparent, and the muddy walls had fallen away until there was no mistaking what Sanner lay on his back laughing up toward.

Chekov rolled over and followed his gaze upward. "Daylight."

"The last of it, at least. God, that looks good."

Chekov reached up to dim his helmet light, the better to appreciate the ruddy sweep of clouds just visible through the sinkhole above them. "It also looks far away." He tried to visually estimate the height from where he lay, but found it surprisingly hard to do while on his back.

Sanner reached to sink his fingers into the nearest wall. The opposite wall was more than a man's height away, but looked to be coated in the same slimy, dripping mud they'd just squirmed through. "This crap isn't very climbable, either," Sanner decreed, wiping his hand on the leg of his jumper. Some of his puckish humor returned with a crooked grin. "Wanna try standing on my head?"

Chekov didn't need a better height estimate to know the answer to that. "I don't think we'd be tall enough." He pictured Sanner standing, then multiplied the image two more times. "But more of us might be."

"Look at us! We're in the circus!"

Even though Sanner and Tomlinson differed in height by only a couple of centimeters, Yuki Smith wobbled atop their shoulders with a good bit less stability than Chekov had hoped for. But the top of her head came within two meters of the surface, and there were enough tree roots and vegetation overhanging the lip of the sink-hole to make up for the rest of the distance. They didn't technically have to reach the surface with their pyramid in order to get themselves out.

Sanner grimaced and slewed against Tomlinson as Smith shifted her weight yet again. "I don't think we're gonna make it."

"I'll make it," Chekov told him. He hadn't crawled all the way back to the upper cavern and led Tomlinson and Smith out here just to fail now. He tied another knot in the rope Sanner had looped around his waist. "If you would, Lieutenants..."

Sanner and Tomlinson shifted slightly to make a stir-rup with their hands, and Smith whooped delightedly as she teetered. Chekov wasn't sure if he should feel reassured by her fearlessness, or alarmed by her complete lack of concern for the stability of their structure. He decided his nerves would be steadier if he settled on the former. At least Sanner had been smart enough to suggest they all put out their carbide lamps until they were done climbing on each other. They could avoid burning each other in embarrassing places even if they couldn't manage to effect a graceful escape from this cave.

Planting one foot in the stirrup, Chekov stretched his arms up to catch at Smith's hands as he heaved himself upward.

She caught him with surprising strength and ease, and guided him to place his feet atop hers on the other men's shoulders. For one uncomfortable moment, Chekov realized how close they all were to overbalancing and tumbling back down into the bottom of the sinkhole. Smith braced her back against the muddy wall behind her, and Chekov was forced to reach past her shoulders to steady himself when Tomlinson and Sanner staggered under their combined weight. *I'm an idiot!* he thought angrily. *Not only will this stupid idea never work, we're just going to end up with four more injured party members to try and drag out of this cave!* Then Smith's hands closed on his waist, and she hefted him high enough to plant one hand on her head and one knee on her shoulder. From there, he moved as quickly as he could into a standing position and stretched overhead to reach for what looked like the most secure loop of exposed root.

His fingers clawed at the mud five or six centimeters below the handhold. "I can almost..." He willed himself to reach farther, almost lifted up on one foot to extend his length. *I am not going to strand us down here for the sake of a few centimeters!* "Stand on your toes," he ordered abruptly.

Sanner made an explosive noise that might have been a laugh. "Stand on *what?*"

"I'm serious!" He only needed the tiniest bit more height. "Stand on your toes!"

Someone grumbled something Chekov couldn't quite understand from the bottom of their pyramid, then the whole human structure shifted a little aimlessly. Chekov felt himself swayed back away from the wall, and his heart leapt up into his mouth as he grabbed for whatever purchase he could find on the crumbling soil face. The root which had hovered just beyond his reach suddenly seemed to surge up in front of his face. He grabbed it, grabbed at another shorter root less than an arm's length away, and heaved himself up toward the precious surface. "Push!" he shouted down at Smith. "Push me up!"

Her hands clamped onto the bottoms of his boots, shoved—and he was up. The grass at the edge of the sinkhole gave spongily beneath his hands and knees. He crawled another body's length away, pursued by images of collapsing the rim back down on the others and plunging them all back to the floor of the hole. When he reached a distance where the ground felt hard and dry and unyielding, he rolled onto his back with a groan. Beautiful stars, beautiful warm breeze, beautiful dry, clean grass. It was all he could do to keep from stripping out of his cave suit just to feel the balmy flush of dry air across his duty uniform.

"Hey, Ensign? You okay up there?"

Chekov suddenly remembered Smith and the lieutenants still down in the sinkhole, balanced precariously one on top of the other. He rolled to his knees and began working at the knot in the rope around his waist. "Everything's fine!" He hoped Smith could hear him. He didn't want to venture closer to the crumbling lip of the sinkhole if he didn't have to. "I'll tie off the rope."

The roots that had helped him to the surface supported a thick, twisted tree that seemed to grow upright only so it could bow back down and sweep the ground with its crown. Smaller siblings peppered the undulating rocky landscape, their broken-backed shapes recognizable in the dim starlight only because the rocks that crouched alongside them weren't swaying in the night breeze. Chekov leaned his weight into the last pull on the knot, to make sure his handiwork would hold. "The rope's secure!"

That was when he saw the footprints.

Not footprints, really, but mud scars and dents of deliberate disturbance on the opposite side of the sinkhole's mouth. As though someone else had clawed his way to the surface, tearing loose grass and rocks as he labored to drag his body over the edge to freedom. Someone without the support of a human pyramid beneath him. Someone who had performed the miracle of making the horrible slippery climb without help.

Chekov pulled off his helmet and turned up the drip on his carbide lamp. Acetylene hissed with renewed vigor, and the small flame he finally ignited leapt suddenly bright in front of the round reflector. He walked around the sinkhole to train the light more fully on its torn-up edge, then began a careful scan of the ground nearby. He could orienteer, but he was no tracker. What might have been a footprint leading away from the cave exit wasn't always followed by another, and they sometimes seemed to point in contradictory directions. But the splayed, muddy handprint he found on a boulder ten meters away from the edge was unmistakable.

He heard someone tromp up behind him with a confident, unhurried ease he was already learning to recognize.

"Everything okay?" Smith asked, leaning over his shoulder with a friendly intimacy she didn't seem to realize.

Chekov barely noticed her closeness. "I don't know..." He nodded toward the handprint still pinned by his helmet light.

Smith grunted in surprise. "Do you think that's the captain?"

Chekov shook his head slowly, then allowed, "It must be," because that was what his stomach had told him from the beginning. He lifted his eyes to the still, moonless darkness beyond the reach of their lights. "But where does he think he's going?"

Chapter Ten

"UHURA TO *Enterprise.* Come in, *Enterprise.*"

A roar of static filled the storage tent where Survey Team Three had left their main communicator, wedged between the sample crates and supplies they had hastily dumped into this shelter when they relocated their base camp. As Uhura had cleared a path to it through the mess, she had found a spare photon lamp and now had it jacked up to its highest illumination, as if that could somehow erase the memory of too many dark hours underground. The volume on the communicator was also turned up as far as it could go. Uhura was so tired that she couldn't make her eyes focus on the flickering bars of the frequency monitor, so she was trying to make her ears do the work instead. Unfortunately, even loudly amplified static had a tendency to become tedious after a while. Every time Uhura caught herself drifting off, she jerked upright in the hard metal seat and forced herself to send another hail. She was beginning to doubt the ship could hear her any better than she could hear it, but the activity at least kept her a little more alert.

The tent flap opened with a hiss of parting electrostatic seals, letting in a swirl of Tlaoli's dusty air along with a figure so caked in dried mud that his once salt-and-pepper hair had become a solid, grizzled gray. Deep furrows of weariness added to Zap Sanner's appearance of having prematurely aged, but the cave specialist's eyes still held their usual cheerfulness.

"Hey, Lieutenant," said Sanner. "We've got some soup and coffee going over in the mess tent. Why don't you come get some?" He grinned and jerked a thumb at the communicator. "I bet you'll be able to hear that from there just as easily as you can here."

"Sorry." Uhura dialed the volume down to a normal level, and only then realized that the static roar had given her a headache. She rubbed at her forehead and grimaced as she felt mud crumble and sift down between her fingers. "I assume you finally got Crewman Davis up to the surface?"

"Yeah. Once you've got enough rope and pitons and come-alongs set at the top, you can haul damn near anything out of a cave." Sanner gave her a quick, embarrassed look. "Uh, sorry, sir. I didn't mean—"

Uhura smiled and shook her head at him. She had no trouble believing that the captain had scaled that brutal vertical slope on his own, but she wasn't ashamed of waiting until Sanner had rigged a sling and pulley system to help her scramble up to the top. She knew that physical courage was part of what made Kirk a natural and inspiring leader, but right now, Uhura was willing to settle for just being the highest-ranking officer in the group.

"How is Crewman Davis feeling?"

"She's pretty out of it," Sanner said bluntly. "Wright found a working set of medical instruments here and got the subcranial bleeding stopped, but she says Davis needs microsurgery within a few hours."

"And we have to get her to the *Enterprise* for that." Uhura gave her static-clogged communicator a frustrated look. She still remembered the surge of hope she had felt when they had retraced their rugged hike through the karst to Team Three's relocated base camp, and she'd seen that its power generator was still up and running. She'd thought that with the more powerful base communicator here she might actually have a chance to reestablish contact with the ship, but it looked as if Tlaoli's static interference had expanded to clog the entire subspace spectrum.

"Any luck yet?" Sanner asked, following her gaze to the communicator.

"No. I haven't gotten even a flicker of signal to focus in on, much less a response."

The furrows in his mud-caked face deepened a little more. "You don't think the *Enterprise* left the system, do you?"

Uhura felt her head shaking before she'd consciously decided to do it. "Commander Spock would never leave us stranded down here, knowing we were in trouble."

"Yeah. Especially not with Captain Kirk..." Sanner's voice trailed off uncertainly, and Uhura winced. If and when the *Enterprise* ever responded to her hail, she wasn't sure how she was going to explain what had happened to the captain. *First he disappeared into thin air, then we think he came back with amnesia and ran away from us, and now he's probably out wandering around on a dangerous karst plateau in the middle of the night.* It was almost as if the Psi 2000 virus had chased them back through space and time, creating yet another insane crisis, but this time without the man who'd extricated them from the last one.

"Hey," Sanner said, awkwardly. "Don't worry, Lieutenant, we'll find him as soon as it's light out. In the meantime, you really should get something to eat. Can't you set that thing to hail the ship automatically?"

"I'm afraid they won't be able to separate a normal hail from the subspace interference. I've been using a rolling frequency assignment to find out which bands are penetrating the noise best. Then I'll pulse those manually to send the Starfleet code for 'emergency pickup.' "

"Can't you just set the transmitter to pulse that signal on all bands, all the time?"

"Yes, but..." Uhura's voice trailed off. She was still thinking like a ship's communications officer, she realized, assuming she had to be present at the com in order to elaborate on the simple emergency signal. But the *Enterprise* already knew what the situation was down here on Tlaoli. Even an automated and coded message sent from the location of the base camp would be enough to tell Mr. Spock they had managed to escape the cave. "You're right, Mr. Sanner. Hang on a minute while I program that in."

"No problem," he said, and grinned again. "I told that kid Chekov to guard our share of the food with his life. I'm pretty sure he took me seriously."

Somewhat to her own surprise, Uhura felt laughter bubble up through her exhaustion. "Shame on you, Zap. It's his very first landing party—he's going to take *everything* seriously."

"Well, somebody has to cure him of that." Sanner unsealed the tent seams again and held one wall up for her to pass through. Uhura stepped out and paused, waiting for her eyes to adjust to the profound darkness of night on an uninhabited planet. It didn't take long to notice the light spilling out from the open mess tent, or the tantalizing smell of coffee and bread and vegetable soup that came with it. Uhura was halfway there before she even noticed the dim lemony glow on the opposite horizon.

"Zap, what's that light out there?" she demanded, pulling the cave geologist to a halt. He glanced in the direction she pointed, scrubbed a hand through his beard and muttered under his breath as if he were counting something.

"Moonrise, I think," he said eventually. "Sun won't be up for another three hours or so."

Uhura followed him into the mess tent. "Do you think the moon would give us enough light to look for Captain Kirk?"

Sanner shrugged. "Depends on what phase it's in. We'll have to ask Jaeger about that." He suited his action to his words by raising his voice to a cave-piercing bellow. "Hey, Karl! Will the moon be bright enough for us to start looking for the captain right away?"

Jaeger glanced up from the mess tent table on which he had spread several topographic and geologic maps. "That depends. Do you care if you fall into a sinkhole or two along the way?"

"Never mind." Uhura crossed to the food service unit in the corner, where the quiet, dark-haired ensign was guarding a steaming kettle of soup and half a loaf of rehydrated bread as conscientiously as if they were made of dilithium. The soup had a scorched taste, as if it had been heated up too quickly, and the bread was slightly soggy, the way rehydrated food always was. But after the tense and exhausting hours she'd spent underground, Uhura had no complaint to make about either. Even the coffee, brewed bitingly strong the way security guards always seemed to make it and poured out with an apologetic smile by Yuki Smith, tasted like pure ambrosia—at least, once Uhura had surreptitiously mixed in several teaspoons of sweetened dry cocoa that she found on a lower shelf.

It was a measure of Uhura's hunger that she didn't really notice the level of noise and activity in the mess tent until after she'd spooned up the last of her soup. Then she looked around in some surprise. She was sure she had remembered to issue official permission for her subordinates to get some sleep in the hours before dawn. After the long and arduous journey they'd made through Sanner's umbilical exit from the cave, and then the nerve-racking scramble up the muddy slopes of that final sinkhole, she thought most of them would have been thankful to head for the camp's dormitory tent. But aside from the injured crewman Davis and her attendant medic Wright, not a single member of Survey Team Three or the cave rescue party appeared to have heeded her suggestion. Uhura was so new to the idea of being in command of a mission like this that it took her a moment to realize that it was probably her own example of staying awake and at work that had inspired their behavior.

At one table, Sanner, D'Amato, and Palamas had cabled their scientific tricorders into the base camp's generator and were extracting the data they had gathered before the power failure, arguing vigorously about its internal errors as they did so. At another table, Chekov and Smith had gone to help Jaeger sketch out yet another reconstruction of the alien cave system, this time overlain directly on a topographic map of Tlaoli's surface. And in an empty space near the entrance, Martine and Tomlinson were assembling scaffolding and power supplies into something that looked like a small siege tower. Uhura got up and went to join them.

"What are we building, Lieutenant?" she asked, peering up at the apparatus he was attaching to the top of the structure

"A light flare, sir." Tomlinson showed her the bank of photon lamps he had lashed together. "Angela and I thought if the captain was wandering around at night, not sure where he was, and he saw a really bright light..."

"Good idea," Uhura agreed. "But will it be visible all the way back at the cave exit where we lost him?"

"If we calculated the voltages right, it should be," Martine answered. "We've jacked the power up with a couple of heavy-duty electron accelerators, but these photon lamps are combat-rated and they should be able to handle the load. We'll point them straight up, of course, so nobody gets blinded."

Uhura shot her a quick look, trying to decide if that had been a joke, but both weapons officers gazed back at her gravely. "Very good," she said, for lack of anything more intelligent to say. "Um...is it ready to go?"

"Yes, sir."

"Then let's take it out and set it up."

That at least, seemed to have been the right thing to say. Martine stopped fussing with the wiring and Tomlinson clambered off the scaffold and whistled for Chekov and Smith. The two younger crew members came over as if they'd been half-listening for his signal, and the three of them heaved the small tower up to their shoulders while Martine and Uhura lifted the tent flaps out of their way. A few steps past the tent wall, they plunked the light flare down again.

"It doesn't really matter where we put it, since it's pointing straight up," Tomlinson explained to Uhura. "Now, all we have to do is make sure we don't blow out the main power circuit when we first turn it on."

"I'll turn off the food server, and tell those guys inside to unplug their tricorders," Yuki Smith said and slipped back into the tent. When she came back, the four scientists trailed after her, D'Amato with his unplugged tricorder still clutched in his hands. "Okay, everything's off."

Martine finished connecting the flare's power cables to the main generator feed while Tomlinson climbed up the scaffold again to check the photon lamps. "Ready to go," he reported as he vaulted off. There was a pause, and Uhura realized everyone was looking at her expectantly.

"Power it up, Mr. Martine," she said, with more confidence than she felt. She had never realized before that part of being in command was taking responsibility for the ideas and decisions of your crew as well as your own.

"Aye-aye, sir."

There was an ominous crackle from the midsection of the tower—Uhura hoped that was just the accelerators jacking up the voltage—then a fierce white column leaped high into Tlaoli's night sky. Even at its margins, the glare was strong enough to make Uhura blink and turn away. After a moment, her eyes adjusted well enough to see not only the flood-lit sprawl of the base camp but also the rocky rim of the dry canyon in which it was located. Tlaoli's lemony little moon had just finished lifting over that rocky horizon, but its light paled to dim ivory beside their flare.

"Lieutenant." That was D'Amato's diffident voice, somber and pitched low enough that only Uhura could hear. "I'm not sure this is such a good idea."

"Why not, Mr. D'Amato?"

The geologist held out his tricorder, on which small

lights were blinking furiously. Its display panel showed a single blue curve that was dropping, slowly but steadily.

"What's that?" Uhura asked.

"Total power consumption here in the base camp," D'Amato said. "Unless this contraption of Tomlinson's is reducing our generating capacity, which seems unlikely, the curve implies—"

"—that something is draining our power," Uhura guessed. "The alien caves?"

D'Amato nodded. "The power loss isn't very noticeable, this far away. At least, not yet. But apparently we're not really safe even here, sir. We're still not outside the reach of whatever force is coming from inside those caves."

"Will running the flare make our power loss worse?"

D'Amato queried his tricorder, then shook his head and showed her its unhelpful splay of extrapolated curves. "Hard to tell, sir. All this subspace interference is still messing up the analytical circuits. It might be doing that. And we might lose power at exactly this rate without running it at all."

Uhura frowned and tried to weigh various scenarios of failure against each other. No power meant no more hails to the *Enterprise,* but no light flare meant no chance of bringing Captain Kirk in tonight, before he could stumble back into the clutches of whatever alien weapon or transporter they'd encountered back in that cave. If they were going to lose power anyway, there was no reason not to run the flare, but if they could conserve power by shutting everything down right now...

"Sir, I hear something," said a polite Russian voice from behind Uhura. She turned and found Ensign Chekov standing with one ear cocked toward the light-slashed sky. "I think it's a shuttle."

Like any good communications officer, Uhura could make her voice ring like a bell when she needed to. "Quiet, everyone!" she commanded. Silence dropped over the base camp, except for the annoying crackle of the high-voltage accelerators. Uhura was about to order Tomlinson to turn them off, too, but then she heard what Chekov's less distracted ears had already caught—the distant but unmistakable wail of a shuttle dropping at high speed through a planetary atmosphere. Uhura glanced up at the sky, then realized how useless it was to look for a shuttle's blinking lights past the white column of light they had sent fountaining up into Tlaoli's sky. That thought led to another, more urgent one.

"Tomlinson, Sanner, Chekov, Smith—get this thing out into an open space!" Uhura ordered. "If the shuttle's using it to home in on us—"

She didn't need to complete that sentence. The four crewmen picked up the light flare by its makeshift legs and marched in double time out toward the edge of camp, while Martine frantically strung out power cables behind them. "Almost out of line," she warned as they passed the supply tent.

"Set it there, on the edge of the open space." Uhura cast a glance back toward D'Amato. "Is the power holding out?"

He nodded. "It's not dropping any faster than it was

before. Or any slower." D'Amato glanced up at the approaching drone of the shuttle. "I just hope the same power draining effect doesn't hit the shuttle when it starts getting close to us."

It certainly didn't seem to. With a confident, roaring swoop that told Uhura who the pilot was likely to be, a slice of shadow detached itself from the dark eastern sky and flickered into a big silver cargo shuttle as it passed through their fountain of light. It swung around and hovered in the light just long enough for them to read the name *Drake* on its blunt hull, then settled down in the open space with a thump violent enough to suggest the pilot hadn't been completely sure where the ground was. There was a pause before the shuttle's hatch swung open to let out a wiry, blinking figure.

"This had better be the new base camp for Survey Team Three," said Dr. McCoy's familiar caustic voice. "Because I'm not getting back in that shuttle until there's enough light for Lieutenant Sulu to notice that not a single damned one of his instruments is working."

It was strange, Sulu thought, how out of place he felt down here. It wasn't just that his uniform was clean instead of mud-caked, or that his skin wasn't dark with bruises. He'd been just as clean and healthy at the first two landings he'd made on Tlaoli, and it hadn't seemed to separate him from the weather-beaten survey teams he'd picked up there. But there was something almost claustrophobic in the way the survivors of the Tlaoli caves moved around in small groups, never alone. There was some bone-deep terror that haunted them, a shadow that darkened even their initial shouts of welcome and relief.

None of their halting explanations of the alien technology they'd encountered had really explained that fear to him, either. All Sulu had been able to gather was that some kind of alien transporter system had been activated by draining the power from their instruments. He'd told them about the power loss the *Enterprise* had experienced after trying to transport them, and they agreed that it probably explained why it had gotten so much colder and more dangerous in the caves after that. But Sulu still didn't understand why the alien force had flung only Captain Kirk and one hapless young ensign through space, when it clearly had the power to haul down entire 190-ton starships. Or why Ensign Chekov had lost only a few hours of his memory after that experience, while Kirk might have lost all of his.

The dark-haired young man had been standing quietly at the edge of the group when they'd broken the bad news about Kirk's absence, and Sulu had to clamp his teeth down hard to bite off the comment he otherwise would have made. But he still couldn't erase the uncharitable feeling that it was rotten luck to have lost the ship's captain instead of a brand-new and unknown crewman. He'd wondered at the time, catching a sidelong glimpse of the ensign's bleak face, if the young man thought the same thing.

Now he stood next to Uhura and that same silent ensign, hadn't watching the rocky western horizon for the first nebulous glow of sunrise. Around them, the base camp bustled with activity despite the predawn darkness: scientists downloading their data onto lightweight cubes so they could leave even their tricorders behind; weapons officers and security guards deactivating the gear they were leaving behind; McCoy and Wright exchanging curt medical comments as they operated in what had been the camp's mess tent. The photon light flare that had led him through the moonlit jumble of the karst plateau to the base camp had been switched off moments after they'd landed, to preserve power for McCoy's emergency surgery. The internal clock that most pilots developed told Sulu it wouldn't be long now until dawn.

Uhura apparently felt the same way. "If Dr. McCoy's not finished operating by the time the sun's up…" she began suddenly, then trailed off as if she was still deciding exactly how to end that statement.

Sulu smiled at her in the darkness. After the months they'd spent working together on the main bridge crew, he already knew what she was thinking. "I can take a quick trip aloft to look for the captain," he finished for her.

"But only if McCoy's not ready to go," Uhura warned him. As the group's commanding officer, she had reluctantly decided that Sulu's first priority after sunrise was to evacuate the wounded and exhausted members of Survey Team Three, and bring down a fresh crew of security guards to conduct a more effective search for the captain. She had impressed Sulu both by ignoring the howls of protest this brought from her junior officers, and never disclosing how painful he knew the decision to delay searching for Kirk must have been for her. But with the hours to sunrise running out fast and no sign that the emergency surgery in the mess tent was close to being finished, he'd been hoping Uhura would allow him to conduct at least a quick and limited search. Apparently, he wasn't the only one with that thought.

"Sir." There was a pause, as if young Ensign Chekov had to gather up his courage to add anything to that monosyllable. "Sir, if Mr. Sulu takes the shuttle up, couldn't we climb one of the karst mounds near here and watch him? In case he spots the captain right away?"

" 'We?' " Uhura gave him a stern look. "Mr. Chekov, Dr. McCoy's medical scan showed enough microscopic scarring in your lungs to prove that you practically drowned when you fell down that waterfall—"

"—but he also said I hadn't suffered any permanent damage, sir," Chekov said stubbornly. "And, sir, Crewman Smith and I are the ones who tracked the captain out of that sinkhole. We know which direction to look for him."

As justifications went, it was pretty feeble, but even Tlaoli's dim moonlight was enough to show them the shadows of guilt and remorse that looked out of the younger man's eyes. Sulu knew how he would feel, if he had been the undeserving survivor of that alien force field. He cleared his throat to catch Uhura's attention.

"If that photon flare managed to draw the captain in close to us last night, Smith and Chekov might not have to travel very far to find him," Sulu said. That wasn't a very strong argument, either, but the speaking look of gratitude he got from the ensign made him add, "There's no point in me spotting him from the air if we don't actually go get him."

"True," said Uhura, frowning. "But we don't have any way to communicate with the shuttle. If you spot the captain, how will you let Mr. Chekov know?"

"Double-dip," Sulu said. He could see the first tinge of sunrise bleeding into Tlaoli's western sky now. "The energy fluxes down here bump me around a lot, but they never throw me the same way twice. If Mr. Chekov sees the shuttle rise and descend two times over some part of the karstland, he'll know I saw Captain Kirk there."

"And we'll only go to get him if it looks like he's within an hour's walking distance," Chekov promised recklessly. "Otherwise, sir, we'll mark his location and come right back to camp."

Uhura sighed. "I know I shouldn't let you two convince me, but..." She glanced over her shoulder at the creeping light of dawn. "Lieutenant Sulu, go get the shuttle ready. Mr. Chekov, take Smith and Tomlinson, and climb up the nearest karst mound. And I don't want anyone to fall. That's an order!"

"Aye-aye, sir." Chekov answered with such youthful and serious sincerity that Sulu couldn't help exchanging smiles with Uhura before he turned away and headed for the shuttle.

That young Russian would make a reliable crewmate one of these days, the pilot thought as he climbed into the cockpit. Once he lost his rookie nervousness, and got a rudimentary sense of humor, he might even be good enough to end up serving on the bridge.

Chekov didn't envy Lieutenant Sulu the piloting feat he'd volunteered to perform.

"Was that a dip?" Tomlinson asked anxiously. Squinting into the rising sun, he rose up on tiptoe as though the additional centimeters would improve his view.

His own eyes still locked on the shuttle, Chekov shook his head. "No, sir. He's only jockeying for altitude." Even as Chekov spoke, the shuttle executed an elegant swoop along the slope of one towerlike hill, then rode her own velocity a half-kilometer higher in the parchment-yellow sky.

As part of Starfleet Academy's major in Astrogation and Piloting, Chekov had taken a short course in shuttle piloting. The portly craft at their disposal had been old, ill-used models no longer safe for extra-atmospheric flights, and most of the students in the program had secretly suspected they weren't all that noble for local usage, either. The morning winds that swept San Francisco Bay had tossed the clumsy ships about like soccer balls, more than once threatening to deposit one atop Mt. Tam or crash them all into Alcatraz. At the time, the flights had been a little bit scary, but also challenging and fun. Chekov often imagined that this must be what it felt like to ride a starship through an ion storm, or weather the conflicting gravity wells of a trinary star.

Now, as he watched Lieutenant Sulu coax a decidedly unaerodynamic craft to stay aloft with hardly any sensors or flight controls to speak of, Chekov understood why no one else on the *Enterprise* had much hope of becoming chief helmsman anytime soon.

"I hope when he does finally see the captain, it's closer to our hilltop than that one." Yuki Smith trooped up to join them, as good-natured as always despite the rugged climb. As strong as she was when it came to lifting and hauling, she apparently couldn't climb the nearly vertical karst terrain quite as easily as Tomlinson and Chekov. "That's more than an hour away, isn't it?" She seemed to direct the question toward Chekov, if only by virtue of being tight against his shoulder when she asked it. "And if we can't walk there in an hour, we're not allowed to go. Right?"

Chekov tried not to let the worry churning in his stomach sour his tone. "Once we start walking, it won't matter how far away it is. It's not like the ship can stop us by beaming us up or anything." He remembered Sanner's grim promise in the cave passage. *We're not leaving anybody down here.*

The shuttle banked to widen her sweep, and Chekov turned a slow circle so as not to let the ship out of his sight. He nearly bumped into Tomlinson when the weapons officer made no corresponding move. He smiled down at Chekov, but didn't step aside.

"If I were you, Ensign, I'd be careful who I let hear me talk like that." The lieutenant's demeanor was just as friendly and relaxed as it had always been, yet Chekov heard the edge of something more serious than casual conversation. "At best, ignoring Lieutenant Uhura's orders is willful disobedience. At worst, it could be considered mutiny."

Chekov understood how Tomlinson meant it—not as a warning, but as a bit of fraternal advice from someone with more years on a starship to a woefully inexperienced comrade. And he was even fairly certain that

Tomlinson understood that he'd said what he did out of loyalty to Kirk, not defiance of Lieutenant Uhura. But neither realization kept the blood from his face or the mortification from his voice. "Yes, sir. I understand, sir." He forced himself to add, a little stiffly, "Thank you, sir," because the tiny part of him that wasn't writhing in humiliation truly did appreciate what Tomlinson had tried to do.

Still smiling, Tomlinson gave him a clap on the shoulder as though they'd only been discussing some unlucky sporting event. "Lighten up," he suggested. "You're gonna be out here a long time."

At first, Chekov had assumed Tomlinson meant out in space, on a starship, serving Starfleet—all of which Chekov did hope to be doing for quite some time yet. But later he wondered if the lieutenant hadn't experienced some sort of unexpected psychic insight, and instead had meant they would all be trapped on Tlaoli for days or weeks or years to come. It was the sort of thing that started to occur to one when unimaginable disasters followed on each other fast enough.

Smith caught their attention with an excited whoop. "I think he's found him!" She jumped up and down a few times, pointing out toward Sulu's shuttle as it cinched around in an ever tightening turn. "Just above that little forest, or stones, or whatever," she rushed on. "I think he dipped!"

Chekov and Tomlinson hurried to flank her at the edge of their knoll. Some distance ahead, still blanketed in shadow from another of the steep hills and blurred by the heavy mist, a broken landscape of some kind of complex shapes lay across the ground like pieces of a three-dimensional jigsaw puzzle that no one had been able to finish. Chekov understood Smith's confusion. He couldn't tell, either, what made up the irregular structures, or even how far away they were. He was willing to guess, however, that it was under an hour's quick hike.

The shuttle's nose dipped downward once, twice, directly over the center of the broken landscape. Smith whooped again, and they all three flailed their arms to let Sulu know they'd seen his signal. The energetic signaling felt both silly and invigorating. Kirk wasn't lost. He was on the planet, only a brisk walk away. Everything was going to be all right after all. Chekov caught himself laughing along with Smith as they started down the slope toward Sulu's signal.

None of them actually saw the shuttle go down. Chekov saw it bank away to the south in a loop that took it far behind them, heading back toward the base camp, he assumed, to let Uhura know that the rescue party was on its way to retrieve the captain. It had occurred to him to wonder if Sulu would be able to return with the others if it turned out the captain needed something like medical assistance from Dr. McCoy, if he could actually put the shuttle down in the terrain toward which they were headed or if they'd have to somehow drag Kirk free of it before counting on any outside help. He turned to voice this concern to Tomlinson just in time to glimpse a strange, brilliant flash of light explode like a halo beyond a row of ragged dark hills. Then a clap like thunder rolled over them and echoed away, passing back and forth across the valleys until it seemed like it would never die.

After a very long moment, Tomlinson was the only one to recover his voice enough to speak. "Oh, God, what now?"

Chekov knew the answer with a sick certainty that frightened him. "I think we just lost the shuttle."

Chapter Eleven

IN ANY OTHER CIRCUMSTANCES, Uhura thought somberly, Tlaoli's karstlands would have been beautiful. In one direction, huge monoliths of limestone rose from a mist whose drifting movement gave them the illusion of advancing like waves on a storm-beaten sea. At their feet, the mist had cleared away enough to reveal a rocky gray plateau so broken by crevasses and solution cracks that it resembled a maze, or a jigsaw puzzle scattered on a gigantic scale. Beyond that, an army of smaller rock formations marched off toward the horizon, so hunched and gnarled with erosion that they looked like petrified versions of the weather-beaten trees living in their shadows. Feathery plumes of mist crowned the largest tree-fringed hollows, marking places where the caverns below blew cold, damp breath up into the morning air through sinkholes and solution pipes. It was the kind of landscape that could have taken your breath away.

If you hadn't already been hammered into numbness by repeated blows of shock, disbelief, and despair.

"The last time we saw him was just over that little ridge, the one that looks like a row of teeth." Tomlinson took a careful step forward on the slick stone of their karst mound and pointed the direction out to Uhura. She turned to look that way, measuring the distance with the part of her brain that remained coldly alert and functional despite this latest disaster.

Uhura's first, almost hysterical, impulse had been to deny it, to refuse to believe Chekov when he'd come back to the base camp with the news that the shuttle had gone down. Oddly enough, it had been the stifled edge of fear in the young ensign's voice, the desperate look in his own dark eyes, that had steadied her enough to thrust that impulse aside and acknowledge reality. Sulu had admitted that he was flying the shuttle on a razor-thin safety margin, with unreliable instruments and unpredictable changes in altitude caused by Tlaoli's strange power fluxes. It shouldn't really have come as a surprise that he had crashed, but once again Uhura had let herself be lulled into a treacherous sense of hope.

Dr. McCoy had just come out of the mess tent to report that his emergency operation on Davis had been a success when they had seen the joyful flurry of leaps and arm waving atop the karst mound to the north. Everyone watching from below knew that meant the unseen shuttle had made a find. Even though they had all seen the bright glint that flashed across the sky, their celebratory cheer must have drowned out the distant explosion that followed. Even the sound of running feet hadn't alarmed them—after all, wouldn't one of the crewmen sent to watch the *Drake* come hurrying back to tell them how far away Captain Kirk had been spotted? But even before she saw Chekov's grim face, something about the sound of his labored, almost sobbing breath as he approached warned Uhura that the news would be bad.

Now, after a near-vertical climb up a fractured limestone cliff that had seemed more of an annoyance than the terror it might otherwise have been, Uhura couldn't even decide how bad the news actually was.

"Why isn't there any smoke coming up from the crash site?" she demanded.

Silence fell over the karst mound, profound enough to let Uhura hear the rustle of wind through the bonsai trees many meters below. Tomlinson stared over his shoulder at her as if he'd been stunned by the question, while Smith and Chekov exchanged baffled and forlorn glances, like cadets caught unprepared by a pop quiz. It wasn't until Jaeger hurtled over the edge of the fractured rim-rock with a painful gasp, followed a moment later by the man who had hoisted him up that slope, that anyone even acknowledged Uhura's question.

"Wind couldn't be blowing it away," Sanner said, leaning down to haul Jaeger to his feet. "Look at the mist from those cavern vents down there—straight as a plumb line."

"Maybe the shuttle landed in a pond or something," suggested Smith. "That could explain—"

Her voice hadn't carried much conviction to begin

with, but it shriveled away entirely at the explosion of snorts she got from the two cave geologists. "There's no standing water that high on a karst plain," Sanner informed her. "The water table's hundreds of meters below, down at the feet of those big towers over to the east."

"Oh." Smith took an abashed step backward, teetering for a moment on the edge of the mound before Chekov grabbed and steadied her. "Of course."

"I think…" Jaeger unfolded one of his topographic maps, smoothing it down across the rippled gray surface of the karst mound and anchoring it with chunks of rock. A dirt-stained finger traced a path from the round contours of their current perch to the more linear elevation lines that marked Tomlinson's little ridge. "Yes, look. That sinkhole over there—" He stabbed at another set of concentric circles, these marked with slashes like inward-pointing teeth. "—is where we first entered the upper level of the caves. That means the hollow where you saw the shuttle disappear—" His hand swept over another section of the map, where the contour lines spread further apart. "—sits directly over the ice cave where we first lost Captain Kirk."

"Damn."

That was Zap Sanner, expressing himself with his usual irreverence. For once, Uhura felt as if the cave specialist spoke for all of them. She cleared her throat, but it still took an effort to put the horrible thought she'd just had into words.

"You think Lieutenant Sulu flew his shuttle into that same alien force field we encountered in the ice cave?"

Jaeger peered up from his map, gray eyes glittering in

211

his bruised and slashed face. "There might be other possible hypotheses," he said dryly. "But have you ever heard of something called Occam's razor, Lieutenant?"

"The simplest explanation is usually the right one," blurted Yuki Smith, as if to atone for her previous mistake.

"Yes," said Jaeger. "Precisely."

Uhura squinted past the jagged ridge rocks, but the rusty glare of Tlaoli's morning sun drowned any hint of blue light that might have rippled in the shadowy hollow beyond. It was no wonder Sulu had flown into the alien force field unwittingly. Uhura just hoped Captain Kirk hadn't stumbled back into it unwittingly, as well.

Although if he had....

"We know Ensign Chekov went from the ice cave to the upper breakdown chamber where the survey team was stuck without lights," Uhura said, abruptly. The conclusion she had just come to was so disquieting that she wanted to make sure she verified each logical step with her subordinates. "And we're pretty sure that's where the captain was sent as well, right?"

"He couldn't have gotten past us if he'd materialized anywhere else," Jaeger agreed.

Sanner nodded. "And it sure looked like someone crawled out of that sinkhole ahead of us."

"Someone did," Chekov said flatly, then added a belated, "Sir."

"Then we have to assume the upper chamber is where the alien force field always sends people." Uhura made the only decision she could, given the evidence they had, although it took all her willpower to actually say it.

"We'll have to go back into the cave and look for Sulu there."

Tomlinson let out a sound halfway between a groan and a grunt of surprise. "Lieutenant, you don't think the *shuttle* could possibly have gone down there, do you?"

"I don't know what that alien installation can and cannot do, Mr. Tomlinson," Uhura said. "But that cavern was certainly big enough to hold a shuttle."

"Provided it didn't try to materialize around one of the flowstone columns," Jaeger commented. "Or take enough kinetic energy with it to flatten it against a wall."

Uhura sighed. "I know there's no guarantee we'll find Lieutenant Sulu down there, Mr. Jaeger, much less alive. But if there's even a small chance he was sent there, then he's trapped underground without any caving equipment, and probably without power or lights, either. We *have* to make sure we're not leaving him there like that."

That stark statement left a trail of unhappy silence after it, broken eventually by the youngest member of their group. "Sir," said Chekov. "I'll volunteer to go back underground with you."

Smith glanced over at him, then let out a large, resigned sigh. "Me, too."

Uhura couldn't quite summon a smile, but she at least managed to give them what she hoped was a kindly look. "Actually, I need you two and Mr. Tomlinson to look for Captain Kirk up here, since you were the ones who saw where Lieutenant Sulu signaled that he found him." She lifted her gaze back to the karstlands, where the morning mist was breaking into glittering strings and shreds. "Take Martine or D'Amato with you, and keep a tricorder turned on while you walk out there. If you see it start to lose power, or get a ridiculous error reading, I want you to turn around and come back immediately. I don't want to send anyone else through that alien transporter if we can help it."

"Aye-aye, sir," chorused Chekov and Smith.

Tomlinson, however, had served for longer on the *Enterprise* and had a rank technically equal to Uhura's, even if he was considerably junior to her on the command list. "Who will you take down into the caves with you, sir?" he demanded.

"Mr. Sanner, of course." Uhura glanced over at the cave specialist. She needn't have worried—Sanner was already tugging the topographic map with its superimposed sketch of the various cave levels away from a reluctant Jaeger and muttering something about counting cave reflectors. "And either Lieutenant Wright or Dr. McCoy, whoever is willing to come and provide medical care, in case..." Uhura trailed off, unwilling to tempt fate by putting her worst case scenario into words. "We shouldn't need any more people than that, as long as we leave the ropes up on the edge of the sinkhole to get us out."

"Getting *us* out won't be the problem," Sanner said. "And if we got Davis out with a fractured skull, I'm pretty sure we can take Mr. Sulu out no matter what's happened to him." The cave geologist surprised Uhura with a snort of wry but genuine laughter. "What I want to know, Lieutenant, is how you think we're going to get the *shuttle* out if it's down there."

"We're not," Uhura said frankly. "But if it is there,

Mr. Sanner, we just may use its warp core to take that alien force field out, once and for all."

Tlaoli's sun was not as bright as many, or as hot as some. The polished brass disk that had finally lifted itself above the farthest ridges of exposed rock barely warmed the air, and the tentative fingers it reached between monolithic shoulders of rock were too pale and watered down to burn away the mist that still swirled catlike around their ankles. No wonder the vegetation consisted of nothing more than stunted trees and scrubby grass, Chekov thought. The anemic morning fog looked to be all the moisture the karstlands got, at least during this time of year, and if Chekov understood what Jaeger had said earlier over their reconstructed maps, even that little bit of moisture was sucked beneath the surface into the caves below almost as soon as it touched the ground. It struck him as almost absurd to realize he had nearly drowned only a few dozen meters beneath a veritable desert.

"Careful." Yuki Smith nudged him, none too gently, out of the path of another sinkhole. He'd seen it, just as he'd seen the dozen others she'd felt the need to steer him around, but he thanked her anyway. Apparently, the security guard was convinced no one could monitor their direction on a hand compass and watch where he was going at the same time.

Behind them, Robert Tomlinson and Angela Martine muttered over tricorder readings, running just as much risk of stumbling into a sinkhole as Chekov did, as far as he could see. He spared a glance over his shoulder to make sure they'd navigated themselves safely past that particular obstacle, then turned his attention back to his compass and the bearing he hoped was taking them closer to Captain Kirk.

"I hope their tricorder is as good as you are at finding trouble before we step into it," he commented to Smith. He felt a little awkward making small talk with someone he hardly knew, but Smith insisted that they'd become good friends during the hours of cave travel he no longer remembered, and he *had* climbed on top of her head. It seemed the least he could do.

Apparently, he could have done it more quietly.

"You worry about your end of the hike, Ensign," Tomlinson called forward to him. "We'll worry about ours." Staring fixedly at the tricorder screen, he pulled Martine to a stop before waving at Smith and Chekov. "Hold up."

They halted obediently enough, although Chekov kept himself half-oriented toward the compass heading they'd been following, as if he'd suddenly forget which way they'd been going.

Martine shook her head at the tricorder readings without waiting for Tomlinson to elaborate on why he'd stopped them. "That's not a big enough error," she said. "It's not outside our standard deviation."

"But it's bigger than we've been getting," Tomlinson argued. "And Lieutenant Uhura said we should turn back at the very first sign—"

"She said we should turn back if the error readings became ridiculous." Chekov gritted his teeth against the embarrassment of everyone turning to stare at him, but didn't back down. "I'm sorry, sir, I didn't mean to interrupt." Which wasn't entirely true. "But the possibility that we're close to the alien transporter's range of affect is remote, sir." He held out his compass toward them as though the bobbing needle there would make everything clear. "Mr. Jaeger's maps of the cave system—"

"They're your maps, too," Smith pointed out, but Chekov only nodded absently in acknowledgment.

"—indicate that the alien force field most likely originates south-southwest of the base camp. We're maintaining a strict easterly heading to reach the rock formations where Mr. Sulu saw the captain. While I appreciate that Lieutenant Uhura wants to be careful, we're much more likely to fall down a sinkhole right now than walk into the alien energy field."

"That's assuming the force field hasn't expanded enough to intersect our route," Tomlinson said, a little grimly.

Chekov nodded. "Yes, sir, it does. Because if the field is maintaining a spherical shape the way Mr. Jaeger speculates it is, then by the time it reached us out here it would have already passed over the base camp and everyone else in the party." He felt immediately awkward when his extrapolation flashed alarm across the others' faces. It occurred to him for the very first time that what he viewed as practicality might come across as coldness to others. He wondered if he should do something about his tendency to give that impression, then decided he'd worry about it once they'd located the captain and gotten everyone safely back on board the ship. "It's just, if we're going to assume the worst, then there's no sense going on. If not..."

The lieutenant sighed and pushed the tricorder into

Martine's hands as though too frustrated to watch it anymore. "All right, good point." It struck Chekov that being in charge of a party didn't necessarily mean you always knew what to do. "Let's keep going, then. If we get any ridiculous error readings..." He glanced aside at Martine, mirrored her grin despite himself, and sighed again. "We'll ask Mr. Chekov then whether or not we're allowed to worry."

The sun kept them company as they threaded between sinkholes and twisted trees. Chekov tried to keep them on as straight a course as possible, given the landscape, but twice had to back them out of a confusion of collapsing ground and find a way around to solid footing again. When they finally reached the broken forest of stone where Sulu had spotted Kirk, it came upon them suddenly, like a beach giving over to the sea. For some reason, Chekov had assumed they would have to climb down among the standing stones, into the solution cracks like mice between house walls. Instead, the exposed rocks suddenly towered over them like giants at parade rest, and they were on the bottom without even trying.

Tomlinson and Martine drew alongside Chekov and Smith, and Tomlinson shaded his eyes to squint up at the jigsaw of broken plateaus. "So I wonder if the captain took the high road or the low road."

At least with four of them they didn't have to make the same decision. They split along separate fractures, Tomlinson and Martine seeking out the steep trails that would take them to the top of the rocks while Chekov and Smith wound through the lower valleys. They each had a whistle from the cave rescue supplies, but Chekov did what he could to keep everyone in sight, even if only occasionally. No matter how certain he'd sounded about it being safe to continue, even he couldn't shake a sick feeling of dread that one of them would stumble into the alien transport system and disappear without the others realizing.

Stripes of pale sunlight rimmed the tops of the maze-like cracks, painted on almost ruler-straight above the shadows cast by the rocks on every side. Chekov couldn't believe the sun wasn't higher by now. Surely it was at least mid-morning. But the uneven floor that wound and cut its way through the stones was still chilly in its darkness. It was almost like wandering through the caves again, only this time without the warming nanosuit or the reassuring presence of Sanner at his back.

"What are we going to do if we find him?"

Chekov jumped aside, falling back against one of the walls with his heart hammering. Smith drew back from the narrow crack through which she'd spoken, her face almost vanishing into the shadows. "Sorry about that."

Chekov tried to cover his startlement by straightening and clearing his throat. "I just didn't expect the rocks to talk."

She giggled, a discordantly girlish sound, and came forward again to frame her face in the crack. "I'm serious, though. If the captain is running away from us, and he doesn't know who he is... What are we going to say to him? I mean, what's going to make him hang around and listen?"

Chekov didn't know how to answer her. He hadn't gotten that far in his own thoughts. Amnesia or no, he couldn't quite believe that Captain Kirk retained no sense of himself, no rationality or dignity or sense. Even if, for some reason, the captain thought he was being pursued by enemies, surely his first sight of them would tell him that they were friends and he was safe.

If not....

"I don't know," he admitted at last. "We can't very well chase him."

"Actually I'm more worried about catching him. He's a strong guy, you know."

That was something else Chekov had never really thought about, but he was sure Smith was correct. This whole rescue operation was beginning to look more uncertain with each question the security guard posed.

High above them, and some distance ahead, a whistle shrilled in silver-bright alarm. Smith pulled away from her peep hole, out of sight, and Chekov jerked a guilty look back over his shoulder toward where Tomlinson and Martine must have gotten well ahead of them. "They've found something!" The captain. They must have found the captain.

He tried to mark the whistle's direction based on the slant of the sunlight and the rise of the stones, but wasn't entirely certain he could maintain his orientation while jogging through the rock maze in search of a way through. Several twists and turns out of sight to his right, he could hear running footsteps, irregular on the rocky ground. He opened his mouth to warn Smith to be careful about hurrying so fast toward their destination lest she lose her footing and break a leg. Before he could do so much as call her name, though, a running figure plowed around the rocks in front of him and crashed them both into the dirt.

Chekov knew the instant it happened that he hadn't collided with Smith. He had a quick impression of slender youthfulness and ratty civilian clothes just as he and the stranger went tumbling, and while his imagination wasn't quick enough to assign any meaning to this impression, he at least understood that it wasn't Smith. Rolling, Chekov shot out a hand to grab a flailing ankle when the other person tried frantically to kick himself free and get up again. "Stop! I'm not—"

The boy didn't wait to find out what Chekov was or wasn't going to do. Lashing out with his free leg, he kicked the ensign hard twice, once on the wrist and once further up the inside of his arm. But as much as that hurt, it wasn't the boy's blows or even the violence of his cursing that shocked Chekov into releasing him. It was the fierce hazel eyes that burned in the handsome young face, and the unmistakably Kirk-like set of his fourteen-year-old jaw when he finally wrenched himself loose, got up, and ran.

Uhura had thought that going back into the caves of Tlaoli would be one of the hardest things she'd ever had to do. Intellectually, she knew that squirming down through the twisting passage that had led them out through the rubble pile would be physically dangerous and emotionally draining. But when the time came to take that first step down into darkness, all she really felt was numb and exhausted. After nearly twenty hours of constant toil and danger, Uhura's mind no longer seemed able to envision possible disasters, and the jangle of stress hormones in her bloodstream had lost its sharp edge. She followed her own orders as automatically as if they had been given by someone else, setting one foot below another on the swaying cat's cradle of ropes that dangled down into the muddy sinkhole, until she stood beside Sanner at the bottom.

"Heigh ho, heigh ho," said the cave geologist with a crooked smile, while they waited for McCoy to join them.

Uhura tried to find a smile to match his, although she suspected it looked more like a wince. "And just who are you calling a dwarf?"

"Hey, I think I'm pretty bashful." He reached out and adjusted Uhura's water drip until her carbide light glowed a little brighter, then grunted in satisfaction. "You want to make sure you can catch all the reflectors ahead of you. There should be twelve of them."

Uhura blinked at him, startled back into alertness. "I'm going first?"

Sanner nodded. "That passage is too narrow to pull someone through. If Dr. McCoy gets stuck, I'll need to push on him from behind."

"I'm not going to get stuck." A wiry figure in anomalous gold jumped off the last rung of ropes and came sloshing through the mud to join them. Ensign Davis's cave jumper had been the one that fit McCoy best for height, although it stretched a little tightly across his shoulders and sagged in a few other places. "I feel like a greased pig already, with all this mud I'm wearing."

"If you think you're muddy now, just wait until you see the soil zone we're going to crawl through," Sanner said cheerfully. He consulted the folded map he had pulled from his jumper's chest pocket. "All right, it's three hundred meters from here to the edge of the rubble pile. If anyone gets stuck, just yell for the person behind you to come up and push. Ready?"

"Hell, no." Despite his wry words, McCoy had been the one who'd insisted on coming with them, even using his authority as the ship's chief medical officer to over-rule Wright's protests that she knew the caves better. He followed them willingly enough down the sinkhole, al-though he couldn't refrain a snort when he saw the ankle-high wedge of darkness that was their entrance. "I can't believe you got Yuki Smith out through that crack," was all he said, however.

Uhura caught a last glimpse of Sanner's grin as she lowered herself to her hands and knees. "I pushed, Tom-linson pulled," Sanner told McCoy, his voice fading be-hind her as she squirmed through the jagged opening. "And to tell you the truth, I think that opening might have been just a little wider by the time—"

The passage twisted a meter past the entrance and Uhura lost the sound of the others' voices. The tightly clinging walls of the passage echoed back her own sounds to her with claustrophobic intensity—the scrape of her gloves as she hauled herself around projecting rock corners, the thump of her booted feet pushing off any ledge or wall they could find to propel her forward, the hiss of her strained breath.

It seemed forever until Uhura saw the first glint of a cave reflector, guiding her past a vertical crack that looked far too narrow to represent a viable alternate route. The second reflector warned her away from an even less appealing solution cavity along a bedding plane, but the third one was mounted at a place where the passage widened for a deceptive moment, then split into two halves. Uhura turned her carbide light back and forth several times, but there was no mistaking it. Sanner had posted the cave reflector squarely over the more narrow and sloping of the two passages.

"Hey." A groping hand caught at her ankle, withdrew, and then gave an inquiring rap on one boot sole. "Something wrong?" McCoy asked.

"I'm trying to make sure..." Uhura squirmed one outstretched hand back to her face, tugged off the glove with her teeth and licked at the tips of her finger. She stuck her hand forward again and realized at once that she hadn't needed to make her skin wet to feel the sucking indraft of warm outside air being pulled into the cavern below. It blew strongly against her unprotected skin, and to her surprise it pulled into the narrow uphill slant of the fork. "All right," she said, and twisted to her left to fit her shoulders through the crack.

She realized almost at once that had been the wrong decision, since another twist of the passage put her on her back instead of her stomach, without even enough room to spin herself around. By then it was too late to back out—she could hear McCoy bumping and cursing his way through after her. Fortunately, this was the section of cave whose roof was snarled with tree roots, allowing Uhura to pull herself hand-over-hand along it instead of crawling. It would have been the easiest part of the trip so far, if the roots hadn't made the ceiling so soft and crumbly that at every other pull clots of dirt and mud scattered across her eyes or nose or mouth. Somewhere along the way, Uhura lost the glove she had been carrying between her teeth ever since she'd stripped it off to check the draft, but by then she barely cared.

The cave passage angled down again, this time steeply enough to dump her in a slithering rush into a larger, shoulder-height chamber. Uhura barely remembered to pull herself out of the way before McCoy came hurtling through after her, upside down and coughing. A moment later, Sanner's carbide glow descended the slope right-side-up and a lot more sedately. He emerged with a loopy grin that made Uhura want to smack him.

"Boy, you guys make good time!" said the cave geologist. He dug around in his chest pocket, then tossed Uhura her abandoned glove before she could make any of the crushing remarks that came to mind. "I'm going to tell that kid Chekov that he's a slug compared to you."

McCoy paused in wiping mud from his face to give the other man a sour look. "I don't care what you tell Chekov," he said. "Just tell me that we're almost to this big upper chamber of yours."

"About halfway," Sanner estimated. "But there's no more spots quite as tight as that. Want me to go first now, Lieutenant?"

Uhura finished pulling on her glove and opened her mouth to say "Yes," but what came out instead was a decisive, "No." It startled her a little, because it wasn't what she would have expected of herself, but she had to admit that she liked being in the lead. The constant need to look for cave reflectors kept the crawl from becoming too monotonous, and the knowledge that McCoy could easily push her through any spot where she happened to get stuck made the constricted twists and turns of the cave passage seem a lot less claustrophobic. "I don't mind going first," she said, smiling under her mud mask when she realized it was actually true.

"Onward and downward, then." McCoy tightened the strap of his cave helmet under his chin. "Although I'll warn you—if we find Mr. Sulu drinking coffee at the base camp when we get back, I'm going to dump him down this sinkhole just on principle."

The sound of Sanner's guffaw followed Uhura into the next winding section of the cave. The passages here were generally wider, with only occasional places where what looked suspiciously like blocks of broken roof crimped the space down to a few dozen centimeters in height. Uhura wriggled through easily enough, although she tried not to think about how hard it must have been for the sturdier members of the original cave party, Tomlinson and Smith and Wright, to make this trip the first time through.

After the last of the pinches, a final cave reflector glittered over a spot Uhura remembered: a jagged hole in the passage floor that opened like a narrow downspout over the rubble pile below. She crawled over to the edge of it, angling her carbide light into the rush of arctic cold air that came blasting up from the darkness. The drop was at least three meters down to the unstable footing of the breakdown pile that filled the back end of the big cavern. Uhura grimaced, but when she pulled her head back out, her light splashed over the slim length of rope Sanner had left dangling from a couple of pitons at the top. She scuttled around to that side of the hole, tested the rope with a jerk, then swung herself down onto it just as McCoy's carbide light appeared on the far side of the opening.

"What, don't we get to slide down this drainpipe, too?" he asked tartly.

"Not unless you want to start an avalanche when you land," Uhura retorted. McCoy crawled out to the edge and watched her rappel downward, grunting when he saw the size of the breakdown pile below. With the glare of his carbide light added to hers, the immense size of the column-filled cavern below began to reveal itself. Uhura could feel the cold biting harder at the skin of her face and neck as she entered the main chamber, and she fervently hoped that didn't mean the alien force field had grown to envelop this end of the cave system, as well.

It wouldn't make sense for it to do that, Uhura assured herself, as she found her footing on a large boulder and released the rope for McCoy to use. After all, if the purpose of this system was to transport people here, it wouldn't also take them *from* here. Although it made Uhura wonder why, with the sophisticated energy-gathering technology these unknown aliens had apparently been able to construct, they had used their force field simply to send people from one end of an hour-long walk to another. Or had this once been part of a much larger transportation system, similar to the continent-wide transporter systems back on Earth, that had simply eroded through countless millennia down to just this last functioning piece?

Sanner followed McCoy down the rope and added his

carbide glow to theirs. The combined illumination lit the cavern all the way to its end, painting long, thin shadows like prison bars on the floor from the cathedral-like columns that supported its arching roof.

"No shuttle," said the geologist, unnecessarily.

"No," Uhura agreed. She lifted her voice to a ringing shout. "Sulu! Lieutenant Sulu, can you hear me?"

Only silence answered her. The cold must have frozen even the water dripping off the columns, which had previously filled the chamber with a sound like tiny aqueous chimes.

"Want to go down and look around?" Sanner asked after a while. His voice sounded distinctly more glum than it had a moment before.

"Not yet." Uhura reached up to twist the control knob on the water reservoir of her carbide lamp. A memory of waiting in the darkness of alien conduits and seeing an indigo-blue light glowing behind its ice-covered walls had sprung unbidden into her mind. "Turn off your lights for a minute."

McCoy gave her a scandalized look. "Lieutenant, are you nuts?"

"You can only see the alien force field if your eyes are adjusted to total darkness," Uhura explained. She heard the last of her acetylene gas hiss into the combustion chamber, then her side of the rubble pile suddenly became a little darker. Sanner was already extinguishing his own carbide light, and, a moment later, McCoy grumbled and reached up to dim his, as well. Their lights went one right after the other, wrapping them in utter, stifling darkness.

With neither sound nor light to orient herself, Uhura

felt oddly less sure of her balance on the rubble pile, although she knew for a fact that she'd wedged herself securely between two boulders just a moment before. Only the hard press of rock against her back and the bite of cold air against her skin kept her from feeling as if she'd entered a sensory deprivation tank.

"Over there," said McCoy, in an unnecessary whisper. His hand brushed across Uhura's shoulder as he tried to point in the darkness. "That one big column—is that the light you meant?"

Uhura touched the doctor's hand to see which way it was oriented, then put her own hand against Sanner's shoulder to point the way for him. She kept it there to steady herself as she turned very carefully to look in the direction McCoy had indicated. Her eyes registered light almost immediately, but it took her a moment to actually focus on it. The cloud of golden sparks flitting like fireflies around one of the columnar cave formations was so different from what she'd expected to see that Uhura wondered if she'd have noticed it anywhere near as quickly as McCoy had.

"Actually," she said wryly, "no. That's not what we saw before at all."

"But maybe it makes sense," Sanner said. "The blue light was the part that made you vanish. Maybe the part that makes you appear should be another color."

"Maybe." Uhura dug her teeth into her lip, straining to see what kind of pattern those golden shimmers were making in the darkness. "Dr. McCoy, do you see...?"

"Yes, I do." McCoy began scrabbling with his carbide

229

light in the darkness. "Dammit, how do you get this thing back on?"

"Here, let me—" Sanner reached across Uhura to adjust the water drip and ignite the flame. The glow of McCoy's lamp dazzled Uhura blind for a moment, but her eyes adjusted fast enough to see the questioning look on one man's face and the grimness she'd been afraid of on the other's.

"What's the deal?" the geologist asked, glancing back and forth between them as if their silence had alarmed him. "What the heck did you guys see?"

"A human shape," Uhura said, trying to keep her voice calm and unshaken. "The lights were outlining it, as if it was just starting to appear." McCoy was already scrambling down the rubble pile, and she snapped her own helmet alight, then levered herself out from between her boulders to follow him. "The problem is, it's appearing right in the middle of that rock column."

Chapter Twelve

THE SWARM OF GOLDEN SPARKS inside the stone column grew brighter, tracing more and more clearly the outline of a human body trapped inside solid rock. Uhura scrambled recklessly down the pile of cave rubble, her boots skidding off one frost-slicked boulder after another. She could see the jerk and bobble of McCoy's carbide lamp become a swift, straight line when he reached the bottom of the breakdown pile, then disappear entirely as he approached the glowing pillar.

A fierce golden-white fire seemed to have ignited inside the rock formation, brilliant enough to illuminate the breakdown cavern all the way up to its sparkling ice-crusted roof. The light also showed Uhura the smooth pavement of water-laid flowstone that surrounded the column, with not a loose stone or broken stalactite in sight. She skidded to a stop at the foot of the breakdown pile, looking for a sharp-edged chunk of rock she could use as a hammering tool.

"Don't bother with that." Sanner vaulted down off a boulder somewhat higher than her head. Uhura glanced up to ask what he meant, and saw that he was already striding across the cavern toward the pile of gear Survey Team Three had stacked into a makeshift bed for the injured Davis. The cave specialist threw off the emergency blankets and dove into the backpacks below like a terrier digging for a rat, tossing out sample bags and surveying markers until he finally emerged with a rock sledge in one hand and a prybar in the other.

"*This* should let us break through that rock formation." Sanner handed the bar to Uhura and hefted the sledge onto one shoulder, grimacing in a way that made her wonder if he'd hurt himself coming down the rubble pile. "And I complained about Jaeger's damned handprints..."

Uhura opened her mouth to ask him what was wrong, but a shout from the heart of the cavern interrupted her. The gold light was bright enough now that, when she turned, Uhura had to squint against it to see McCoy. The doctor had plastered himself up against the rock column and was using some kind of antique medical sensor whose cables ran from his ears to a metal disk that he held pressed against the stone. He paused for a moment to peer out into what must have looked like darkness to his light-blind eyes, then beckoned when he spotted them.

"Hurry up," he yelled. "We've got to get him out of here!"

Uhura leaped to follow Sanner as he ran toward the

glowing column. As they got closer, she could see that the light was coming from deep inside the rock, turning the outer layers of flowstone into a translucent alabaster shell. A blurred but familiar face was visible beneath the stone.

"Is Sulu alive?" she asked.

"I can hear him breathing." McCoy moved the metal disk to another part of the flowstone casing. "The transporter must have taken the stone out when it put him in. But he sounds ragged, like he's gasping. There might not be any air in there with him."

"All right, you guys, stand back." Sanner hefted the sledge as they obeyed him. "God dammit, here goes a thousand years of laminar accretion," he said regretfully, and swung.

The first blow rebounded off the stone with a crash that stung Uhura's ears and made her eyes blink shut involuntarily. She saw McCoy wince and yank the cables out of his ears. A network of little cracks appeared on the glowing surface, radiating out like rays from the dent Sanner had made, but nothing broke or fell. The cave geologist stripped off his cave gloves, spitting on his hands despite the bitterly cold air, then hefted the sledge and swung again. A louder crash was followed by a fierce crackling sound. Uhura threw a worried glance at the ceiling, but a moment later a shard of flowstone detached from the face of the rock formation and came clattering down at her feet.

"Pry bar." Sanner held out his hand like a surgeon demanding an operating tool. Uhura handed it to him, then began clearing away the curving fragments of flowstone as he pried them off the column, one by one. Their outer surfaces were ridged and crenulated with layered travertine, she noticed, but their inner surfaces were oddly concave and smooth. Uhura ran her gloved fingers over one and frowned.

"Zap, wait a minute," she said. The geologist levered off one last milky fragment of rock, then stepped back to catch his breath. Uhura took his place beside the column and lifted her hands toward the much clearer figure of Lieutenant Sulu.

A smooth curve of almost invisible transparent metal met her palms inches away from the pilot's face. To her surprise, it wasn't anywhere near as cold as the cavern's bitter air. Even through her insulated gloves, Uhura could feel that it was warm and humming with the vibration of some inner force.

"I don't think this is a rock formation," she said over her shoulder. "I think it's some kind of stasis chamber."

"One that got covered up with travertine in the millions of years since the aliens left?" Sanner glanced around at the other pillars throughout the room, spaced with what now looked to Uhura like suspicious regularity. "Do you think they're all—?"

"Could be." McCoy had plastered himself against the luminous curve of the alien stasis chamber, cables plugged back into his ears. "Sulu's still breathing—in fact, it sounds like he's breathing a little easier."

"He's not awake, is he?" Concern brought Uhura up next to the doctor, slitting her eyes to peer into the fierce alien radiance. The pilot's eyes were serenely closed, but there was something about his face that was beginning to bother Uhura. She studied him closely, noticing a network of lines like fine scars around his eyes, his mouth, between his dark eyebrows. Or were those...wrinkles?

"What's that uniform he's wearing?" Sanner peered over her shoulder. "That's not the one he had on back at the base camp."

Uhura craned her head to look down into the remaining shell of stone, and blinked in surprise. She had watched Sulu climb into the *Drake* a few hours ago in a clean gold uniform tunic and regulation trousers. Now, he wore a scuffed and stained combat jacket, camouflaged in an odd combination of violet and green, over a black and gray jumpsuit whose silver piping traced a strange, silhouetted version of the familiar Starfleet insignia on the front of its neck-hugging collar.

"What the hell—" McCoy shouldered both of them aside as he slid himself around the edge of the chamber, staring down at Sulu's right arm. "Look at his hand!"

Uhura scrambled back up on the pile of fallen shards, then gasped as she caught a glimpse of what the doctor was staring at. What had once been Sulu's right hand hung below the blood-stained sleeve of his jacket, but it was barely recognizable now. Blood rilled up and was somehow invisibly wicked away from that awful tangle of shredded tendons and shattered bone. Every few seconds, some part of it was gently moved and pressed against another. Muscles seemed to swell and knit across those joinings, then atrophy away again, allowing the bones to be moved to a different location. Uhura glanced up at the pilot's serene, sleeping face, then back at the ruined hand again, not understanding how both could belong to the same body.

"The chamber's trying to fix him," said Sanner excitedly. "It must have him sedated or something, and now it's trying to put his hand back together. It's not a stasis chamber, Lieutenant! It's a healing device."

"An *alien* healing device." McCoy watched the gentle manipulations of Sulu's wounded hand, then startled Uhura with a curse. "Dammit, that's the second time it put his first metacarpal into the correct CM joint and then took it away again. I don't think it knows what the hell it's doing!"

"It must be programmed to heal according to an alien body plan," Uhura said in dismay. "And it's trying to match Sulu to that."

"But if it can't..." Sanner glanced worriedly at the bloodstain growing darker on the pilot's right sleeve. "And he keeps on bleeding like that..."

"He'll die." The doctor banged a fist on the glowing curve of transparent metal separating them from the injured pilot, cursing again when his blow rebounded harmlessly. "Can we break through this thing?"

"With a phaser, maybe," Sanner said. "Not with a sledge and a prybar."

"*Look!*" Uhura stiffened, feeling the back of her neck prickle with horror even in the bitter cold. "What is it doing to him now?"

The phantom swelling of muscles had stopped, and now, one at a time, the broken bones and hanging tendons looked as if they were melting into mist. Uhura heard McCoy take in a sudden sharp breath, then let it out in a long sigh of regret and resignation.

"I guess it's not such a bad doctor after all," he said gruffly.

"But—" Uhura watched the alien chamber remove the last jagged fragments of bone from the pilot's crushed wrist, but it wasn't until it begin sealing the fractured ends of his radius and ulna that she understood. "It amputated his hand?"

"Yes," McCoy said. The blood had stopped dripping from the edge of Sulu's jacket and new skin crept out from under it, sealing across the severed bones. The doctor sighed again. "Which is exactly what I would have had to do, if I'd been the one to treat him."

"But what happened to him?" Sanner demanded. "If all the alien transporter did was take him out of the shuttle and send him down here, how did he get his hand crushed? How did he get dressed in those clothes?"

Uhura had lifted her gaze to the pilot's sleeping face again, and not only because it was easier to look at than the useless stump of his right arm. "And how," she asked slowly, "did he get to be twenty years older than when he left camp this morning?"

Chekov hesitated for only an instant—just long enough to think, *I don't understand! We both went through the same alien force field, and I don't feel any younger*—then blasted frantically on his whistle and scrambled to his feet.

Tomlinson materialized at the lip of one rock plateau before Chekov had even let the whistle fall from between his teeth. "Did you see him? Did he get past you?" Chekov nodded miserably, but Tomlinson barely paused long enough to notice. "Angela saw him. It isn't the captain, and I don't know how he could have gotten here—"

"It *was* the captain." Chekov interrupted without considering protocol, or even realizing how absurdly sure of himself he would sound. "It was Captain Kirk."

"Did you *see* him?" Tomlinson asked again, more peevishly this time.

"Did *you?*" Chekov countered through his stung pride.

At almost any other time in Chekov's life, he would have been acutely aware of the impropriety of snapping at a senior officer that way. Right now, he only knew a profound annoyance when the lieutenant screwed his face into a scowl and gestured dismissively down at him. "We can argue about this later. Which way?"

Chekov bit off the impolite retort that first boiled up, and instead pointed down the winding passage ahead of him before breaking into a run himself.

He was surprised how familiar the shadowy twists and turns seemed—he hadn't thought he was paying that much attention when he first navigated his way into the karst maze. Maybe it was all the practice tracking and backtracking through the cave system. While Chekov knew they had been on Tlaoli for less than twelve hours (and he had apparently completely forgotten at least three of those), it felt as if he'd been finding his way through some rocky passage or other for days and days. He barely had to glance at the cracks that splintered off to left and right to remember which ones circled back to meet him, which narrowed down to impossibly tight fissures or dead ends.

What if Kirk slipped through one of those? The thought brought him to a sudden halt at the mouth of one dark, knife-thin passage. No matter what Tomlinson believed, Chekov knew they were no longer looking for a powerfully built adult male, with all the attendant assumptions about where Kirk could have climbed to and how he could have got there. An athletic young boy on the brink of manhood could slip into some frighteningly small spaces. Chekov realized with a start that this same boy had already sped through the crawlway that had challenged him and Sanner for hours. And the boy had done it without having to remove any of the roots and rocks that Chekov and Sanner had been forced to rearrange in order to fit through the same space. If Kirk—*this* Kirk—decided to dart into one of these tight side passages, there wasn't a one of them on the landing party who could possibly follow him.

Another whistle shrieked far off to his left, this one warped by its passage in and around the twisted mazework. Cursing, Chekov backed out of the narrow deadend, ducked right to circle one of the pillars, then cut as directly toward the sound as he could manage.

The little path he finally followed brought him closer to the top of the maze than he expected. He came upon Smith from above, sliding down the sharp water-worn rock at the expense of both his trouser seat and his palms.

The security guard spun to face him as he landed, her dark eyes anomalously wide. "You're not going to believe this—"

"He's young," Chekov cut her off. "He's just a boy. And he's frightened."

She nodded fervently. "Can I still get in trouble? I mean, I hit him! I was trying to stop him, and I hit him! Is he still the captain? Are they going to court-martial me?"

The question was more esoteric than Chekov could handle at the moment. "He's still the captain. But if they court-martial you, they'll have to court-martial us all by the time we manage to catch him." He remembered grabbing at the boy's ankle, and how close he'd come to striking out himself. "I think they'll understand that we're only trying to help him. Which way did he go?"

Smith pointed overhead. "Up the way you came down. You didn't pass him?"

He hadn't. And there hadn't been that many options for where the boy could have gone.

"He's up top," Chekov said with sudden certainty. "He's trying to get past us overhead."

Smith leapt to follow when he scrambled back up the incline. "Mr. Tomlinson and Mr. Martine are up there." She gave him a hard push from behind, then reached for a hand up in turn.

"He may not know that." Chekov hauled her as far up as he could, glad that she was able to pull herself up easily enough once she'd secured a handhold. "And he can't know the topography as well as we do. I don't think he realizes how hard it will be get back off the rocks again." He turned in a quick circle, looking for some sign of the boy's passage.

Smith mimicked his move, but didn't seem to have anymore success. "Where does he think he's going?"

Chekov remembered the terror behind the determination on the boy's face, and tried to imagine what would move a younger version of his captain to feel such desperate fear. "Away from us. Wherever he's going, it won't be back the way he came." He started to whip his compass out of its pocket, then realized he could just glimpse the lumpy tents and ground rover of the survey team's base camp between the misty hillocks. He grabbed Smith's arm. "Come on."

Away. Away from the base camp, away from the caves. Whatever Kirk thought he was running from, he'd awakened in the same big, dark, empty chamber as Chekov, probably with even more fear than Chekov had felt. He'd followed the breeze outside, and had gone to this much effort already to put distance between himself and that place. Chekov had a feeling that was all Kirk knew about where he was going—he was just getting away. He probably wouldn't even think about what to do next until he was far from the danger he'd already faced, and felt a lot more safe.

They found him again about midway across the broken plateau. The cracks had swelled to ridiculous widths, dropping bare rock sides into valleys where so much of the dirt had washed away that you could almost see down into the cave systems below. The boy made a single convulsive move toward the edge when he saw them approaching. Chekov put an arm out to slow Smith, and stopped her when she reached to take hold of her whistle.

"We need to call the others," she whispered. As though they were conspirators and the boy some worrisome kind of spy.

"We need to not frighten him." Chekov hadn't failed to notice the measuring look Kirk cast at the next plateau over. Even Chekov wondered if the boy could clear the gap with a single running leap.

"Please don't try it." Chekov resisted the urge to call him "sir," then felt absurdly disloyal for leaving the honorific silent.

The boy cast a final look over his shoulder before straightening as proudly as any young king. "Why shouldn't I?" His hands worked nervously, unconsciously at his sides.

Chekov risked taking a few careful steps closer. "Because you can't possibly make it. I could land a shuttle in that gap." He felt more than saw Smith move a few steps to his right. A little of the tension in his stomach eased. At least they both understood that they needed to make sure the boy didn't dart past them. Maybe he should have let Smith call the others after all. "I think we have a misunderstanding here. You don't need to be afraid of us."

The last step was apparently too many. The boy flung his hands up in front him, shouted suddenly, "Stop!"

Chekov did.

"Why do you have to find me?" The boy sounded suddenly pleading, and much younger even than he looked. "Just tell them you didn't find me! I promise, I won't tell anybody. My dad is in Starfleet, everybody will believe me. I'll tell them I hid in the woods, and I never saw anything." His eyes stood out unnaturally dark in his pale face. "Please, I just want to go home."

Chekov wished it were that simple for any of them. "You can't go home, not yet."

Tears welled up in the boy's eyes, as though the last shred of his reserves had abruptly eroded away. He was suddenly shaking too hard to remain standing. Sinking to his knees, he hugged his arms across his chest and lowered his face in what might have been either desperation or shame. "Please..." His voice was so quiet, Chekov could barely make out the words. "Please..." he whispered, almost in prayer. "Please, don't kill me...."

"Something's happening."

Uhura snapped abruptly awake at the sound of McCoy's voice, and only then realized that she had been sleeping. Because there had been nothing else they could do, they'd wrapped themselves in silver emergency blankets and arranged themselves around the glowing alien medical chamber in the upper cavern, waiting for it to release this strangely altered version of Sulu into their custody. Despite the cave's bitter cold, the possible danger, and the shock of what they'd just discovered, the sleepless hours she'd spent on Tlaoli had finally caught up with Uhura. She'd fallen asleep partway through that vigil, so suddenly and unexpectedly that she hadn't even realized it in time to stop herself.

She lifted her head off its lumpy and muddy pillow, then felt that pillow stir beneath her. Uhura grimaced, realizing belatedly that it was Sanner's shoulder she'd been slumped against. Fortunately, the cave geologist must have fallen asleep, too. He woke now, snorting muzzily and blinking out into the darkening glow of the cave. The golden light inside the chamber was slowly glittering away, ebbing down to a last few golden sparks.

"Is he awake?" Uhura asked quietly.

"Not yet." McCoy had shed his blanket and was standing near the column again, using his carbide lamp to peer into its darkening interior. "But it looks like—hey! He's *gone!*"

Uhura scrambled to her feet in a tangle of blankets, hearing Sanner curse and do the same beside her. Two steps brought her up to the pile of shattered travertine that lay around the alien chamber, but even when Sanner added his carbide glow to hers and McCoy's, they saw nothing inside that invisible cylinder of metal now but empty darkness.

"It must transport people out when they're healed," Uhura said, frowning. "That would explain how Chekov and the captain got out into this chamber without breaking through the travertine shell."

Sanner grunted agreement. "I was wondering why we hadn't seen a couple of these columns all cracked apart like Easter Eggs. But where's Mr. Sulu now?"

"Around here somewhere, I bet." Uhura reached up to open the water drip on her carbide lamp to a reckless pour, but the light only spread out a few meters further, leaving the rest of the echoing stone cathedral still bathed in darkness. As far as she could see, however, nothing stirred between the travertine columns that disappeared up into darkness. "Like Chekov and the captain, he might be disoriented, and not really sure what's going on."

McCoy dropped his voice to a murmur. "Uhura, he probably knows you better than any of us. Call for him."

She nodded and cleared her throat to shout, then thought about how tense young Ensign Chekov had been after his journey through the alien transporter system, and lowered her voice to a gentler pitch. "Hikaru, where are you?" Uhura slowly turned, making sure her voice was projected to carry into all the echoing corners and crevices of the cavern. "Don't worry, we're here to help you."

"Uhura?"

The voice was completely familiar, deep and resonant with just that slight hint of a native California accent. But the emotion in it was so foreign that it took Uhura a moment to recognize it as not just amazement but utter, bone-deep disbelief.

She took a step toward the darkness where she thought Sulu's voice had come from. "Yes, it's me." She made an urgent shushing gesture at Sanner when it looked as if the geologist was going to open his mouth. McCoy came soft-footed over to join her, nodding approval when Uhura glanced up at him inquiringly.

"Keep him talking," the doctor mouthed, barely loud enough to be heard over the hiss of their acetylene flames. Then he turned his own carbide lamp off completely and stepped away into the darkness. Comprehension crossed Sanner's face, and he extinguished his light, too, vanishing in the opposite direction from McCoy. Uhura hoped the unusual brightness of her own head lamp would keep the unseen pilot from noticing the loss of the other lights.

"Sulu, how do you feel? You were—you were very badly hurt." That seemed safe enough to say. Surely Sulu would have noticed his amputation by now, although he might not have any more understanding of why it had happened than they did.

"I know." The disbelief was still clear in Sulu's reserved voice, although an odd, wry note had been added to it. "I thought I was going to die back there. Too," he added in what sounded like a significant tone.

"Back in the shuttle, you mean?" Uhura ventured, although even as she said it, she knew it couldn't be true. But her eyes had caught a scrap of movement at the flickering edge of her carbide light's halo, and she was pretty sure McCoy and Sanner must have seen it, too.

Sulu's laugh rolled out into the darkness, unexpectedly bittersweet. It was so recognizably the laugh of a man who'd lived a long time and seen a lot of pain that Uhura winced, but there was still a core of genuine humor buried deep inside it. "I always think I'm going to die in that damned Gorn shuttle whenever I let Chekov fly! But Pavel never lets us down." He paused, then spoke again more somberly. "We were the ones who let him down this time, Uhura. We didn't make it, and now we're where—in Hell? Or is this some kind of alien purgatory that we have to wait in before we're allowed to finally be done with it all?"

"Sulu, we're not dead." Uhura began walking toward him, both because the sudden grim note in his voice alarmed her, and to cover the soft sounds Sanner and McCoy made as they crept closer through the darkness.

She wasn't sure of much anymore, but she knew they couldn't let this altered Sulu, recently injured and disoriented as he must be, slip past them into the alien conduits and be lost. "We *are* in an alien installation, one with medical chambers that healed you before you could die." Uhura took a deep breath, then bravely continued. "How else could your right hand have been amputated and then healed so fast?"

"You know about that?" A quiet step in the darkness, and Uhura saw the slim figure in the mottled battle jacket separate itself from the shadow of a nearby column. "Did the alien medical chambers here heal you, too? Even after I saw you lying there by the gate with that hole blasted through your heart—"

The pain cracked through the calm shell of his voice so sharply and unexpectedly that Uhura winced at the sound of it, even before she absorbed the shock of his words. Before she could say anything in reply, a flurry of running steps and a thud in the darkness told her that one of the unseen watchers had flung himself at the pilot. There was the sound of a struggle, brief and unexpectedly violent, then a painful groan that sounded suspiciously like Sanner.

"All right, all right, I give up! Hey, I was just trying to make sure you didn't go running off and get lost in these caves."

"I don't know you." Suspicion hardened Sulu's voice until Uhura barely recognized it. "Why should I believe you when I don't even believe it's really Uhura who's talking to me?"

"Steady there, son," said McCoy's voice from the other side of the column. "Don't do anything you'll regret later. All it's going to take is a little light to get this all cleared up—"

"Doctor McCoy?" Sulu's voice changed again, this time to a harsh and self-doubting growl. "God, I must be pumped full of torture drugs! I'm hearing people who I know have been dead for years—"

"Let's see if that's the truth," McCoy said calmly and Uhura heard him snap his carbide igniter once or twice. The flame caught and danced to life on the helmet he held in his arms, throwing its pale yellow glow up to splash on the contours of his face. Uhura came forward to join him, pulling her own helmet off and holding it in front of her the same way. It hadn't occurred to her, until she saw what McCoy had done, that the downward glare from her headlamp must have kept Sulu from seeing who she really was.

"Ouch," Sanner grumped in the darkness, but a rustle of cloth and the sound of footsteps told Uhura that Sulu must have released him. The pilot stepped into the circle of light she and McCoy now made, his strange black and violet camouflage jacket breaking up his slim outline when he moved in a way that proved how effective it was. The network of fine lines around Sulu's eyes and mouth had deepened with his baffled frown, but his gaze was steady and sane as it moved from McCoy to Uhura and back again.

"Either it's really you, from back about twenty years ago," he said to the doctor, "or the Gorn have gotten a lot better at synthesizing torture drugs than the last time they caught me." His glance swung back to Uhura. "You look twenty years younger, too, but I'm not—" Sulu lifted his right hand as if to touch his own face, then stopped and stared at the healed stump that used to be his wrist. Uhura watched him worriedly, but all he did was tug down his empty black uniform sleeve to cover the amputated limb, smoothing the fingers of his left hand awkwardly across the glittering silver slashes embossed there. "I'm the same forty-seven-year-old former starship captain who took our last pulse bomb into Tesseract Fortress and never came out again," he said quietly, almost to himself.

"Because you came here instead." Uhura tried to infuse her voice with equal parts calmness and firmness. It wasn't easy, especially when Sulu pinned her with a gaze so self-controlled and keen that she knew he hadn't lied about having been promoted to starship captain. She went on, feeling her way awkwardly through an explanation that she wasn't quite sure she really understood herself. "I think there's been some kind of time slip, some kind of exchange between different versions of you and your younger self. It's stardate 1704.3, Sulu, and we've triggered an alien force field, some kind of transporter device, on a planet called Tlaoli 4. Do you remember any of that?"

"Tlaoli?" The black-clad older version of Sulu shook his head. "I don't remember any planet by that name. All I remember from around that stardate was getting to that blue planet a day after it exploded, too late to rescue the geological team we were supposed to pick up. What was its name? Psi or Phi something?"

"Psi 2000." Uhura exchanged glances with McCoy and saw the doctor looking as puzzled as she felt. "In the history you remember, we didn't arrive in time to visit that planet? You don't remember catching a viral infection there, or Joe Tormolen dying after he—?"

She stopped, because Sulu was regarding her with what looked like suspicion again. "Joe Tormolen didn't die that early," he said. "It wasn't until after war was declared and the *Enterprise* crew was split up and sent off to the front. He was on board the *Delphi* when the frontier fleet tried to stop the Gorn from invading the Prellant system. I was in command of the *Hotspur* by then, with you as my com officer and half my crew made up of *Enterprise* ensigns and cadets yanked out of the academy for war duty. And you—" He turned to McCoy grimly. "—you were already dead."

"No," Uhura said. "No, that's not—that can't be our timeline. In our timeline, we made it to Psi 2000 before it blew up, but we lost Joe Tormolen to the virus he caught there. And then we had to cold-start the engines, which threw us back in time three days..." She trailed off, seeing from the dubious look on the older Sulu's face that he didn't find this alternate history particularly credible or convincing. Uhura took a deep breath and started again. "We came down here on Tlaoli 4 to rescue a survey crew who were trapped in the caves. While we were here, we ran into some kind of force field, one that seemed to be part of some kind of ancient alien transporter system. It made the captain and Chekov vanish, then made them reappear here, in this cavern. As a side effect, it seemed to cause them to lose some of their memory—"

"Chekov is here?" Sulu took an eager step forward, his lined face lighting with the first hint of gladness Uhura had seen there. "Did he come through this alien machine of yours, too? Is he all right?"

Uhura bit her lip, wishing she didn't have to disappoint him. "He's here, yes, but the Chekov I mean is the young ensign who belongs to this timeline. He's always been here, the same way you were always here until just a few hours ago."

Sulu nodded, his face growing still and thoughtful again. "The younger version of me, you mean. A different younger version that I can't remember having been."

"Yes." Uhura glanced at McCoy and got a silent nod of encouragement. Either the doctor still thought she was the best one to deal with this version of Sulu, or he didn't want to upset the former pilot by forcing him to talk to a man he considered long dead. "That younger version of you was still aboard the *Enterprise* when we lost Chekov and the captain. You came down to the planet in a cargo shuttle to take us back to the ship, but the captain was still missing." Uhura swallowed down the bitter taste of the words she had to say next. "I allowed you—I ordered you—to take the shuttle up to look for him. And you got caught by the alien force field yourself. We came down here to this cave because we thought it might send you here, where Chekov and the captain had been sent. We didn't know it would heal you. Or that you wouldn't be the same Sulu that had vanished."

The older man in the battle jacket remained silent after she stopped speaking, but he no longer looked suspicious. His dark eyes crinkled thoughtfully, if he were mulling over the ramifications of what she had just told him. Uhura wondered what kind of life this alternate Sulu had lived that allowed him to accept this bizarre twist of fate with neither denial nor protest, but instead with what looked like stoic resignation.

"Which captain?" he asked at last.

Uhura stared at him through the cavern's shifting shadows, unsure of what he meant. "Which captain of what?"

"Of the *Enterprise.*" Sulu gave her another of those sharp, probing gazes that his younger self had not yet developed. "Which captain of the *Enterprise* did you lose in this alien transport device? Pike? Hoffman? I know we only had him for a few months, but I think that was around stardate 1700 or so. Or is it that idiot Mitchell?"

Uhura had opened her mouth to answer, but the reference to the former first officer of the *Enterprise,* who in her timeline had died on an alien planet several months ago, left her speechless. McCoy, on the other hand, was startled out of his tactful silence.

"Gary Mitchell was never the captain of the *Enterprise,*" he said bluntly. "And neither was anyone named Hoffman. The captain we're talking about is James Kirk."

Only silence followed his statement. Uhura felt a sudden rush of odd sensations: a strange, hollow shakiness in her arms and legs, a sickening swoop in her stomach, a leaden pounding that began to thrum inside her ears. It took her tired brain a moment to realize that all of these were symptoms of terror, and another moment to grasp that the terror emanated not from any part of the alien caves around her, but from the completely blank look on the face of the Sulu who stood before her. Because she knew, even before he stirred and answered McCoy, exactly what he was going to say.

"I don't know anyone named James Kirk," the older Sulu said. "He may be captain of the *Enterprise* in your timeline, but for all I know, in mine he never even existed."

TO BE CONTINUED
in
BOOK TWO: *FUTURE IMPERFECT*

Look for STAR TREK fiction from Pocket Books

Star Trek®: The Original Series

Star Trek: The Next Generation®

Star Trek: Deep Space Nine®

Star Trek®: Stargazer

The Valiant • Michael Jan Friedman
Double Helix #6: The First Virtue • Michael Jan Friedman and Christie
  Golden
Gauntlet • Michael Jan Friedman
Progenitor • Michael Jan Friedman

Star Trek®: Starfleet Corps of Engineers (eBooks)

Have Tech, Will Travel (paperback) • various
  #1 • *The Belly of the Beast* • Dean Wesley Smith
  #2 • *Fatal Error* • Keith R.A. DeCandido
  #3 • *Hard Crash* • Christie Golden
  #4 • *Interphase, Book One* • Dayton Ward & Kevin Dilmore
Miracle Workers (paperback) • various
  #5 • *Interphase, Book Two* • Dayton Ward & Kevin Dilmore
  #6 • *Cold Fusion* • Keith R.A. DeCandido
  #7 • *Invincible, Book One* • Keith R.A. DeCandido & David Mack
  #8 • *Invincible, Book Two* • Keith R.A. DeCandido & David Mack
  #9 • *The Riddled Post* • Aaron Rosenberg
  #10 • *Gateways Epilogue: Here There Be Monsters* • Keith R.A. DeCandido
  #11 • *Ambush* • Dave Galanter & Greg Brodeur
  #12 • *Some Assembly Required* • Scott Ciencin & Dan Jolley
  #13 • *No Surrender* • Jeff Mariotte
  #14 • *Caveat Emptor* • Ian Edginton
  #15 • *Past Life* • Robert Greenberger
  #16 • *Oaths* • Glenn Hauman

Star Trek®: Invasion!

#1 • *First Strike* • Diane Carey
#2 • *The Soldiers of Fear* • Dean Wesley Smith & Kristine Kathryn Rusch
#3 • *Time's Enemy* • L.A. Graf
#4 • *The Final Fury* • Dafydd ab Hugh
Invasion! Omnibus • various

Star Trek®: Day of Honor

#1 • *Ancient Blood* • Diane Carey
#2 • *Armageddon Sky* • L.A. Graf
#3 • *Her Klingon Soul* • Michael Jan Friedman
#4 • *Treaty's Law* • Dean Wesley Smith & Kristine Kathryn Rusch
The Television Episode • Michael Jan Friedman
Day of Honor Omnibus • various

Star Trek®: The Captain's Table

Star Trek®: The Dominion War

Star Trek®: Section 31™

Star Trek®: Gateways

Star Trek®: The Badlands

Star Trek®: Dark Passions

Star Trek® Omnibus Editions

The Captain's Table Omnibus • various
Star Trek: Odyssey • William Shatner with Judith and Garfield Reeves-Stevens
Millennium Omnibus • Judith and Garfield Reeves-Stevens
Starfleet: Year One • Michael Jan Friedman

Other Star Trek® Fiction

Legends of the Ferengi • Ira Steven Behr & Robert Hewitt Wolfe
Strange New Worlds, vol. I, II, III, IV, and V • Dean Wesley Smith, ed.
Adventures in Time and Space • Mary P. Taylor, ed.
Captain Proton: Defender of the Earth • D.W. "Prof" Smith
New Worlds, New Civilizations • Michael Jan Friedman
The Lives of Dax • Marco Palmieri, ed.
The Klingon Hamlet • Wil'yam Shex'pir
Enterprise Logs • Carol Greenburg, ed.